MW00653898

Every Time
I Fall

Every Time
I Fall

New York *Times* Bestselling Author
LEXI RYAN

Every Time I Fall © 2021 by Lexi Ryan

All rights reserved. This copy is intended for the original purchaser of this book. No part of this book may be reproduced, scanned, or distributed in any printed or electronic form without prior written permission from the author except by reviewers, who may quote brief excerpts in connection with a review. Please do not participate in or encourage piracy of copyrighted materials in violation of the author's rights. Purchase only authorized editions.

This book is a work of fiction. Any resemblance to institutions or persons, living or dead, is used fictitiously or purely coincidental.

Cover design © 2021 by Hang Le

Cover photo © 2021 by Lindee Robinson

Ebook ISBN: 978-1-940832-19-7

Print ISBN: 978-1-940832-21-0

❀ Created with Vellum

ABOUT THE BOOK

New York Times **bestselling author Lexi Ryan brings you** *Every Time I Fall***, a sexy standalone romance about a woman learning to love herself and the guy who's loved her all along.**

He's my brother's best friend.

The hot guy with the heart of gold I've never let myself want.

Guys like Dean don't go for girls like me.

Curvy. Thick. A big girl. Whatever label you put on me, I know who I am and what it means. And that's fine. I'm content to be Dean's buddy and nothing more.

Or so I thought. But when Dean finds out about my bedroom issues and decides to help me fix them, everything changes.

He swears there's no such thing as "bad in bed" and pleasure is all about chemistry. I'm not convinced, but he intends to prove it. With his mouth. With his body. With his dirty texts and whispered promises.

I know from the first kiss that I'm going to fall hard. That this can't last, and the end might break me. But, for these days and nights with Dean, all the hurt might be worth it.

For every woman who's ever avoided the mirror, hidden from the cameras, or had to fight to love herself in any way. You are worthy of love and happiness without changing a damn thing.

CHAPTER ONE

ABBI

*T*he air conditioning in Smithy's bar feels like the sweetest reward for my short walk through the Georgia humidity, and the clamor of the busy establishment instantly makes me smile.

Dean Jacob—my brother's best friend and the hottest guy in all of Orchid Valley—is sitting at the bar, and by some miracle, the barstool next to him is vacant. Dean's broad shoulders, thickly muscled arms, and single dimple usually mean there's a woman or three fighting for any available space near him. Never me, though. Dean might be a good friend, and he might make for some seriously enjoyable scenery, but I've never been foolish enough to think I'm the kind of girl he'd pick for his next flavor of the week.

I take the spot next to him, just happy for a little company and two-for-one martini night. I'm a big girl, and I can handle drinking alone from time to time, but it's always better with a friend.

The corner of Dean's mouth hitches up in a crooked grin when he notices me, and I warm inside. I needed to see a friend tonight. "Hey, Abbi." He looks me over and his smile falls away. "You're all flushed and stuff. You okay?"

All flushed and stuff probably means my cheeks are bright red from the late August heat and humidity. While other girls look dewy and fresh when they get warm, I look more like I've run my fastest mile and have *serious* regrets.

I push the frizzy tendrils from my face. "I'm fine. What about you?"

He shrugs. "Fine, I guess."

I arch a brow. "Not very convincing, Dean."

He takes a pull from his glass—a light-colored draft beer, an IPA if I had to guess—and shakes his head. "Nah, everything's good. I just . . ." He shrugs again, and some instinct has me looking over his shoulder toward the other side of the bar, where Amy Matthews sits with a man I don't recognize. Amy used to be married to my brother, Kace, but that's old news at this point. Kace has moved on, falling madly, deeply in love with Stella. Amy moved on long before that with many men, something I wouldn't judge her for if Dean hadn't been among her conquests.

"Ugh." I scowl. "Please tell me *she's* not the reason for your grumpy mood."

He doesn't have to follow my gaze. I can tell by the tense line of his jaw that he knows who I'm talking about.

"Aaaaaabbi," Smithy croons, tossing a couple of napkins on the lacquered bar in front of me. "Where've you been, girl? I've missed you!"

I grin at my stoner friend. Smithy's rocking a full beard

2

these days and he's recently put his long, light brown hair into dreadlocks. While I appreciate dreads on many people, they somehow just make Smithy look unshowered. "I've been busy," I lie.

Saturday nights off used to be reserved for girls' nights and lemon drop martinis at Smithy's. They were for laughter and cutting loose from the week before. These days, when I get the rare Saturday night off, I spend it alone in front of the TV and questioning all my life choices while my friends are busy with their amazing boyfriends.

Savvy and I are the last single girls standing. I adore Savvy. She's fun and feisty and not afraid to speak her mind. But I, the head chef at the nicest restaurant in Orchid Valley, don't actually have all that much in common with fitness instructor Savvy Downing. So aside from the rare occasions when Stella and Brinley pull themselves away from their men to meet up for a drink, I rarely spend time at Smithy's these days. I'm trying to change that.

"I couldn't pass up two-for-one martini night," I say with a genuine smile.

"Damn straight," Smithy says. "Lemon drop for you and your date, or will the lucky guy be drinking another of my martini selections tonight?"

My cheeks flash hot. "Um, well, it's just me tonight, Smith. Is that a deal breaker on the special?"

"Two-fisting it, eh? I *likey*. No problem at all."

I made the right choice coming tonight. Another lonely night in my apartment, and I might've caved and downloaded Random again.

I shudder at the reminder of what gems of "dates" that app brought to me last time I tried. "You didn't look this fat in your picture," the last guy said. "Why are you trying to fool guys like that? Think we won't notice when we meet you in person?"

I dumped a very expensive drink down his shirt and walked out. I'd rather wash my papercuts out with lemon juice than use Random to find a date again.

"Want some cheesy tots too?" Smithy asks.

I shake my head. "Not today. I already had dinner." My chicken marsala might be all the rage with patrons of The Patio, but it's nowhere near as satisfying as Smithy's cheesy tots, and now I'm disappointed in my choices. I'd never admit it out loud, but in general, *all* of Smithy's food is more satisfying than the fancy stuff I make for my customers. You just can't beat bar food for comfort eating.

When Smith walks away, I turn back to Dean to see his attention has shifted to Amy again. "She's not worth it."

"I'm aware of that," he mutters, but after a beat he rolls his eyes and sighs. "I mean, I know *intellectually.*"

It was one thing to see Kace hung up on Amy after she left him—I mean, they were married. They had a child together. But seeing Dean hung up on her bothers me way more than I ever thought it would. I'm not sure I totally buy into whatever bro code says you can't sleep with a buddy's ex—there are exceptions for everything—but I don't trust Amy's motives. She used Dean for the rush of a wild, forbidden fling even though she knew he had feelings for her. Smacks of selfishness to me.

I wasn't a fan of Amy's before, but after the shit she pulled with Dean, I only tolerate her because she's the mother of my amazing niece. I love Hope way too much to screw her up with family drama.

"I think you need a rebound fling," I tell Dean, pulling my attention back to him.

He arches a brow. "And are you volunteering?"

I snort. "Yeah, right, Dean." I've known him all my life. I knew him when he was an awkward preteen and his voice was changing. I knew him when he was chasing cheerleaders in high school. And I knew him when he went off to college and came home with more muscles than my hormonal teenage self could handle. As a heterosexual woman, it's no surprise that I find Dean attractive—with his dark hair, soft brown eyes, trim beard, and *that dimple*— but as the chubby little sister of his best friend, I notice his attractiveness on an objective level and nothing more. I don't let myself notice the way his jeans hang low on his hips or the way his shirt stretches across his pecs. I definitely don't let myself gawk when he's shirtless at my brother's pool. I mean, almost never.

He shrugs. "It was worth a shot."

I feel heat creeping up my neck and pray my cheeks are already red enough from the heat to cover the visible signs of my embarrassment. I'm not one of those girls who knows how to tease about sex or who can flirt just because it's entertaining. Hell, I can't even flirt when I want to.

Smithy slides my drinks—plural—in front of me, and I grab one with greedy hands and take a long, boozy drink.

Dean watches me with wide eyes. "You okay there, champ?"

I sigh. "I'm just missing the good old days when my girls didn't ditch me for their guys."

"Brinley and Stella stood you up?" He rotates his stool to face me. "What the fuck for?"

I shake my head. "No, no, nothing like that. They just don't have time for girls' night anymore." I wave a hand. "Forget I said anything. How was your day?"

"It was fine. Long." He closes his eyes and rubs his temples. When he opens his eyes again, I realize they're red and a little puffy, as if he hasn't been sleeping enough or he's been stressed. Is he still losing sleep over Amy or is something else bothering him?

I nudge my second, untouched martini toward him. "Want a drink?"

He grins. "Don't mind if I do." He takes a large gulp then coughs, his eyes watering. "Holy shit. You didn't tell me that was mostly vodka."

I roll my eyes. "It's a martini. *Of course* it's mostly vodka. The only time martinis aren't mostly vodka is when they're mostly gin."

He coughs again and waves a hand in front of his watering eyes. "Noted. *Jesus.* It looks so sweet and harmless with that sugar on the rim. I thought it'd be like lemonade."

Laughing, I flick my tongue out to catch some of said sugar from my own glass but stop when I notice Dean watching me. I don't want him thinking I'm such a sugar addict that I have to resort to licking the rim of my martini between sips, even if maybe that's a little true. I put the glass down.

His gaze flicks back up to meet mine. "If you're jealous of Brinley and Stella's dates, why not get one of your own?"

"Where?" I ask without thinking. "Just pick one up at the store?"

Dean chuckles. "It's been known to happen. What about that app my sister used to use?"

"Random?" I shudder. "I tried it a few times and have promised myself and my future children that I'll never lower myself into that cesspool of dating despair again."

He makes a face. "That bad?"

"Whatever you're imagining, add in unemployment, body odor, and a porn addiction."

Dean coughs on his martini again. "Jesus. Really?"

"And worse," I mutter. Good thing it's two-for-one martini night. If we're going to rehash my dating life, Smithy's gonna need to keep them coming.

Dean's phone buzzes, and he pulls it from his pocket, reads the screen, and taps out what I'm assuming is a reply to a text before putting the phone facedown on the bar. "Well, I can't do anything about Brinley, but I'll talk to my sister."

I gape at him. "You will do no such thing!"

"It's not cool to ghost your friends just because you're dating someone new. I taught her better than that."

I roll my eyes. "She's not ghosting me, so back off, Friendship Police."

He stops his martini halfway to his lips and points at me. "I'm just looking out for you."

I grin. "I can handle myself."

"No doubt." He drains his martini so quickly that I fear a contact buzz. His phone rattles against the bar again, and he flips it over and repeats the same routine from less than a minute ago.

"Who's blowing up your phone?" I glance over my shoulder to where Amy's sitting in a booth with the guy she was talking to earlier. "Is it her? She's texting you while she's on a date with someone else? Gross."

Red crawls up his neck, and he studies his hands—his big, strong hands.

Sighing, I pull my gaze away before my thoughts can stray to forbidden territory—like how those hands might feel on cool skin or tangled in my hair. My libido wakes up at all the wrong moments.

He shrugs, nudging the empty martini glass to the side and reaching for his abandoned beer. "We're still . . . friends, I guess."

"Friends." I wonder if I'm immature, because I can't imagine being friends with someone so soon after they broke my heart. Hell, Cody broke up with me five years ago, and I *still* can't imagine being friends with his cheating ass. "Are you sure that's a good idea?"

He shrugs. "It is what it is. And before you say so, I do realize I made my bed and now I need to lie in it or whatever."

"I'm not judging you for getting your heart broken. Not at all. You deserve better than her. So much better."

"Right." He grunts. "People always say that to the person who was dumped. I'm pretty sure if that were true, I wouldn't be single right now."

"You're insane if you actually think she left you because you're not good enough for her. Do you think *Kace* wasn't good enough for her?"

He swallows. "Well, obviously not. They just fizzled out. But that isn't what—" His phone buzzes again, and this time as he reads the screen, he actually scowls before he puts his phone back down.

"Abbi!" someone calls, right as I open my mouth to ask Dean about his latest text.

I turn to see Vincent Brunetti strolling up to the bar, a tight smile curving his lips that, on a woman, might be described as *prissy*. On Vince, the description still holds. This guy's been trying to get me to go out with him for years. At this point, I don't think it even has anything to do with attraction. I've accidentally made myself a challenge, and after a lifetime of getting everything he wants handed to him, Vince can't stand that I keep saying no. He tugs on the lapels of his suit coat as he looks me over. "Can I buy you a drink?"

"She has a drink," Dean says.

I nudge him to get him to shut up. Vince is just trying to be nice. "I'm all set. How are you, Vince?"

"I'd be better if I had you keeping me company tonight." He nods to an empty booth across the room, where a pitcher of beer sits next to a tray of pizza. "What do you say? Impromptu date night. Let's do it."

"I'm sorry. I can't. I have to leave soon." A total lie. I fully intend to nurse this martini until it's time for round two, but I'm not in the mood to deal with his whiny brand of "persuasion" at the moment.

"Someday, Abbi girl," he says, waving a finger at me. "Someday, I'm gonna talk you into going out with me."

"Maybe," I say. "But not tonight."

"I'll take *maybe*," he says, backing away. He bumps into a waitress, causing the tray of drinks in her hand to topple over.

Cringing, I wave to the girl behind the bar to hand me some towels.

"Aw, shit," Vince says. "Did I do that?"

The waitress forces a smile over her scowl. "It's fine. I've got it."

"Cool, cool," he says, and trots off to his booth.

She takes the towels from me and waves me off, so I return to my stool.

"*Maybe?*" Dean says next to me. "You gave that guy a *maybe?*"

"Well, I . . ." I did. I'm not exactly interested in a relationship with Vince, but I'm positive he wouldn't say no to a casual fling. Since I don't have any hopes riding on a relationship with him, it could be the perfect opportunity to grow more comfortable with the things a girl my age should already be comfortable with. Vince might not be my type, but it'd beat another lonely Netflix night.

"What's that look?" Dean asks.

"I'm just . . ." I tug my bottom lip between my teeth. "Maybe I *should* go out with Vince."

Dean coughs on his beer. "You're fucking kidding me, right? Dude's a total tool."

I shrug. "There's not exactly a long line of guys begging to buy me a drink."

"It's because they don't think you're interested. You might as well have *leave me the fuck alone* tattooed on your forehead."

"If that's true, Vince hasn't seemed to notice."

"That's *why* Vince notices. He loves that about you. If he got you to date him, he'd have something no other guy in this town can have. He eats that shit up."

Something no other guy in town can have. I glare at him. It's one thing to soften the truth. It's another to spout total bullshit. "Don't condescend to me."

"I'm not. That's who Vince is."

That isn't what I meant, but I just shrug and sip my drink.

Dean's phone buzzes again, and he sighs as he looks at it. "It was good to see you, champ, but I've gotta head out." He slides off the stool and looks me over as he slides his phone into his pocket. "No dates with Brunetti, got it?"

I roll my eyes. "If you promise not to hook up with Amy."

I can tell by his grimace that he can't make any such promise, and my stomach sinks. Dean deserves better than a cheating thrill-seeker who doesn't return his feelings.

He bops my nose with one finger. "Don't worry about me, 'kay?"

Too late. "Be safe," I murmur, and my chest actually aches as I watch him walk away. I tell myself I'm only worried about him. I want better for him than a woman who will lead him on and break his heart over and over again. This tug is *concern.* It's definitely not jealousy, definitely not longing for the guy I know better than to let myself want.

DEAN

The biggest mistake I ever made was falling in love with my best friend's ex-wife. My second biggest mistake was caving to loneliness one drunken night after we'd called it all off. In a moment of weakness, I texted to let her know I was DTF, no strings necessary, and now we're back to the same fucked-up patterns we had months ago.

I pretend to sleep while she sneaks out of my bed for the thousandth time. I could sit up and turn on a light so she doesn't have to stumble around in the dark. I could tell her to cancel the Uber I already know is on its way to my door and confess that I only do this because I'd rather have her scraps than nothing at all.

Instead, I bury my face in my pillow and listen to the sounds of her leaving—too afraid that my battered ego and splintered heart might shatter if I had to see the pity in her eyes.

I need to cut this off. I need to say no the next time she asks me to meet her for a drink, the next time she texts to say her date is boring and she can't stop thinking about me, the next time she calls and tells me exactly where she wants my hands and mouth . . .

"Move," she whispers to my dog. "Go on. Get out of the way."

Trixie whines. She's always loved Amy more than Amy loved her. I know what that's like. But unlike Trixie, I won't beg. I stay perfectly still until the bedroom door clicks closed behind Amy.

Only when I hear the thump of the front door opening and closing do I roll to my back and turn on the light to face my empty bedroom. The mess of discarded clothes on the floor—including the black satin underwear she left behind—the empty bottles of wine, and the lamp we knocked to the floor in our haste to get to the bed.

I climb out of bed to clean up and ignore the weighty sense of déjà vu settling over me.

"You deserve better than her. So much better." Abbi's words echo in my head. A lie delivered with such conviction that I would've believed her if she'd been talking to someone else.

This is my life. Inviting Amy in, hoping she'll stay, and finding myself alone to pick up the pieces. I close my eyes and promise myself, yet again, that this is the last time.

CHAPTER TWO

ABBI

"*I*s that my brother's arm?" Stella asks, shoving her phone in front of my face. "Please tell me that's not my brother's arm."

I drop my rag and take the phone, frowning at it under the fluorescent kitchen lights. "This is Amy's Instagram," I say needlessly.

"Tell me I'm losing my mind," she says, tossing her long red hair over her shoulder. "Tell me that's not Dean's arm."

Frankly, I'm surprised Stella follows my ex-sister-in-law on any social media, but I sigh and study the picture and the big hand and muscular forearm wrapped around Amy's middle. Amy cropped his face and body out of the image, but I know without a doubt that hand and arm belong to Dean Jacob. The caption reads, *Moms Just Wanna Have Fun! Great weekend with great friends but glad to have my baby girl back home.*

"So?" Stella asks. "I'm losing my mind, right? Tell me it's not Dean and I should mind my own business."

I give her a weak smile. "You should mind your own business?" I say, but it comes out sounding like a question, because I don't really agree. Amy broke Dean's heart over the summer, and I don't blame Stella for wanting her to keep her distance.

"The other part, though?" Stella asks. "That it's not really Dean?"

I shake my head. "Unless you want me to lie to you . . ."

She groans and snatches her phone back. "I'm trying *so hard* not to hate her. She's Hope's mom, and I *need* us to have a good relationship, but . . ."

"She makes that extremely difficult," I supply, and Stella nods. Poor girl. I have to give her props for trying to make nice with her boyfriend's ex-wife. "What is Dean *thinking?*"

"He's not. Obviously." She shakes her head. "Anyway, why are you here?" She props her hands on her hips and takes in the empty kitchen.

"I have a meeting," I say, grabbing my rag to finish sanitizing the stainless-steel counter, where I just prepped a new variation on my much-loved artichoke chicken flatbread.

Stella folds her arms. "A meeting, or an excuse to be a workaholic?"

I shrug. "Little of column A, little of column B."

It's Monday afternoon and The Patio is closed today, but I've come in for a special meeting with one of my wine suppliers. Even if Frankie hadn't emailed asking to change the time, I still would've probably found myself here. The kitchen is my happy place, and when the restaurant isn't open, I can play with my *true love*—chemistry. By which, of course, I mean baking.

I used to be embarrassed about that, about being a big girl who likes to cook and bake—who wants to be a walking cliché?—but when I dropped out of college almost five years ago, necessity won out over pride. I took a job as a sous chef. I worked my way up to head chef the way someone my age can only do in a town as small as Orchid Valley, and I've never looked back.

Stella laughs and shakes her head. "I'm clocking out. Do you need anything before I go?"

In addition to being my friend and my brother's girlfriend, Stella is the receptionist at The Orchid, the day spa that houses my restaurant, and she's as responsible for holding this place together as my other best friend, Brinley, who's the owner.

"Not a thing," I say. "What about you? Need anything? I have some cookies in the walk-in."

She presses a hand to her stomach. "No. I ate a brownie and a sea salt caramel cookie while at reception, and I enjoyed them way too much. I'm cut off."

I laugh. "Glad you liked them."

She arches a brow. "Liked? They were amazing. I had . . . mouthgasms."

I laugh. "Mouthgasms?"

"Yeah. I feel like I should at least buy you dinner or something."

Laughing, I take my bucket of sanitizing solution to the sink and dump it. "What are you and my brother up to tonight?"

She sighs. "We have Hope, so I think we're going to talk Dean into having dinner with us."

"That's nice," I say, trying to keep the frown from my face.

"Maybe? He's not been doing so great since Amy dropped him, and Kace is worried about him. But now I'm going to be all awkward avoiding the subject of Amy and what he did this weekend."

I keep my mouth shut, determined to neither confirm nor deny her suspicions.

"He needs a good woman, ya know? Someone who can remind him what it's like to be treated with respect and value. Amy just—" She snaps her mouth shut and shakes her head.

"You can say it. You know how I feel."

"Nope." She flips her hair and rolls back her shoulders. "I will not talk trash about my boyfriend's ex. I won't do that to him or to Hope."

I get it. I feel the same way, but as we already established, Amy makes it difficult. Especially if she's messing with Dean's head again.

"And anyway," she says, "Dean makes his own choices. It's not like Amy's some evil seductress who's got him under her spell. He knows how she feels and what she does and doesn't want and chose to be involved with her anyway." She glances at her phone. "Apparently, *continues* to choose, I guess."

"So true," I mutter. It's easy to cast Amy as the villain here, but if she's being upfront with Dean and he's choosing to sleep with her anyway, isn't that Dean's problem? "I think you're a better person than I am, Stell."

She shakes her head. "Nah, but I'm trying to be decent."

"Abbi?" someone calls from the hall.

I gasp, eyes flying to the clock. I wanted to be at my

desk when he arrived, to be doing paperwork so it didn't look like I made a special trip into work just for him. Even if I did. "On my way," I call back. I toss my rag in the bin and turn to give Stella a quick squeeze. "That's my meeting, but tell the boys I said hi."

Stella arches a brow and tries to peek around me. "Who's the cutie?"

"Wine distributor," I say, hoping my voice doesn't give away any of my nervousness. He isn't just a wine distributor. Frankie Perez has a smile as warm as the sun and a tendency to aim it right at me. I look forward to his visit every month.

He's one of the few guys I can comfortably flirt with. And if he didn't live in Atlanta, maybe I would've had the courage to ask him out by now. But probably not.

"Hmm," Stella says, biting back a smile. "Okay, then. I'll see you soon."

I take a deep breath and head to my office at the back of the kitchen, where Frankie is waiting, a leather messenger bag slung over his shoulder.

"Abbi!" His brown eyes are pools of melted chocolate as he looks me over, and when he looks at me again, he's grinning. "Thanks for coming in on your day off."

I wave a hand. "I needed to do some paperwork anyway." Kind of true, but there's always paperwork.

"I have a few things to go over with you," he says, pulling a manila folder from his bag. "If this is an okay time."

My smile falls away, but I quickly replace it. Usually, Frankie's in no hurry to get out the door. I can always count on him to ask about my mom, whom he met at a wine-tasting event we did here at the spa once, or my latest offerings at the restaurant. He'll typically entertain me with some story about his home-brew experiments or the best new restaurants in Atlanta.

But none of that today, I guess.

I pretend I'm not disappointed and lead him into my office, where we go over my order and some changes his company is making to bulk order pricing. It's over far too quickly for something I've looked forward to all day long, but I don't let my disappointment show as I stand to show him out.

"This is the last time you'll see me in this capacity," he says, tucking his folder back into his messenger bag.

My heart sinks, and this time I can't keep the disappointment from my face. This guy is so sweet. He's kind of like a big teddy bear—on the shorter side, with a barrel chest, dark hair, and dark eyes. He's a little goofy and awkward around my employees, but always smiles when he sees me. He makes me feel cute in a way girls like me don't usually get to feel. "Why's that?"

"I've taken a new job." He nods. "All the traveling gets really old."

"I'm sure," I say. *Failing.* I'm failing at keeping the disappointment from my voice. And how lame am I that this once-a-month sales call is the most exciting part of my romantic life? Okay, that's just sad. *Social life*, maybe? Even that's a stretch. It's not like we've ever been involved. I might've imagined we could be . . . someday . . . but the most physically intimate we've ever gotten is an accidental brush of fingers when I'm signing my order.

This isn't romance. It's just Frankie selling me wine, but his flirty eyes and warm smile are the closest thing to romance in my life.

"I'll miss having an excuse to see you all the time," he says, and my stomach jumps. He grins. "But . . . after I finish training in Atlanta, the new job will actually mean me living in Orchid Valley."

"Really?" I squeak. *Down, girl.* I have zero chill.

His grin widens. "Really. I'll be moving into those new downtown condos in six weeks and opening a tasting room for Montgomery Wines. I wouldn't mind having a friend to show me around town." He cocks his head to the side. "Maybe someone who can introduce me to the best place to get a beer or a nice meal."

Oh, God. I can't decide if I'm grateful I get to see him again or if I'm terrified I'll no longer have the security blanket of professionalism as an excuse not to make this into what I've wanted since the first time I met him.

The truth is I suck so badly at real relationships that I've avoided them altogether since I dropped out of college and moved home almost five years ago. So, yeah, chalk this one up to *terrified*.

"You know where to find me." My voice squeaks again. Oh my God. I'm a mess. He's going to think I'm crazy and then straight-up avoid me.

"Yeah." He steps a little closer. He smells warm and spicy, like pine and coriander. "But maybe I should give you my number, just in case?"

My heart is hammering so hard. "Sure. Just in case."

He pulls his business card from his wallet and hands it over to me then winks as he shoves his wallet back into his pocket. "I'm looking forward to it, Abbi."

"Me too."

Six weeks. I have *six weeks* to figure out how to do this

dating thing. Six weeks to figure out how to not scare him off if anything ever happens between us.

⚜

DEAN

My phone buzzes for the third time tonight, and I ignore it. I already know it's my sister. *Come have dinner with us. We love you. Don't shut us out.*

I can't face them until I take care of something else, so here I am, at The Terminal on a Monday night. I feel like a traitor even walking into this place. I don't like this bar, but I like Amy's reasons for wanting to meet me here even less —she doesn't want to risk my friends seeing us together. Doesn't want to risk word getting back to Kace that we're messing around again. If that red flag hasn't made me back way the fuck off this relationship, I'm not sure anything will.

Amy grabs my hand and pulls me into her booth at the darkest corner of an already dark bar. "Does anyone know you're meeting me here?"

I sigh. *Why am I doing this?* "No." Though I all but told Abbi I was meeting up with Amy on Saturday. Fuck, maybe I wanted her to talk me out of it. I don't know.

"My date was a total bust," she says. She leans on my shoulder and grins up at me. If I didn't already know from her texts that she's half-drunk and a lot horny, I'd know now. I'm pretty familiar with her fuck-me eyes at this point.

"That's what you get for dating losers," I say, and she laughs as if I'm joking. I'm not. We both know I'd prefer she date *me*. At least, I *think* that's what I want, but my bitterness lives beside my love for her, and it's starting to overshadow it.

"I know he wanted to fuck me, but I couldn't stop thinking about you."

The dark cloud hanging over me rumbles with thunder. I shouldn't have come. I should've done this over the phone. "I don't want to hear about how you almost fucked some other guy tonight, Amy."

"Even if the whole reason I didn't was because I wanted *you* instead?"

Yeah, even then. I just shake my head. I had a couple of drinks at Smithy's before heading over here, but my buzz is fading, and I need another drink if I'm going to get through this night without turning pathetic, without forgetting the promises I've made to myself.

"Are you thinking what I'm thinking?" she asks.

I grimace. "I guess that depends."

My stomach is in knots, and I can't blame the alcohol— though, to be fair, there's been far too much of it in my life lately. I can't even blame giddy anticipation, because I know how the next few hours go down. She'll look at me with her pretty baby blues and flash me a series of those smiles I'm too weak to resist on a good day. Then she'll go home with me and we'll make love—only it's not making love, because mine is the only love in the equation. It's taken me weeks to realize this. Amy's just getting off. She's snuggling against me now because she wants me to drag her to the bathroom and fuck her against the door, not because she wants all my tomorrows.

No, all she'll want tomorrow is to ghost me until the next time she decides she needs my dick.

The idea of it depresses the shit out of me. "Amy, this

isn't why I agreed to meet with you. I'm not taking you home tonight."

She trails a finger across my beard and to my mouth, hooking her finger in my bottom lip. Under the table, her hand is on my leg, and it inches up, up, up, until the side of her palm brushes the hard length of my cock through my jeans. "You didn't have any complaints Saturday night."

Saturday was another mistake, but I don't want to argue about it. Mostly because my argument makes me feel really fucking pathetic. If she comes home with me, I'll want her to stay, and if she sleeps next to me, I'll want her to give us a fucking chance. *If you give a mouse a cookie* . . .

Amy's made it clear she's not interested in a relationship, and I'm only hurting myself by pretending I'm okay with that. Hope springs eternal, and each time she comes back to me, I hope maybe *this* is the time she'll want more than another night in my bed.

I grab her hand from my thigh and return it to her side.

"You have needs," she says. "More than the average guy your age, to be honest. And until you find someone else, don't you need me?"

"It's a bad idea," I say, and my words come out rougher than I intended, rough enough that if she were a little more sober, she'd hear the truth behind them.

I'm still in love with you. I can't do casual with you. I'll always want more than you're interested in offering a guy like me. Watching you walk away again might break me.

"Pleeeease." Her lips graze the side of my neck. It feels so damn good, and I want what she's offering—to lose myself in sex, to feel her in my arms again. Not to be *alone*.

When her mouth skims over mine, I can taste the satisfaction in her smile, a sweet shot that could chase away my bitterness. If I let it.

I hate myself for being so damn tempted, and even more for giving in to temptation so many times. I'm an idiot, and the fact that she thinks we'll be hooking up again tonight is all my fault.

I pull my mouth away from hers and put space between us in the booth. "I can't do this anymore. I'm happy for you and I'm glad single life is all you dreamed it would be, but I'm not interested in being your standby fuck."

"But just one more time," she says, leaning closer.

"No." Standing, I shove my hands in my pockets, because I don't trust them not to reach for her. "I can't do this anymore. We want different things, and every time I watch you walk away, it kills something inside me."

Her lusty expression falls away and is replaced by annoyance. "I've never lied to you about what I want."

I shrug. "Maybe. But it's time for me to stop lying to myself."

CHAPTER THREE

DEAN

"You look like hell. If you're here for booze, you need to go somewhere else."

I glare at Smithy. First, it's Friday night and this is a fucking bar. Drinks are literally the reason people come here. Second, he's denying me a drink before I even get started, and that's just insulting. "Wanna tell me what this is about?"

He folds his arms on the bar top and lowers himself until we're eye to eye. "It's about you finding your way home with a certain toxic ex every time you drink in my bar. I've made an executive decision not to be part of that."

I don't bother denying it, nor do I bother explaining that half the reason I look as shitty as I do right now is because I've spent the whole damn week trying not to text her, trying not to crawl back for scraps again. "She's not toxic," I say, sliding onto the barstool despite his dickish behavior. Maybe I *should* go somewhere else.

"Can't tell by looking at you. How about some dinner?" he asks, brow arched. "Unless you can tell me the last time you ate solid food—and protein bars don't count."

I roll my eyes. "Dinner would be great, Smith. Thanks so much. Do I get to order, or would you like to continue treating me like a child and pick out my meal for me?"

"Oh, I'm fucking picking it." He pours me a glass of water. "But you can choose what dressing you want on your side salad."

My stomach churns at the idea of eating a salad, but I mutter, "House," as he plops the tall glass in front of me.

Smithy's right. I'm a fucking train wreck. I started my day with a protein bar because I was too exhausted and hungover to consider anything more substantial. Instead of taking the day off and getting my life together, I put in a twelve-hour day. Lately, I've been donning my toolbelt and using manual labor to get my mind off my heartache, even though Kace and I haven't *had* to work in the field for years. Which is pretty much every day. I met the crew at the lake-side house at seven a.m. and worked until long after everyone else had clocked out for the day, losing myself in the monotony of drywalling. The only time I took a break was at lunch, when I stopped for an hour to do my favorite five-mile loop through the park and down a protein shake and an apple—which is absolutely solid food, *thankyou-verymuch.*

Now it's nearly nine p.m., and I know if I go home, I'll end up in bed with Amy again. Either she'll show up, or I'll text her and suggest something I know she can't resist—like fucking me. Unfortunately, she absolutely can resist what I really want from her—a real relationship. Commitment. Love.

Smithy might be trying to save me from myself, but he doesn't realize the only reason I'm here tonight is because I'm actually *less* likely to cave if I'm here than if I'm alone at home.

I drag a hand over my face and sigh before forcing myself to drain the glass of water.

Within minutes, Smithy's back with my dinner. The dude must know I've been having stomach issues, because instead of bringing me my usual buffalo chicken sandwich, he brings me the chicken breast wrap. I might not have any appetite, but at least I can manage this. "How long are you going to keep doing this to yourself?" Smithy asks.

"I don't know what you're talking about," I mutter, then take a bite of the wrap. It tastes like ash in my mouth.

"She must have one hell of a unicorn pussy if you're still this fucked up."

I drop my food to my plate and glare. "Don't talk about her like that," I growl.

Smithy throws up both hands. "Hey, no offense. I've had a taste of unicorn pussy. I get it." Grinning, he leans forward. "Dated this girl back when I was on the Patriots practice squad. She was almost sixty and a preschool teacher, but she did this thing when I was fucking her, like . . ." He squeezes and opens both fists simultaneously to illustrate.

I cringe. "Please stop."

"And her mouth . . ."

I put down the wrap and cock my head to the side. "Do you want me to eat or hurl?" I ask. "It can't be both, so you're gonna have to choose." Then I cringe again as I'm assaulted with an unwanted mental picture of twenty-two-year-old Smithy with a sixty-year-old preschool teacher with a "unicorn pussy." "Damn you," I mutter.

Smithy shrugs. "Okay. Then let's talk about you. Let's talk about how the only time you're not in here, you're working or chasing that—"

I glare, and he winces.

"Right. You." He points at the food. "You're losing weight and drinking too damn much."

"You own a bar. You should be glad I'm drinking."

"You're one of my best friends. I know you don't have a drinking problem, but you do have an *Amy* problem." With that, he slides down the counter to help another patron, leaving me to contemplate my food and my general loneliness.

I never did agree to have dinner with Kace and Stella this week. I don't remember a time when Kace Matthews wasn't my best friend, and right now all I really want is to crack open a beer with him and tell him exactly what's eating me. But I can't. You don't get to sleep with your best friend's ex-wife and then complain about how she's treating you. Kace and I already had it out about this, and he was cooler about it than I deserved, but he thinks I let things end this summer, and I can't face the disappointment in his eyes if he knew the truth.

Maybe I could talk to Smithy, but having *him* be the one to call me on my shit decisions is making my pride bristle uncomfortably. Marston, Brinley's husband, is a nice enough guy, but we're not close enough that I want to pour my heart out. It's just not that easy for me to open up like that.

Maybe it's ironic, but this is the reason I always end up texting Amy. Loneliness and desperation make the perfect self-sabotage cocktail. And there were certain things I could talk to her about without feeling judged. I didn't have to worry if her knowing about my shit father figure, for instance, would scare her off. Amy has her faults, but she always let me have mine too. I needed that.

By the time Smithy makes it back to my end of the bar, I've eaten half my wrap and a few bites of salad. It's probably the most substantial thing I've managed all week. "Listen," I say as he refills my water. "I want to get over her. I'm working on it."

Smithy rocks back on his heels and folds his arms. "You're like a junkie who swears he wants to get clean but keeps surrounding himself with the good stuff."

I grunt. That analogy seems . . . well, fitting. "I can't help that our lives overlap."

His lips twist. "But you can help how much time you spend alone with her."

I study my water, watching air bubbles rise to the surface of the glass. I don't know how Smithy knows so much when we've been semi-secretive about the whole thing, but somehow it doesn't come as a surprise. Smithy knows a frightening amount about what goes on in this town, and though he says it's because people talk a lot in bars, I know there's more to it than that.

"And you can also control whether or not you *dip your wick*, if you know what I mean."

I rub the dull ache in my temples. "The nuns at St. Mary's know what you mean, Smith."

"Did I ever tell you about the time I banged that nun in Jersey? At least, I think she was a nun, but maybe it was just a stage costume." He chuckles. "Anyway, do you really want to be her booty call? Because she might not realize what she's doing to you, but it's pretty fucking obvious from where I stand."

I cringe. Shit. It was bad enough when I was Amy's dirty little secret, but everyone knowing I'm her toy might be even more mortifying. "I'm working on it," I say. "Seriously, I want off this ride. It's breaking me." It's the most vulnerable thing that's come out of my mouth in weeks—since the day she broke up with me the first time, and I got loaded and poured my heart out to my little sister.

"Have you tried dating anyone else?"

I bark out a laugh. "Seems kind of shitty to go out with one woman when I'm fixated on another."

He nods. "Yeah, I get that, but it might be the easiest solution. Put yourself out there. Get yourself some strange. Right now, your little copilot thinks Amy's unicorn pussy is the only pussy in the world. Remind him there's other pussy to be had."

I drag a hand over my face. "One, never call my dick 'little' anything ever again. Two, please stop saying pussy."

Smithy chuckles, and I grin. It's hard to take yourself too seriously around Smithy. My smile falls away when I see Amy standing at the pool tables. She's fresh-faced and smiling tonight, and the joy in her eyes reminds me of the good times. Loneliness curls up in my stomach like a cat in a windowsill, just making itself at home. Maybe Smithy's right. Maybe I am an addict.

I try to focus on my food. Try to ignore the feeling of her eyes on my back.

My phone buzzes, and I unlock it and open the message without thinking.

Amy: I'm sorry about Monday.

Shit. Apologies from Amy are rare, but she knows I have a weakness for them and is a master at manipulating me to get what she wants. Or maybe I'm just jaded.

> Dean: What are you apologizing for?
> Amy: For being heartless. I don't mean to be
> like that.

I stare at my phone for a long time. I can't help but feel like she doesn't really get it, even after all this time, but I'm not up for trying to explain myself again, either.

> Amy: And you can give me your apology any
> time you want.
> Dean: What am I apologizing for?

I glance over my shoulder to see her laughing with her date before she bends over the pool table to take a shot. When he takes his turn, she pulls out her phone again, and I turn away. Moments later, my phone buzzes.

> Amy: For rejecting me in my hour of need?
> For leaving me wanting? For sending me
> home to take care of myself when I blew
> off my date to be with you?

Yeah, she definitely doesn't get it.

> Dean: Taking care of your needs isn't my
> responsibility.
> Amy: Ha! Well, you can make it up to me.
> Come to my place tonight.

Dean: We've been over this. I'm done.

Amy: That's what you always say . . . <winky
   face>

Dean: I'm in love with you. I need more from
   you than sex.

Amy: So this is an ultimatum?

Dean: Call it whatever you want. It's where I
   stand. And I know where you stand, so
   I'm not sure there's anything more
   to say.

I stare at my phone, willing her to reply. Willing her to finally offer me more. She doesn't, and every time I look over my shoulder, she's snuggling closer to tonight's date. The sight gnaws at my gut. I can't decide if she's trying to make me jealous or if she really believes that doesn't fuck with me.

This is better. I need to cut ties. No more fooling myself into believing she has more to offer than she really does.

As I force myself to look away for the tenth time, I notice Abbi Matthews sitting in one of the back booths, smiling up at Vince Brunetti. Oh, *hell* no.

ଛ

ABBI

"What about tomorrow night?" Vince asks, his eyes slipping down to my breasts for the hundredth time since he took up his position at the end of my booth two minutes ago. My shirt's not even low-cut, but Vince's gaze is so searing that I feel exposed anyway. And a little dirty.

"Vince . . ." I sigh, shifting in my seat. "It's just that I'm not looking for anything serious." *Not with you, at least.*

"I'm okay with casual," he says, licking his too-pink lips. "Casual can be a lot of fun."

I should say yes. I should go out with Vince and get practice dating. But what I really need is practice doing the *other stuff* that comes with dating, and Vince . . . well, I just don't think I can do it.

"Have you ever been *taken care of* by a real man, Abigail?"

"Pretty sure she's trying to let you down gently, Vince," Dean says, sliding into the booth across from me like he belongs there. "Take the hint and back off."

"Oh," Vince says, backing up a step. He waves a finger back and forth between us. "I see what's going on here."

I wait for Dean to explain that we're just friends, but he folds his arms, leaning back in the booth and holding Vince's gaze in a way that can only be described as hostile. Apparently, Dean's playing the part of protective big brother tonight. *Lovely.*

Now I feel like everyone in the bar is looking at me—looking at *us* and wondering just what Vince is implying. And probably feeling sorry for me for thinking I have a chance with Dean.

"Does Kace know about this?" Vince asks. "Somehow I don't think he'd appreciate you fucking around with his little sister when we all know you have no intention of making an honest woman out of her." An *honest woman?* What is this, 1892? I barely hide my eye roll, but then Vince adds, "Especially when we all know you were fucking his wife."

Just like that, Dean's out of the booth and in Vince's face. "What'd you just say?"

Vince's ruddy cheeks turn bright red as he stumbles back. "Nothing. I don't know what I'm talking about."

Dean moves to follow him before I make it out of my side of the booth and grab his arm. "Don't. Please?"

Dean doesn't take another step, but there's so much fury in his eyes, I'm not surprised when Vince back-pedals all the way out the front door.

"I'm sorry." I squeeze his wrist one more time before pulling away. Dean is warm and strong, and since I turned fifteen, I've made sure to never touch him more than necessary, to never let physical affection betray the depth of my emotional affection.

Dean glares at the glass door until Vince disappears from sight. Only then does he turn to me. The moment his eyes connect with mine, all his rage melts away and is replaced with apology. "I'm the one who's sorry. He made it sound like you're . . . like we . . ."

Is he embarrassed at the prospect of someone thinking we're messing around? Disgusted? I bow my head and slide back into the booth. "It's fine," I mutter. "I don't think anyone actually believes we're having a secret affair."

"You can't be seriously interested in that guy," he says, taking the bench across from me. *Really?* He's going to stay and chat after *that*?

"I'm not."

"You're interested enough to make him press you. That's new."

"I wanted to be interested, but it turns out I'm not." *Especially now.* Bringing up Amy was low, and implying that Dean slept with Amy while she and Kace were still together was even worse. Dean's made mistakes, but he'd *never* do that.

He drums his fingers on the table, studying me. "I need you to explain that to me. Why would you *want* to be interested in Vince if you're *not* interested in Vince?"

"I just . . ." I look around to make sure no one can overhear our conversation. "I'd just like to get comfortable with . . . *stuff,* ya know?"

Dean arches a brow. "Stuff?"

"You know, like, dating stuff."

He folds his arms on top of the table and leans forward, head cocked toward me. "You're going to have to explain. What *dating stuff?* There's nothing to learn. Pay if you want; don't if you don't want. Go to coffee if that sounds good, or dinner if you prefer. It's all personal preference. There's no wrong way to do it except any way that makes you uncomfortable. Come on, furries are a thing. You can't fuck this up."

I snort-laugh and shake my head. "Not *that* dating stuff," I say, but honest to God, I don't know why I'm still talking. If this were a text message, I would've killed it with the delete key *way* back there.

Dean's eyes go wide. "Physical stuff?"

Alarm bells blare in my head. *Delete, delete, delete.* "I'm bad at it, okay? So bad that my worries about it mess with how I act beforehand." *God, why am I still talking?*

"Bad at what, exactly?"

I squeeze my eyes shut. "Why are you doing this to me? Do you hate me? Do you want me to look for the closest rock to curl under?"

"I'm serious." He smiles, all traces of the Vince-induced rage gone at the mere whiff of making me uncomfortable. *Butthead.* "I want to know what it is you think you're so bad at."

"All of it," I blurt, mostly because if I have to be uncomfortable, he should be too. Serves him right. "Sex."

"You think you're bad at . . . *sex.*" He says the words as if he's repeating something absurd. Like the way you'd repeat someone who insists that cats walk on two legs or that boxed mac and cheese is better than homemade.

"I *know* I'm bad at sex."

"I— What—" He shakes his head. "Can we back up a little?"

"Nope." I shake my head. "We're just going to pretend this conversation never happened. No backing up, no starting over, no remembering it at all. This didn't happen. I wasn't even here. This was all a figment of your imagination."

Dean chuckles. "No. You're not getting off the hook that easy. You just told me you were considering going out with Vincent Brunetti because you want to get better at sex." He presses a palm to his chest. "Now I feel like it's my duty to make sure you find a better"—he clears his throat and grins—"*tool* for the job."

I fold my arms on the table and bury my face in them. "Someone wake me up. I'm having a terrible nightmare."

CHAPTER FOUR

ABBI

*D*ean nudges me with his elbow. "Abbi, come on. Talk to me."

"Smithy!" I call, barely lifting my head when I see my friend pass our table. "I need more alcohol. Stat!"

Smithy stops, tray full of beer pitchers resting on one hand. "You're gonna have to be more specific, baby girl. Alcohol is kind of what we do here."

I look to Dean. "What's a good way to get drunk fast?"

His eyes go wide. "Faster than those martinis you drink?"

"Yes! Faster than that."

He chokes on a laugh. "Uh, shots, I guess?"

I nod. "Let's do it." I raise my hand. "Smithy, three shots of tequila."

"Holy fuck, what are you doing?" Dean mutters.

"If you insist on continuing this conversation, I'm going to do everything in my power *not* to remember it. Thanks."

Dean smirks. "Bring her the salt and the limes too," he says without taking his eyes off me.

"Sure thing," Smithy says, already moving on to deliver the beer.

Dean's still staring at me, so I respond the mature way and hide my face in my arms until Smithy returns with one of the boards used for beer flights. There are four small glasses on the board. Three shots of golden memory eraser all in a row, one glass of lime wedges, and in the fifth spot he has a salt shaker.

I lift my head as Smithy slides it in front of me, but before I can grab a shot, Dean reaches out and drags the board in front of himself.

"Those are mine," I say, though I'm already having second thoughts about the wisdom of *three* shots. One I can probably handle, but three? Chances are I'll be sharing with Dean, anyway. Either that or leaving a shot or two untouched.

"Oh, I'll give them to you," he says, picking up one and examining it in the light. "One shot in exchange for one piece of information."

"It doesn't work that way. I bought those."

"I don't care." Grinning, he nods to my hands. "Lick your wrist."

"What?" I gasp.

"For the salt, prude."

I narrow my eyes and hold his gaze as I swipe my tongue across the inside of my wrist before sprinkling the skin with salt. "Does this mean I get my shot?"

"In a second."

I sigh. I could leave. There's no one here forcing me to be subjected to this. I could go home and get drunk and not have to worry about Dean prying embarrassing secrets out of me. But drinking alone is depressing, and I don't want to go home. I want to figure out how I'm going to use the next six weeks to become less awful at dating and, yes, at sex. I want to feel excited rather than terrified of a potential romantic relationship with Frankie. Maybe Dean will have some advice.

It's probably stupid to try, because I *am* bad at sex, and nothing I can do in the next six weeks is likely to change that. If Frankie and I do end up in bed, that'll be the end of it. It always is.

"When was the last time you had sex?" Dean asks.

My cheeks are *on fire*. "You did not just ask me that."

"I did. Now answer."

"Eighteen months ago," I mumble.

His eyes go wide. "Excuse me?"

"Eighteen. Months. Ago." I snatch the shot from his hand, lick the salt from my wrist, and toss back the tequila. I grimace at the burn as it goes down. "Jesus," I sputter, reaching for a lime. "It's been a long time since I've done that."

"Not as long as it's been since you've done something else," Dean says, handing me a lime.

I glare. "Shut up." I shove the lime into my mouth.

He chuckles. "God, you're adorable when you're flustered."

I try to grab another shot, but he slides them out of my reach. "*Vince* is the tool?" I ask. "Really?"

He chuckles again. "Answer another question, and I'll give you another shot. Easy-peasy."

I glare at him then point to the shots. "Fine, but you're paying for those."

"No problem. So you haven't had sex in a year and a half?"

"Is that your question?"

He considers this for a beat before shaking his head. "No. My question is . . ." He swallows, and his tongue touches his bottom lip in a way I'd find incredibly *hot* if this were anyone else. On Dean, I can only acknowledge it's hot *objectively speaking*. "Did you like it?"

I look at my lap. I'm still in the black pants I wore to work today, and they're tight around my too-thick thighs. I'm so embarrassed to be having this conversation with Dean. "It was okay," I say without looking up.

He coughs. "Right."

I snap my head up, ready to punch him if he's mocking me. "What?"

"Nothing about sex should be *okay*. Was any of it good?"

"I mean, it was all fine. I just . . ." I bite my bottom lip. There's no way to finish that sentence that doesn't make me want to crawl under my blankets and never come back out.

"You didn't like it." I glare, and he holds up his hands. "With all due respect, *why* do you think you're bad at it?"

"It was made clear . . ." I shake my head, scowling when I realize Dean's still staring. "Would you stop looking at me like that?"

"Like what?"

"Like I'm some weird insect you found crawling in your kitchen."

He chuckles. "Abbi, I'm *not* looking at you like you're an insect. I'm offended."

I roll my eyes. "You know what I mean."

He shakes his head. "I still don't believe it."

I set my jaw and give him my best glare. "Believe it, okay? Or don't. I don't care. Please drop it."

"I don't think you understand," he says. "What I don't believe is that a woman as confident and self-assured as you would believe she's bad in bed."

The only parts of my life where I could be accurately described as "confident" and "self-assured" are in the kitchen and with my friendships. Those words are galaxies away from bedroom-Abbi, and they'll never exist in the same universe as naked-Abbi. Sighing, I shake my head. "Well, it happens, right? So here I am."

"I don't think it really does, though. I don't believe *bad in bed* is actually a thing."

"Okay." Leaning forward, I drop my voice. "Let someone who has *way more* experience with this let you in on a sad truth: bad in bed is *totally* a thing."

"Nah." He drapes his arm across the booth seat and leans back. He snags a shot from the tray and tips it to his lips, sipping it like it's fancy bourbon. "Physically incompatible partners are a thing. Not every pair has chemistry. Bad experiences, those definitely happen. Then there's the unenthusiastic or selfish partner—that's a thing too—or one who's detached for one reason or another, though generally both of those also come down to a lack of chemistry."

"Semantics," I mutter.

"But semantics *matter*," Dean says. "To say someone's *bad in bed* implies that no matter who that person took to bed, the experience would be a bad one."

"Yes, I'm aware of the literal definition," I mutter. I keep slinking lower in the booth, but despite cashing in on every wish I ever failed to make in my twenty-five years, I simply don't disappear.

"That's just a bunch of bullshit right there," he says. "I don't buy it."

"And I don't want to be having this conversation. Just pretend I never said it."

"I can't. I'm sitting here with you, and instead of having a drink with my bud Abbi, I'm drinking with my bud Abbi who believes she's bad in bed."

I narrow my eyes. Am I drunk? Can you get drunk off one shot? "We're the same people."

"This revelation really bothers me, Abs."

"Why?" I growl. Dean's not cruel, so I know he isn't trying to make me feel uncomfortable, but I don't understand what his end game is here. "Why do you even care?"

"Well, first of all, I'd like to put my fist into the face of whatever guy put the idea in your head."

"It wasn't their fault," I blurt.

Dean's brows shoot up. "More than one asshole. Good to know."

"Listen, my prior partners can't be held responsible for what I do or don't know, or for how I act or look in the bedroom."

He holds up a hand. "Okay, now we're onto something. What you do or don't know is experience versus inexperience, which is another thing that definitely exists, but it doesn't make someone bad in bed. If I'd never kissed someone before, it's pretty unlikely I'd knock your socks off the first time I put my tongue in your mouth, but give me a few tries at it, and I'll get better. That doesn't make me a bad kisser, just an inexperienced one." He leans forward. "The same goes for other things."

"Listen, I know I'm not exactly the kind of girl guys dream about having in their beds. And I know—"

"Wait. Hold up. *What?*" Bless his heart, he's staring at me as if what I just said isn't *completely obvious.*

This is what turns perfectly normal women into reclusive cat ladies. Moments like this. I want to crawl out of my skin. "Don't make me do this."

"No. For real, back up." He drags a hand over his beard and blows out a breath. "You think guys don't *want* you? Because they don't flirt with you?"

"I'm not doing this. I can't. Tequila be damned." I grab my purse and throw some cash on the table. "I'll see you later. Please don't mention this conversation again. Better yet, forget it altogether." I slide out of the booth and stride toward the door as fast as my short legs can carry me.

"Abbi!" Dean calls behind me. I hear him mutter a curse then, "I'll be right back, Smith."

I don't stop. I keep going, pushing through the door and back out into the sticky, hot evening. I'm not built for Georgia summers, and I totally envy girls like Brinley who can deal with the heat by wearing thin, flowy dresses with nothing on under them. Those dresses make me feel terribly self-conscious. They show every roll at best. At worst, they make it look like I'm expecting a baby. So for me it's T-shirts and leggings or cropped jeans, because I haven't been brave enough to include shorts in my wardrobe since junior high. But tonight, my pants feel way too thick and tight on my skin. I'm burning all over from embarrassment.

"Abbi!" Dean calls again, catching up to me on the sidewalk. "I'm sorry, okay?"

It's not until I see the tenderness in his eyes that I

realize how close I am to tears. I walked here and my house is straight ahead, but I turn down the alley and lean against the side of the building, swallowing hard as if that'll keep the tears at bay. I do *not* want to cry about this right now. Or ever.

I know my little problem can't be all about my size. I know for a fact there are big women in this world whom men *enjoy* sleeping with. I just need to learn how to be one of them.

"Hey," Dean whispers, propping one arm against the side of the building by my head. He leans forward and looks down into my eyes. "I didn't mean to make you feel shitty, and I'm sorry I handled that so badly."

Dean's almost a foot taller than me. I always dreamed I'd end up with a guy like him, someone built enough that I don't feel massive next to him in bed—not that I ever gave those dreams much thought. There's a food chain in dating, and I've known my place in it since puberty. But as he looks down at me with those deep brown eyes, I can almost imagine what it'd be like to be with him. I can almost imagine what it'd be like to have his flirty smiles directed at me.

The problem is I don't want to imagine it. I don't want to fool myself into thinking I'm something I'm not.

I press my palm against his hard chest, trying to nudge him back. "It's fine. I just don't want to talk about it."

Dean stays put for a long beat as he scans my face. When his phone buzzes, he sighs and retreats two steps. "But I think maybe you should."

Never. "Just not right now," I say, forcing a smile.

He nods. I expect him to walk away and drop it forever, so I'm surprised when he wraps his hand around my wrist as if he doesn't want me to go yet. He searches my face. Is there something more than concern in those eyes? Do they study my lips longer than necessary?

He smells so good, like hickory and sage and a cool night bundled up by a fire, and I'm aware of every beat of my pulse against his fingertips. "What?" This moment isn't what my mind wants to make it into, and I need one of us to say something that distracts me from the dark brown of his eyes and how soft his lips look.

"I've told you this before, but you deserve—"

"Dean? What are you doing out here?"

The sound of Amy's voice is enough to make me jerk away—from his smell, from his touch, from those eyes that see too much. "Later," I rasp. I duck under his arm and stride past Amy and toward my house, and when I hear her speak again, I pretend I don't hear. But even when I'm home in the safe solitude of my apartment, her words echo in my mind like a punch to the gut.

"You can't stand that close to a girl like Abbi," she told Dean. "You'll give her ideas and make her want things she can't have."

"Don't worry, Amy," I say, staring at my reflection in the foyer mirror, noting the pink flush in my puffy cheeks. "I know exactly what I can and can't have."

DEAN

I'm a mess. Standing next to the woman I love, the one I just bared my soul to over text message, and watching the one I've wanted for way too long walk away.

Stella says it's a form of self-sabotage, the way I latch on
to women who don't want me, who'll never give me what
she seems to think I "deserve." Stella's a good sister who
only sees the best in me, but she doesn't understand that a
lot of women want better than a guy like me.

"You can't stand that close to a girl like Abbi," Amy says,
pulling attention off Abbi's retreating form. "You'll give her
ideas and make her want things she can't have."

I frown at her. "What the fuck does that mean?"

She rolls her eyes and waves it away. "Never mind. I'm
only out here because we need to talk." She swallows.
"About what you said in your text."

My chest blooms with hope. "Yeah? What do you
think?"

"I think we've had this conversation before," she says,
sounding resigned and . . . hell, frustrated. I can't blame her.
When we started sleeping together again, I told her I could
handle a fling. I was lying. I thought we both knew that,
and I'm irritated with myself that I expected her to ignore
my words and read my thoughts.

"Well, I guess there's no need to have it again, then."

I start to walk away, but she stops me with a hand on my
arm. "You don't really want me, Dean."

"The fuck I don't." Spinning around, I shake off her
touch. "Do you want me to prove it? Tell me how. I'll get
right to it."

She folds her arms. "I know your type. You're attracted
to the rush, the hookup, the quickies in the bar bathroom
and drunken fucks in the back of an Uber."

She's not wrong. I do like those things, and I've enjoyed
them all with her, but that's my *history*, not my *type*. If
anything, my *type* is the girl who just walked away. Nothing

else would explain why I'm still carrying a torch for her four years after she made it clear she'd never settle for a guy like me. "What does any of that have to do with *us*?"

"When we mess around, you're getting fun, single Amy." She tucks her blond hair behind her ear and gives me a shaky smile. "But I'm only her half the time. The other half, I'm a busy mom. I have to rush home to get Hope to dance practice and then rush to get dinner on the table so we can eat before I give her a bath and get her ready for bed."

I turn my palms up. None of this is a surprise. I know Amy. I know her life and her priorities and have never complained about Hope coming first. "I don't see a problem."

"What is it you think you want? To move in with me? To play daddy?"

Heat creeps up my neck, because . . . yes. That's exactly what I was thinking. "I'm not trying to replace Kace."

"But you would be. Half the week, you'd be the surrogate dad, and your life would be hella unsatisfying."

"I don't see it that way." To be honest, I've pictured everything she's describing. That's part of the appeal. I love fun, drunk Amy. Horny Amy. Naughty Amy. We have a good time. The sex is amazing. But I fell for her because she's more than that. She's a good mom. Despite my track record, I've always wanted a family. I've just never been in a hurry to start one with the wrong person.

"I've given this a lot of thought," she says, turning her head toward the Friday night traffic passing through the town square. "That's why I've never offered you more than a fling, why I always said this had to be a no-strings arrangement. My life is what it is, and I can't bring you into Hope's world and have you break her heart the day you realize that's not the life you want."

I swallow. It makes sense that she's trying to protect Hope. It's the kind of mother she is. This isn't necessarily about me and what I do and don't have to offer. "What if it *is* the life I want?"

She sighs and turns back to me. "How could it be? Most days, it's not even the life I want. That fact destroyed my marriage. I won't let it hurt Hope too."

"You really think that little of me?" I shove my hands in my pockets. I need a fucking drink. The ups and downs of this conversation are destroying me. "I'd never hurt Hope."

"Not intentionally," she says softly.

I hate that we're standing on a busy street right now. I hate that I can't pull her into my arms and make her all the promises she needs to hear. But I'm not sure it'd matter anyway.

"It'd be different if you had a different track record, but you don't know what it's like to date someone boring— someone you didn't meet at a bar, who spends more time at home than out being fun, who's a little frumpy because she has to prioritize real life over her appearance. You've never dated someone like that."

My blood runs cold. "You're saying you won't give me a chance for something real because my prior girlfriends were too *fun*?"

"I'm *saying* you need a reality check."

"That's really fucking screwed up, Amy." Screwed up. Insulting. And evidence she doesn't feel the same way about me that I feel about her. I tilt my face toward the sky and squeeze my eyes shut. At least I tried before giving up. "I guess this is goodbye for good, then."

Her hand is warm on my arm, and I wonder at how a gentle touch can hurt so much. "I'm sorry, Dean."

"Me too." I turn back into the bar before I weaken and ask her to reconsider. I did everything I could to prove myself. She's right. It is time for a reality check. If I was what she wanted, we'd still be together now. We wouldn't have broken it off. It's time for me to let it go.

CHAPTER FIVE

ABBI

J'm in a terrible mood. I'm the storm clouds that are so dark they blot out the sun.

I check my phone for the twentieth time and blow out an aggravated breath when I see nothing. Again.

I'm an idiot. One, to think I could just jump into dating without changing anything else about myself, and two, to have agreed to meet Austin, a.k.a. RimsandRepos, at Smithy's, where all my friends can see me get stood up on my first attempt at dating in nine months.

I open the Random app on my phone and tap out a message to RimsandRepos.

> BrownEyedGirl25: I hope you're okay. I'm going to head out. Maybe another time.

I send the message and immediately cringe. Someone

who stands me up and doesn't even bother to message me with an explanation doesn't deserve "another time," but it seems bitchy to just *assume* he stood me up.

> RimsandRepos: Sorry. Something came up. I
> don't think we'd work anyway.

Something came up or he got one look at me and didn't think we'd "work" because of my appearance? My stomach turns sour, and hot tears prick the back of my eyes. I push away my martini. I type and delete a reply four different times.

Wow. Okay. Delete.

Whatever you say. Delete.

You could've messaged instead of leaving me waiting for an hour. Delete.

Whatever. You do you. Delete.

Nope. Sometimes the best reply is no reply at all.

But what if I'm right? What if he came in here, saw me, and ran the other way? It's not like I hide myself on my Random account. My avatar is a selfie of my face, and while I'll admit it's a flattering angle, it doesn't *not* look like me. I don't advertise I'm a big girl on there either, though. Maybe I should. Maybe it should be the first line of my bio.

If you're not man enough for a big girl, don't waste my time.

I wish I had that kind of confidence.

I'm staring at my phone when someone slides into the booth across from me. Not my failed attempt at a date but someone I'm equally uninterested in seeing tonight.

"Hey, Abster!" he says, grinning at me.

I frown at him. Hudson is twenty-two, fresh out of college with an exercise science degree and a new personal training certification. He's a sweet guy, but I'm not in the mood to be proselytized to by someone trying to convert me to the Church of Health and Fitness.

"Haven't seen you at the gym lately," he says, predictably.

"That's because I'm not a member?" I say, but it comes out sounding like a question.

"Whaaaaat?" He shakes his head and presses his palm to his chest dramatically. "Don't tell me you work out at my competitor's gym."

Since the day spa that houses my restaurant has the most popular fitness classes in town, I technically *work for* his competitor, but I don't point that out. "Nope." I force a smile. *He means well, Abbi. Don't tear into the boy.* "I'm not much of a gym rat, to be honest."

"You don't have to be a gym rat to enjoy health and fitness." He props one elbow on the table and leans forward. "Listen, I know the whole group-class scene isn't for everyone. Neither is coming in and grinding on a cardio machine. But if you sign up for a series of sessions with me, I can put together a program for you. Workouts and an eating plan—the whole bit."

Quick. Someone kill me now. I glance toward the bar, hoping to catch Smithy's eye and get him to save me, but he's oblivious as always, flirting with one of his servers.

"I couldn't help but notice you ordered the lemon drop martini," Hudson says, nodding at the barely touched drink. "Now, I know girls like their frou-frou drinks, but there's a good twenty grams of sugar in one of those—and that's assuming the bartender didn't go heavy on the simple syrup. I could teach you how to make better choices without completely eliminating the occasional drink. After a couple of weeks, you'll feel like a new woman."

"I don't want to feel like a new woman. I like the woman I am." I mentally high-five myself for that little lie. At least I *want* it to be true. It's a start.

Hudson throws his head back and laughs. He really is cute. Too bad he's a diet-and-exercise pusher. "So do I, obviously." He winks at me. "But who doesn't want to have more energy?"

I sigh. "I work on my feet forty to fifty hours a week, Hudson. I have no desire to go to the gym before or after work." It's not that I don't move my body outside of work, but I'd rather not get his opinion of my walking and yoga routines. Those are things I do for myself, and I don't need his dude-bro input.

His gaze flicks down my body. "I respect that. Seriously. But I promise I wouldn't make you too sore." He winks again, and I'm so damn confused. Was that an innuendo? Is he trying to flirt with the fat girl, or get her to lose weight? Or is flirting part of his sales ploy? *Yuck.*

"Abbi!"

Hudson and I both turn to see the curvy blonde sauntering toward us, glass of wine in hand. Layla's a big girl like me, but unlike me, she's stunning. She looks like one of those plus-size models—the ones who wear every damn outfit so well that I practically need a pop-up built into my web browser that reminds me the clothes on my screen will *not* make me look as good or feel as confident as the model appears.

Tonight, Layla's rocking a retro polka-dot dress that shows off all her assets, with red Mary Jane heels and matching lipstick. Her platinum-blond hair has been pinned into curls at the nape of her neck, perfecting the fifties pinup look.

I bet RimsandRepos wouldn't have suddenly had something come up if he'd seen *her* waiting for him.

"Hey, hey," Hudson says, sticking a hand in Layla's direction. "I don't think we've met before. I'm Hudson, but my friends call me Hause."

Dear Lord. I cringe. First, I don't believe anyone in the history of ever has called Hudson *Hause*. It's an aspirational nickname at best. Second, I swear he sees dollar signs when he looks at big girls. Luckily, Layla's unlikely to be swayed by his sales pitch.

"Hudson, this is Layla, our new catering coordinator at The Orchid, so she's the liaison between me and Brinley for our large events. Layla, this is Hudson. He works at Mainstreet Fitness and will sell you personal training sessions and protein powders galore the second you let your guard down."

They both laugh at this as they shake hands.

"I didn't mean to interrupt your date," Layla says to me. "I just saw you over here and wanted to say hi." She turns to Hudson. "I'm new in town, so any time I'm out and about and see a familiar face, I turn into an excitable puppy."

"Oh." My cheeks heat as her words register. "This isn't a date. Not at all."

Hudson flashes me a look I can't quite interpret, but it's a pretty fair guess that he too is mortified by the assumption. "I was just saying hi too," he says. He points over his shoulder toward a group of dude-bros at the nearest pool table. "I'll get back to my friends."

"Wait," Layla says as he climbs out of the booth. "Do

you have, like, a card or anything? I haven't found a new trainer since my move."

Grinning, Hudson reaches into his back pocket to retrieve a card. "Absolutely. Here ya go. We can do a one-time consultation to chat goals or set up weekly sessions or anything in between—it's entirely up to you."

"Awesome. I'm into powerlifting. You do that?"

He beams. "Hell yeah. I do a more traditional strength split myself, but I train a few powerlifters. Give me a call, and we'll work something out."

Layla does an excited little shimmy and tucks his card into her purse. "Can't wait!" She watches him go before sliding into the booth across from me. "Girrrrrl, he is so into you."

I laugh and am still laughing when Smithy shows up at my table to check on me and my lemon drop martini. I suddenly feel like draining the whole thing and *every single one* of its twenty grams of sugar. Hudson isn't into me. He looks at me and sees dollar signs.

"What's so funny?" Smithy asks.

Layla says, "I was just—"

"Nothing," I say. I don't need Smithy getting Layla's nutty ideas in his head. "Just girl talk."

Layla arches a brow at me but keeps her mouth shut until he walks away again. "You seriously didn't see that? With the trainer?"

"See what?"

"He was checking you out and doing everything he could to keep your attention on him. There's a *reason* I assumed you were on a date."

I laugh again and take a sip of my martini. Lemony

sweetness. *So good.* "What you saw was Hudson giving me the hard sell. He wants my business, not my body."

She takes a sip from her wine. "He was using his business as an excuse to get closer to your body."

"You're delusional."

"I'm *astute*," she says, winking.

I sigh. "So you lift, huh?"

"Yeah. I love being strong. It's rad."

I shudder. "I think I'm allergic to gyms. I've tried the ones in town a couple of different times and feel like everyone is staring at me. I prefer doing stuff on my own."

She licks her lips, and her perfect red lipstick doesn't budge. I'm pretty sure she's a magical creature. "Well, that's cool too, but don't let your aversion to the gym keep you from sampling a little hot trainer ass." She casts a long, meaningful glance over her shoulder toward Hudson. "Damn, you could bounce quarters off those glutes."

I grin. I really like working with Layla. She's nice and organized and never screws me over by making promises to clients that the kitchen can't deliver on, but I've never hung out with her outside of work. "Why don't *you* go after him?" At least I could picture that.

She shakes her head. "Nah. I'm already taken. My boyfriend is still in Nashville, but he's relocating to Orchid Valley next month to move in with me."

"Wow. Serious, then?"

"Absolutely. I had my share of fun in college, but I'm not about letting men waste my time anymore."

"Good for you," I say, and I mean it.

"If you aren't here for Hudson, what brings you in tonight?" she asks, looking around. "Just chillin'?"

I consider lying—after all, who wants to admit their

date blew them off?—but I like Layla. "I was supposed to be meeting someone, but he didn't show. Or rather . . ." I tap my phone a few times to bring up Random and my chat stream with Austin then hand over my phone.

Layla frowns at the screen. "What the actual fuck? Lame."

Some of the heaviness that's been sitting in my gut lifts away. "Right?"

"You dodged a bullet."

"I keep thinking that he saw me and ran away."

"As if." She hands back my phone then looks me over critically. "He's probably married and found out his wife was gonna be here or something."

I shrug. "Maybe. Who knows?"

"Well, since you don't have Mr. Jackass to keep you company, do you mind if I do?"

"I'd love that."

DEAN

Smithy's is packed tonight—both inside and out. The night air has that perfect crispness that promises cooler days ahead, and I'm in a fucking fantastic mood.

I just landed a new contract at work—the biggest renovation we've done in years, on a historical home that some money-hungry landlord violated by chopping into apartments, and we're renovating it back to a single-family home. On top of that, I haven't talked to Amy all week, which makes two weeks since I've been to bed with her. I didn't even text her to ask how her week went or show up at The

Terminal last night when she posted on her Insta that she was there and looking for company.

I feel almost invincible.

I've spent most of the evening out on Smithy's newly renovated patio nursing a single beer. I've been chatting with Marston and his business partner, Alec, who's visiting for the week, but when I come inside to get a second beer, I see I've been missing the best company of all. Abbi is sitting in a booth at the back with a woman I don't recognize.

Abbi is the reason I got through this week. Instead of thinking of Amy and letting my mind snag on a thousand what-ifs, my thoughts were circling back to Abbi and her belief that she's bad at sex.

Instead of almost texting Amy a dozen times, it was Abbi whose name I kept pulling up on my phone, Abbi whom all my bad ideas revolved around.

My best friend's little sister is off-limits, and I know it. Not just because Kace wants better for his sister than someone like me, but because I put myself out there years ago and she made it clear she had her sights set on a different kind of guy. Any attraction I felt for her, any hope I'd carried around that she might someday return some of my feelings—I locked it away after the night of her twenty-first birthday. Never to be seen or spoken of again.

The only time I slipped was last year at Halloween, and even that barely counts. But now that I know her issues with guys revolve around her self-esteem and some ridiculous notion that she's bad in bed, I can't stop thinking about it. Sure, maybe I'll never be the guy she wants something real with, but I accepted that a long time ago. I'm not exactly looking to get my heart involved right now, anyway. So maybe I'm the perfect candidate to keep her from practicing horrifyingly poor judgment and using Vince Brunetti to find confidence in bed.

"Another beer?" Smithy asks me from behind the bar.

I pull my gaze off Abbi and nod. "The Jackson Brews hazy, if you have any left."

Smithy nods, fills a glass, and slides it across the bar. "I see you checkin' out Abbi's new friend. Hot, isn't she?"

I do a half-turn and look. I was focused on Abbi and didn't pay any attention to her friend. The blonde is Abbi's opposite in almost every way. Her clothes, makeup, and tattoos are flashy, whereas everything about Abbi is a calculated move to keep people from noticing her. I've always known this, but with last week's added little peek into her self-esteem issues, it's as obvious as ever. "Do you know who she is?" I ask Smithy.

"Works at The Orchid. New to town. You should see if she wants to get your mind off you-know-who."

You know who. As if Amy now has the powers of Voldemort and Smithy can't bring himself to say her name.

"The new girl seems more your type than mine," I say, turning back to Smithy before he catches me staring at Abbi. He's far too perceptive, and I have no intention of sharing my plans.

Smithy shrugs. "They're all my type." He winks before heading down the bar to help another customer.

When I turn back to check on Abbi, her friend is climbing out of the booth and swinging her purse over her shoulder. Perfect timing. I wait until she's stepped away before making my way across the room and taking the empty seat.

Abbi looks up at me from where she was tucking her

phone into her purse, and I realize she was about to head out too. "Hey, Dean," she says wearily.

"Hey, Abs." My smile falls away when I realize she's dressed up—a black short-sleeve shirt that falls off one shoulder, and pink lip gloss any man in his right mind would immediately want to taste. "Where are you heading?"

She frowns. "Home. Why?"

I shrug. "Just making sure you weren't going to do something crazy, like have Vince Brunetti help you with your . . . confidence issues."

She closes her eyes, and I see her questioning every decision that brought her to this moment. "You know, I used to be one of those people who didn't believe in regrets. Who thought they were a waste of time. You've cured me of that. I officially have regrets—well, at least one. One big regret."

"Let me guess." I grin. "Not letting me kiss you last Halloween?"

Her cheeks get pink and her brown eyes narrow, and I get all of her attention. Fuck me, but I've always loved riling her up. "I didn't think you remembered that," she says.

I scoff. "Of course I remember it." *That and your twenty-first.* But we don't talk about Halloween, so we *definitely* don't talk about her twenty-first. "I was a little buzzed, but I wasn't hammered. You flat-out rejected me, Abigail Matthews."

"Did you just full-name me?"

"Yeah, that's what you do when you're disappointed in someone, right? Because the nickname can't carry the weight of your disappointment?"

She folds her arms, and her shirt shifts to expose the swell of her cleavage. My mouth goes dry. I've been thinking about her a lot this week—maybe even latching on to thoughts of her. She's my security blanket, keeping me from doing something stupid. "And *why* are you disappointed in me?"

"*That night,*" I say, dragging my gaze back to her face, "I was disappointed that you didn't let me kiss you." I stop at her mouth—full and pink and shiny. "I wanted to."

"Well . . ." She swallows then shakes her head. "It's probably better you didn't, though, right?"

"I don't know." I lean back. "I've told myself that quite a few times, but . . . hell, if I could stop thinking about it, maybe I'd agree."

She squeaks and glances toward the exit, as if planning her escape.

"What are you thinking?" I ask.

"I'm thinking you're confusing me."

I smile. It's a start. "How so?"

"Because." She lifts her chin and levels me with the *fuck off* gaze that serves so well to keep other guys at a distance. "You don't want to kiss me. I rejected you, and you took it as some sort of challenge. If you *think* you want to kiss me, it's only because your fragile male ego can't stand that I passed on the opportunity."

"Hmm." I prop an elbow on the table and lean on my hand. "Maybe you should let me kiss you now, then. Just to test your theory."

She blinks at me, pink creeping into her cheeks. I love frazzling her. "Take my word for it. If you kissed me, that strange impulse would go away before you could say *big mistake.*"

"Doubt it," I mutter. "But maybe we should recap . . ."

"Please don't."

I hold up one finger. "You think you're bad in bed, which isn't a thing, but you persist in believing it despite my clear and rational argument to the contrary."

"I'm pretending you didn't say that, since that conversation never happened."

I hold up a second finger. "And," I say, continuing before I can lose my nerve, "I still want to kiss you. I think the solution is obvious."

"I have no idea what you're talking about." She shakes her head, but her wide eyes give her away. She knows exactly what I'm suggesting. I know she's thought about it too. There's been a spark between us since she came home from college. She thinks I don't notice the way she looks at me sometimes, but I do. Physical attraction has never been to blame for keeping us apart.

I slide out of the booth then scoot into her side until we're thigh to thigh. When I lean down, I let my lips brush the shell of her ear as I whisper, "I think we should both get what we need. I need to kiss you. You need to learn that all it takes to be good in bed is chemistry."

CHAPTER SIX

ABBI

*M*y blood is on fire. His breath feels good against my ear—too good—and I need to remind myself who we are. I scoot toward the wall, putting space between us. My skin feels so hot that I might spontaneously combust.

I swallow hard. We have *never* talked about last Halloween. It happened and was promptly placed in the vault of Things Friends Don't Discuss, where it belonged. Dean was drunk and kept looking at me and I didn't know why, and then at some point we found ourselves alone in this very booth. Side by side, just like we are now.

He was laughing at my costume, a red Crayola crayon. He said most girls use Halloween as an excuse to show off their bodies, and that if any other woman showed up at Smithy's with the same costume idea, she'd wear a red miniskirt and matching tube top and written *RED*

CRAYON on her bare midriff with Magic Marker. Whereas I had dressed in long sleeves and long pants (both red, obviously), wearing an extra-large red pillowcase as a dress and a red poster board dunce cap on my head.

I told him I was sorry to disappoint and I was sure he'd have plenty of other opportunities to see *sexy red crayon*, but my costume was *respectable red crayon*. Then he asked me why I didn't think respectable red crayon was sexy, his lips brushing my ear like they did just now, my heart pounding madly like it is right now. Then his lips were so close to mine that I held my breath for several long beats before I remembered who I was and where we were. Girls like me don't get kissed by guys like Dean.

That voice saved me that night. Without it, I might've thought he was interested in me and not just drunk, horny, and alone. So I laughed in his face, shoved him away, and told him I needed another drink. And then we carried on as if it never really happened.

Whyyyy did he have to crack open the vault? Nothing good ever comes of that.

But the bigger question I can't get out of my head is: he's thought about that night? More than, like, in-that-moment, horny-and-lonely thought about it? I have. A little. Until I made myself stop.

I don't feel these things for Dean. I don't *want* these things from Dean. I don't *let myself.* I have a lot of wonderful things in my life. Hot guys with ooey-gooey hearts might not be on the list, but that's fine. Honestly, I just want a good guy—someone who makes me smile, who shares my interests, whose personality is enough of a turn-on that the superficial stuff doesn't matter.

Dean's gaze flicks down to the space I've put between us then back up to meet mine. "You afraid, Abigail?"

"No." I laugh and sound like a liar.

"I think you are." He shakes his head. "I don't get the feeling that this is a 'Hey, I don't want you, creep, so back off' kind of rejection. I think you're afraid of what might happen if I kiss you." Under the table, he finds my hand with his and strokes my knuckles with his thumb so gently that I practically jump out of my seat. "I think you're afraid to let me prove you're *not* bad in bed."

I close my eyes. I can hardly keep them open, because I want every bit of my awareness centered on his thumb. Stroking. Making me . . . *want*.

"It's your ball," he says. Then he climbs out of the booth, leaving me breathless with flushed skin and a racing heart. He leans over one last time to whisper in my ear, and the brush of his breath is like a caress I've been waiting my whole life for. "It's okay to be scared, but don't let fear keep you from going after what you want."

I KEEP LOOKING at my phone, but it turns out that willing someone to text you doesn't make it happen. I should know, because I've been willing Dean to text me all week.

I just need to know if he meant what he said at the bar on Saturday or if he was going through some sort of Amy detox that made him lose his mind for a minute. I don't know what I'm going to do if he *was* serious, but if he wasn't, at least I can stop thinking about it.

Alas, no text. No call. And tonight, I'm going to see him face to face again because, in a moment of idiocy, I promised my brother I'd come to his house to enjoy the nice weather around his firepit. Ten seconds after making that promise, I realized Dean would probably be there and almost made up an excuse to explain my absence, but . . . part of me wants to see him. Unfortunately, that's the same part of me that thinks a steamy fling with my brother's best friend sounds like a *grand* idea.

I shut down my computer. Time to face the music—just as soon as I change out of the clothes I've been working in all day. I look up from my desk and catch sight of a blond head passing my office. "Layla, could you hold up a minute?" I ask, walking around my desk. "I need to ask you something."

"Oh. Sure." She smiles, and I wave her into my office. "Is everything okay?" she asks as I shut the door behind her.

"Yes. Of course!" I look through my purse for a piece of gum just so I have something to do with my hands. "I just need a favor."

"Sure. Anything."

I swallow. So awkward. "I was wondering if you ever . . ." I clear my throat. "I mean, if you have free time this weekend, do you think you might . . ." *God, kill me now.*

"Oh." She presses a hand to her chest and crinkles her face in discomfort. "Oh my God, I'm super flattered, Abbi, but Brock and I are doing the exclusive thing."

I blink at her twice before I realize what her boyfriend has to do with anything. "Oh, no! I wasn't going to ask you out." My already hot cheeks blaze a degree hotter. Socially awkward much? "Not that you're not attractive, but I . . ." I look at the ceiling and shake my head. "I was going to ask if you had time to maybe . . . teach me to dress like you do. I mean, not exactly like you, because that would be weird, but, like"—I wave both hands up and down to indicate my general lack of style—"something better than this?"

"You don't like the way you dress?" she asks, cocking her head to the side. "You always look cute."

"Thank you." I take a deep breath and blurt out the little speech I've been planning all day. "My fashion choices are mostly driven by the desire to stay hidden, and my New Year's resolution was to be less afraid." Dean's words echo in my head. *It's okay to be scared, but don't let fear keep you from going after what you want.*

"New Year's . . . resolution?" she asks.

I nod.

"It's September."

Cringing, I turn up my palms. "I'd better hurry, right?"

She chuckles then nods. "I get it, and I'd love to, but I'll be out of town this weekend—gotta visit the man before the event schedule gobbles up all our weekends."

"Oh, sure. Of course. No problem."

"But maybe next weekend? You just want to go shopping?"

I nod. "Yeah. I was thinking you could help me pick out a few new outfits and maybe teach me how to do my makeup and . . ." I thread my fingers through my limp hair. "And do something with this?"

"Sounds like fun," she says.

My shoulders sag. "You're a goddess. Thank you so much."

"That's usually what people say to me *after* the date." She winks at me then opens the door, heading out. "I'll see you next week, Abbi."

So . . . *makeover—check.*

Next on the to-do list: seduction lessons with Dean. Maybe. Possibly. Probably not.

❦

DEAN

I'm a direct guy. I've never been one to flirt across a room or a crowded bar with nothing but eye contact. I prefer words. Subtle touches that progress to not-so-subtle touches. *Contact.*

But I guess there's a first time for everything. Abbi and I arrived at Kace's a few hours ago to spend the evening with our friends, and we haven't exchanged a word. The tension between us is undeniable. Or maybe that's all me.

Abbi's dark hair is down tonight, flowing past her bare shoulders to the middle of her back. Her cheeks are flushed, probably courtesy of the cans of sparkling wine she's been mainlining since she saw me arrive.

She's dressed in typical Abbi fashion—black cropped pants and a loose sleeveless top—but her feet are bare, her flip-flops discarded on the patio, and there's something unexpectedly sexy about seeing her curl her toes in the grass.

It's been years since I let myself really *look* at Abbi Matthews, years since I let myself indulge in fantasies of the woman who shut me down in such an epic way on her twenty-first birthday. So naturally, I spent a lot of time *thinking* in that week after offering to show her just how *good* she can be in bed.

A *lot* of time. Some of it's been innocent. Some of it's been straight-up X-rated.

I didn't let myself text her or randomly show up at The Orchid—even though I was tempted to do both. I let her stew in it. I realize I'm playing with fire here. Taking my best friend's little sister to bed just to prove something to her is insane. Add in some history and long-ago-buried *feelings*, and it's probably a recipe for disaster.

For this reason alone, I don't want to rush her. I might be okay with pushing the boundaries of our friendship, but maybe she's not. Hell, maybe I'm imagining the way she looks at me sometimes. Maybe she doesn't want to take me up on my offer because she's not attracted to me.

Only, she hasn't said no yet. And the way she keeps sneaking glances my way tells me I'm not the only one who's been doing some *thinking* this week.

"Kace," Abbi says, leaning on her brother in an uncharacteristically sloppy show of affection, "I'm so glad you bought this place. I swear I want to *live* at your pool next summer. I love it, and I love *you*, brother."

Kace stares at his sister, baffled. "Are you *drunk?*"

"Totally drunk," she says, nodding. "But you said I can crash in your guest room anytime, so it's *fine*."

I bite my lip, but I can't hold back my grin. *I did that.* I love that I've flustered her enough to throw her off her game.

"Would you two get a room?" Smithy says. He gives pointed looks to both Stella and Kace. "The eye-fucking is *out of control.*"

"Jealous, Smithy?" Stella calls.

"Damn straight I am. It's not fair that you get that fine ass in bed with you every night, Stella."

Stella laughs, and Kace smiles.

I'll admit I never expected my sister to end up with my

best friend, but I love seeing them both so happy. I want that for them. I open my mouth to tell Smith to mind his own business when he points at me and then Abbi.

"Those two are just as bad."

"What?" Abbi squeaks, and I have to bite back a grin.

Kace's eyes go wide and his face pales a bit, taking any thrill out of the moment for me. I might be happy to see my best friend with my sister, but clearly Kace doesn't feel the same way.

Kace takes a deep breath and waves a finger back and forth between me and Abbi. "Are you two . . . ? Seriously?"

Abbi's eyes go wide. "No! Why would you—"

Half because I've been dying to touch her and half because I'm a stubborn asshole, I step up behind her and wrap an arm around her waist. I lower my mouth to her ear and feel her shiver in my arms. "See?" I murmur. "Even Smithy can see the chemistry between us. So tell me what it'll be. Are we doing this?"

I search her face. It's been a week, and suddenly I feel like I can't breathe until I have my answer. Until I *know*.

Abbi swallows, but she doesn't take her gaze off me. "There's nothing happening here."

My stomach sinks at the clear rejection. *Nothing changes.*

"The lady doth protest too much," Smithy says. He offers his knuckles to me for a fist bump. I just arch a brow and leave him hanging. Abbi's protests aren't exactly the highlight of my night.

"Weirdos," Kace mutters, but he's already forgotten about us, his focus on Stella.

Abbi steps out of my arms like my touch did nothing for her. Like it meant nothing. And hell, maybe it didn't. Maybe I imagined everything.

CHAPTER SEVEN

ABBI

*M*y stomach flip-flops. I cannot believe Dean just asked me that question at my brother's house, in front of all our friends. If nothing else, this moment in this spot with these people should remind us exactly why we *shouldn't* be considering it.

"Where's your date tonight, Smith?" I ask, just to change the subject. I swear Smithy doesn't miss a damn thing, but right now I wish he would. I wish he'd miss a lot of things.

"No date," he replies, tilting his head back and gazing up at the stars. "Can't risk having a lady friend around when I'm doing Celibate September."

"What the fuck is Celibate September?" Dean asks. He takes a step away from me and shoves his hands in his pockets as if he's totally unfazed by the moment we just had. And maybe he is. Personally, I've been a mess all week while I tried to keep my attraction to Dean from overriding every logical argument against whatever it is he was suggesting.

"Celibate September," Smithy says, lifting his vape pen to his mouth. "You know, like No Nut November, but in September."

"What's No Nut November?" I ask, but I immediately wish I could take the question back. With Smithy, I usually don't want to know.

"Gee, a whole month," I say, sarcasm dripping from my voice. "How will you ever make it that long without sex?"

Smith exhales a plume of vapor, and I sidestep to dodge the potential contact high. Smithy never vapes the legal stuff. "Not just no sex," he says. "None of it."

"What do you mean?" I ask, like an idiot, but at this point I think my mouth would blurt anything to avoid meeting Dean's gaze. Also, there's been some wine involved.

"No shucking the corn," Smithy says.

Dean cringes, and I shake my head. "I don't even wanna know what that means."

"You know, flogging the dolphin, spanking the monkey, poaching the egg, shaking hands with the milkman, polishing the banister, doing some DIY."

"We get it, Smith," Dean says, shaking his head.

Smithy starts waxing poetic about the virtues of celibacy and how great sex is gonna be when he finally "slimes the banana," and I excuse myself and find my way to the cooler on the patio and another wine spritzer. I'm tipsy, but not tipsy enough to hear Smithy's sex conquest stories, which is no doubt where this conversation is headed. Somehow with Smithy, that's *always* where it's headed.

When I stand, Dean's there. And he's staring at me. My

mind immediately leaps to the conversation we had the other night, and I'm again swamped with regret. I should've kept my mouth shut.

"I'm sorry," he says.

I turn around. That wasn't what I was expecting.

"Are you okay?" he asks softly.

I swallow and nod. "Yeah. Just needed a reprieve from Smithy's visuals."

He chuckles, but his expression shifts back to serious. "Maybe I need to apologize for earlier. I shouldn't have been so pushy."

I shake my head. "Why? Don't worry about it. It's fine."

"Really?" He folds his arms.

"Your *willingness* is just surprising, that's all."

"I've been thinking about you a lot this week. And I was getting the feeling that maybe you'd been thinking about me too. Was that my imagination?"

No. It wasn't. But admitting that pretty much means accepting this is going to happen, and there's too big a part of me that's still the girl who got laughed at in high school, the one who had to get creative while changing in the locker room because the other girls would tease her for being heavy. I'm still the girl who got dumped in college after forgetting what everyone else could see so clearly— that my boyfriend, the love of my life, was completely out of my league and only with me because he felt *sorry* for me.

I know Dean isn't lying to me about what he wants. He wouldn't lie to me about this, but that doesn't change that it's so hard to believe. That little part of me will always be waiting for him to break into laughter and tell me his offer was a big joke.

So I don't say anything at all.

He scans my face, his gaze hovering a beat at my lips before lifting to my eyes again. "If this isn't what you want, I won't push this."

"It's not that I don't . . ." *Want?* God. That word makes me feel way too vulnerable. "I'm scared."

He takes a step closer, and I can't breathe. He settles his hand on my hip and squeezes. "Tell me what scares you."

I'm scared you won't like my body. That you'll see me naked and be disappointed. That I'll get naked and freeze up. I'm scared that I'll fall for you. But that sort of vulnerability is a kind of masochism I just don't have the bandwidth for tonight. So I settle for the lame but obvious excuse. "You're my brother's best friend. You're *my* friend."

Swallowing hard, he drops the hand from my hip and steps back. "Okay."

"Okay?"

"I told you I wouldn't push it. I meant it. I'll start getting these ideas out of my head right away." His lips curve into a tight smile. "I've done it before. I can do it again."

He's done it before? When? Halloween?

Then he turns and walks away, and I feel like I've let him down somehow. That makes *no sense.* Dean is amazing. He's gorgeous and sweet and funny, and God . . . if anyone could teach me how to be good in bed, it would be him, right? Maybe he's right. Maybe "good in bed" isn't a thing, but if he could help me gain some confidence, maybe it wouldn't matter that this will probably end with my broken heart. At least after I recovered, I'd have a chance with someone else—a chance to not be *alone* all the time.

I didn't think he'd be leaving until later, but then I see him push through the gate to the front. I chase after him without thinking, breaking into a run after the gate clangs shut behind me.

I catch him at his truck. "Dean. Wait up."

His back is to me, but he stiffens at the sound of my voice, presses a hand to the driver's-side door, and blows out a long breath. "It's fine, Abbi. Seriously, I'm not going to be the asshole who chases after the girl who doesn't want him. I've had my share of that."

My heart pinches. Maybe this doesn't have to be about me. Maybe I'll really be doing him a favor too. Taking a chance, I reach out and press my palm between his shoulder blades, feeling the taut muscles of his broad back beneath my fingers. "Look at me."

Slowly, he turns so he's facing me. He leans back against the car. "Sorry. It's like the harder I try not to be an ass, the bigger an ass I become."

I shake my head. "Don't apologize. Tell me how you're feeling."

He huffs. "Can I not?"

"I want to know."

"Okay." He tips his face up as if he's studying the sky, but I know he's just gathering his words. "I feel a little rejected, embarrassed, and a lot"—he chuckles, and his dimple flashes as he treats me to his crooked smile—"really fucking horny. Because I'm the idiot who thought this was going to happen and who's spent way too much of his week thinking about the possibilities."

Oh. *Oh.* My stomach flutters wildly, and it's hard to breathe. *I spent too much time thinking about them too,* I think, but I say, "You're not an idiot."

"I kind of am, Abs. I misread you, and that's on me."

I step into him, my thighs bracketing one of his legs, and he sucks in a breath.

"What are you doing?" he asks.

"I said I'm scared. That doesn't mean I'm not interested. It just means I'm scared."

His gaze drops to my mouth again, as if he needs to see my lips form the words.

I'm a coward and can't say it, so I take his hand in mine and guide it to cup my face. "And everything you're feeling," I say, leaning into his palm, "I'm feeling those things too."

"You feel rejected? There's not a single part of me that wants to reject you right now."

"Um, no . . . the other part?"

He grins full-out this time. Big, toothy, real. "Horny?" There's so much delight in those two syllables I could smack him.

"It's such an ugly word."

His thumb grazes the line of my jaw as he brings his other hand to my hip. "Nah. It's just raw. Unburdened by pretense. Honest." His smile falls away. "I want to kiss you. *Can* I kiss you?"

My heart, which is already racing, kicks up to a whole new tempo. "On one condition," I say.

"Anything."

I close my eyes, remembering all the times I denied my attraction to him even to myself, all the times I caught myself staring or eavesdropping or *longing*. "If this doesn't feel right, if there's no chemistry for you—for either of us—or if it starts to feel too weird or too scary or anything, then we stop this."

That cute little wrinkle pops up between his brows. "Of course."

"So we'll kiss." I lick my lips. They're already tingling. I want this so much. I'm pretty sure I deserve a reward for not showing up on his doorstep this week. "Just to see if this might work."

He nods. "Let's just see."

"Okay." That word seems to flip a switch in him that brings his smile back and makes his eyes crinkle at the corners.

He slowly lowers his mouth to mine. Ever since last Halloween, I've imagined this. Before that, I imagined it a few times too—maybe not imagining Dean kissing *me,* but what it'd be like to be the kind of girl he'd want to kiss, imagining being that girl and having him kiss me. Then, after Halloween, the fantasy shifted. It was no more welcome than before and completely dangerous. But the idea that Dean wanted to kiss *me?* Not some fictional, skinnier version of me I'm too jaded to believe I'll ever be, but the real, imperfect, deeply flawed *me?* That was heady, intoxicating stuff.

I'd never admit it, but I've had many sleepless nights imagining his big hands holding me and his mouth on mine.

None of those fantasies compare to this.

He sweeps his mouth across mine at first. Slowly. Tentatively. Little jolts of electricity spark in my lips and down my arms. He does it again, and I feel like all the air around us snaps with heat. Chemistry is about desire and longing. It's about moments like this. But I can't help but worry that he doesn't feel it too, that maybe this is just another kiss for him and not something that'll leave him delirious.

I have to trust him when he says he wants this. I have to trust when he says he's been thinking about this—as hard as that is.

He flicks his tongue over my lips, and I gasp and open under him. He groans, slanting his mouth over mine and turning the kiss deeper, fuller.

Some men kiss like they're asking a favor, but Dean kisses like he's making a claim. He kisses the way he lives his life—by going after exactly what he wants and pursuing it relentlessly—and I let him. I glory in being the object of his pursuit, in the way his tongue sweeps into my mouth and his hand plunges into my hair. I revel in the tug of the strands between his fingers and the soft grunt he releases as his other hand pulls my body close.

I want to memorize this moment. The taste of whiskey on his tongue, the smell of his cologne, the hot crush of his mouth on mine.

I'm not ready for it when he tears his mouth away. I don't think I'd ever be ready for it. But he straightens, tips his face up to the sky, and gasps for air.

"Holy shit," he says.

Why? I want to ask. *Why did you stop? Why aren't you kissing me forever?* But I don't. There's obviously a reason, or he wouldn't have done it.

"It's your turn," he says, looking at me. "What are you thinking?"

"I'm . . ." I need to find some courage if I'm going to do this. It's the only way forward. "I didn't want you to stop," I say softly, and I force a smile even though I feel like I'm seconds away from rejection, seconds away from this all falling apart, or from waking up and finding out that every bit of it, down to our Halloween almost-kiss, was a dream.

His eyes scan my face, as if he's looking for the lie. "I didn't want to stop."

"Then why did you?"

He grins down at me. "That was the kind of kiss that makes a man want to fuck you against his car, Abbi, and given what we're after here, I don't think you're ready for that yet."

That liquid heat in my belly goes deeper and hotter and feels like it's flooding my system. My thighs clench. I *am* ready for that. Quite literally *ready*.

Dean cups my jaw, and his eyes are tender as he studies me. "I'm going to head out."

I swallow my disappointment. "Okay."

"Don't drive," he says. "Take an Uber."

I nod. "That was the plan."

"Take it to my place."

My pulse skips then speeds up to triple time. His place. This is happening. "Okay."

"Holy shit." His grin grows. "I swear you won't regret this."

But I'm afraid I might, and as his taillights become red spots in the distance, I already know I don't have the courage to follow through.

DEAN

> Abbi: I can't. I'm sorry. I'm afraid this is a
> mistake.

"Yeah," I mutter. "I kind of assumed as much an hour ago." I collapse onto my couch and lean my head back against the cushions. Trixie hops up beside me, nuzzling my hand to get me to pet her. I scratch her behind the ears until she settles her head into my lap.

I feel like an idiot. This is Abbi. Did I really think she'd go from "I'm scared" to "let's get naked" in the span of an hour?

I'm trying to figure out the perfect reply—something that conveys my disappointment while also letting her off the hook—when my phone buzzes again.

> Amy: I keep thinking about what you said. I don't want to mislead you. I'm not ready for any sort of commitment. But I also hate that giving you up now might mean losing you forever.

Shit. Two weeks. We made it two weeks without texting or talking, and, frankly, it was good for me. I did it wrong the first time. She broke up with me, but I didn't ever let go of the hope that our separation was temporary. I won't make that same mistake this time, so I tap back to my thread with Abbi and reread her message.

My phone buzzes again.

> Amy: You're just going to ignore me now?

I shake my head and tap out a reply.

> Dean: Don't do this. You're only saying any of this because it's late and you get lonely when you can't sleep.
> Amy: See? How dumb am I to move on from a guy who knows me so well?

I start to reply and stop myself. I know how this goes. Amy slowly pulls me into a conversation with little bits of flattery, with breadcrumbs that make me think that maybe —just maybe—she'll give me what I want if I just stick around. I don't want us to be buddies right now. It's easier to keep my distance when I'm a little pissed at her.

It's easier to stay away when you think you might have a chance with Abbi.

Leaving Amy's message on read, I tap back to the text stream with Abbi. I can't stop thinking about that kiss—the taste of her, the little moan in the back of her throat, how soft her lips were.

Even if I were dumb enough to fall into Amy's trap again, I wouldn't want to after that kiss. Not when it felt so right. Not when it was such a long time coming. And maybe that's exactly where I need Abbi focused, as well.

> Dean: The only mistake was making you feel rushed. Don't stress tonight, but don't forget that kiss, either. This is going to happen. And when it does, it's gonna be good.

Her reply comes quickly.

> Abbi: The ego on you.
> Dean: Nah. It's not ego.
> Abbi: Then what is it? Don't tell me.

She follows that text with a line of eggplant emojis, and I grin at my phone.

Dean: Ha! Well, I do have one of those, but that's not what I meant either. My confidence in our chemistry comes from somewhere else altogether.

Abbi: Don't leave me hanging.

Dean: Isn't it obvious? You. That's what's gonna make it un-fucking-forgettable.

CHAPTER EIGHT

ABBI

Sundays are a short day at work for me. We serve Sunday brunch at The Patio from ten to two, then give the place a good cleaning and close up until Tuesday. Usually, the shift flies by, and a day like today—when the weather is beautiful and the place is packed—is usually over before I realize it.

Today it dragged as a certain someone's text played on repeat in my head.

This is going to happen. And when it does, it's gonna be good.

I should've gone to his house last night. Should've ripped off the bandage and revealed all the awkward disappointment that a night with me truly promises.

Hi, my name's Abbi, and I make things weird when I get naked.

As it stands, Dean's starting to make me believe this could be different. That *we* could be different. It's a little like climbing the first hill of the rollercoaster and convincing yourself the drop isn't coming.

I didn't hear from Dean all day, despite checking my phone three times in the middle of the brunch rush. Every time I looked, a mixture of relief and disappointment flooded me. Relief because this is a really bad idea. Disappointment because I want it anyway.

As I drive home from work, I decide I'll text him. I'll feel him out. But I don't get the chance. Dean is sitting on my front porch swing, flanked by two large paper bags. He's in worn jeans and a gray athletic shirt that hugs his biceps and chest, and one look at him makes all of my girlie bits stand up at attention.

One kiss undid *years* of training myself not to notice Dean as anything more than my brother's best friend. One kiss, and all I can think about is when I might get another.

When I climb from my car, he stands and looks me over, causing a long pulling sensation low in my belly.

Lord help me, but I really, really want this man to touch me again.

I swing my door shut and bleep the locks. "What are you doing here?"

"I brought dinner," he says, as if it's a normal occurrence.

I release a nervous laugh as I climb onto the porch. Is he here because he feels obligated to finish what we started? Or does he want to give me the "it was a mistake" speech? Or, oh God, even worse—both? I glance around and decide this isn't the place to figure it out. I live in an old Victorian that's been subdivided into four apartments, and while I like all of my neighbors, a couple of them are big fans of gossiping to my mother. *Small towns. Gotta love 'em.*

"Come on inside," I say, unlocking the door. If they tell Mom that Dean showed up and went into my apartment with me, she won't question it. But if they overhear us talking about him teaching me how to be a decent lay? Well, I'm not sure a person can actually die of mortification, but I'd rather not test that theory.

Dean follows me into my apartment, a bag in each hand, and heads straight to my kitchen. I think he's been here a total of two times, but you wouldn't know it by the way he moves around. He heads straight to my kitchen like he owns the place and begins to pull containers out of the bags. "I wasn't sure what you'd be in the mood for, but then I realized you can never go wrong with bar food and picked up a bunch of stuff at Smithy's." He goes to the cupboard and pulls out a couple of wine glasses and then opens a few more doors until he finds the plates. He retrieves flatware from the drawer and starts filling the plates.

"Dean," I say, tossing my purse on the counter. "What are you doing?"

He looks up from the plate he's currently loading with tater tots. It all smells amazing, but I'm not sure how I'm supposed to eat when we both know why he's here. Or . . . I know the possibilities, at least. And both make my stomach crowded with nerves.

"I'm serving us dinner." He puts the plate down, and his smile falls away. "Unless you already ate?"

I shake my head. "No. I didn't."

He skirts around the island and presses a firm, quick kiss to my lips. "Good," he says, straightening. "So let me feed you."

I fold my arms. "Listen, I know last night we kind of

decided we were going to do this thing, but I think we both know the alcohol was talking. This is a bad idea."

He digs through a couple more drawers until he locates a corkscrew, then he uncorks the wine and fills two glasses to the brim before turning and handing one to me. "Relax. I'm not here to debauch you." He grabs his own glass and murmurs something I think might be "Not that I'd mind."

I drain half my glass before remembering I skipped lunch today and it's gonna go straight to my head. I've never felt so off balance around Dean.

"Sit," he says, waving to the small table and four chairs that make up my dining room. "You've been on your feet all day. I'll bring you your dinner."

I obey, but only because I'm too nervous and don't trust myself to speak. The butterflies in my stomach can't decide if they want to flutter or riot.

Dean slides a plate of tater tots and a buffalo chicken wrap in front of me and then seats himself across from me with an identical dinner. "Now, I'd like to make a couple of things clear."

Here it comes. He's changed his mind. He's come to his senses. I shouldn't be so sick at the thought of him stopping this before it starts when that's exactly what I did last night, and yet here I am. "Okay."

"I wasn't drunk last night. Not even a little. I had two sips of Kace's fancy whiskey and a Diet Coke. Neither of those things had anything to do with my decision to kiss you or ask you to my place. I was really looking forward to you coming over."

"You were?"

He coughs out a laugh. "Yeah. I thought I made that

pretty clear when I had my mouth on yours, but maybe I need to do a better job of showing you next time."

I take another ill-advised gulp of my wine. Maybe if I get the butterflies in my stomach drunk, they'll pass out and leave me alone. "Okay."

"But I think you're right that it would've been a mistake to jump in that fast."

I flinch. This conversation's giving me whiplash. "I . . . Ooh-kay."

He shoves his plate to the side and folds his arms on the table. "You want some confidence in bed, right?"

"In an ideal world." I shrug, as if this is as normal as admitting I'd like to get more sleep.

"And I want . . ." He draws in a long, deep breath and plasters on a smile I don't believe for a single minute. "I *need* to stay away from Amy." He studies his wine for a beat as he chews on his lower lip. "She's kind of toxic to me, and I'm realizing I might need some help not falling back into our old cycle. If that help could come in the form of seducing *you*"—his eyes blaze as he looks me over—"I can't think of a faster road to getting my mind off her."

The heat in his eyes is making it hard to think, but I grapple for rational thoughts. "So I'd be, like, your sober sponsor? Do I need to give you special tokens on every milestone you make it without hooking up with her again?"

He shrugs. "Token or . . . something else." He winks. "My point is, I still want to do this, and I'm hoping you do too, but I shouldn't have rushed you last night. I promise it won't happen again." He pulls his plate back in front of him and picks up his wrap in both hands. Then he eats as if everything is normal. As if we aren't literally having a conversation about whether or not we'll be fuck buddies for a while. "What?" he asks when I don't stop staring.

"I can't . . . You're so casual about this."

He arches a brow. "Am I?"

"Yes. I mean, it's not like we're agreeing to run to the store together. You're acting like you're going to help me pick out a new fridge or something. Is this . . . is it that simple to you?"

He puts down his food. "Not at all. I told you last night that I want you, and I meant it. This isn't charity. We both need this."

"And if it blows up in our faces?"

"In what way?"

What if I fall for you? What if I become delusional and think I could really have you? It's a reasonable fear, given my reaction to him after just one kiss, but I can't admit that if I actually want to consider going forward with this. And I do. Lord help me, I do. "What if it ends badly?"

"Like you break my heart?" he asks, and I actually scoff, the idea is so ridiculous. He shrugs. "All relationships come with risks. Every single one. Friendships can go sour as easily as romances. And this . . ." He scans my face. I wonder what he sees there—wonder how he possibly sees anything that makes him want to follow through with this. "This can be exactly what we want it to be. We're both adults, and we both care about each other enough not to be careless. Am I right about that?"

I bite my bottom lip. I care about Dean a lot. Maybe too much for this. But he's right about Amy. She's toxic for him, and I know he needs to move on if he's ever going to be truly happy. If I can somehow help him with that, I want to. "Yeah."

"I know it's crazy. I do. And if you'd rather go to Vincent Brunetti for what you need, I'll back the fuck off, but I'd feel much better about this if you put your sexual confidence in my hands. Never mind the fact that you'd be helping me too."

"Right. Your Amy repellent."

He shrugs, and I cringe, suddenly remembering what she said to him outside the bar and imagining the things she'd say if she found out.

"You can't tell her," I blurt. "You can't tell Amy—or *anyone*—that we're doing this. They wouldn't understand, and it'd be really embarrassing to try to explain I'm so hopeless in bed that I had to talk my friend into fixing me."

He shakes his head. "We've been over this. You're not hopeless in bed."

"You don't know that," I say, wagging a finger at him. "You're so sure right now, but just wait until you experience disappointing sex for the first time and lie there thinking, *Oh my God, she was right the whole time.*"

"First of all, I've definitely had disappointing sex before. *That* is a thing. And second of all, it won't happen, but if it does, I promise to shift all my efforts from growing your confidence to teaching you how to rock my world, okay?"

I laugh so suddenly that I snort, and the sound just makes me laugh harder. "Oh, God. This is so ridiculous. I can't believe we're contemplating this. I can't believe we're having this conversation."

He props his elbows on the table. "I think you're forgetting something."

"What's that?"

He stands just enough to lean all the way across the small table and plant his mouth on mine. The kiss is brief, nothing like the exploration against the car last night, but it's sizzling, and by the time his mouth disconnects from mine, I'm ready to follow him across the table.

Dean's lips quirk into a cocky grin that shows off his dimple. "You're forgetting we have chemistry," he murmurs, shifting his attention back to his food. "Now eat something."

DEAN

Abbi picks at her food, looking at me every other second like she's afraid I might jump her. It's not doing great things for my ego, so I search for a topic that might help her relax.

"Tell me about how things are going at The Patio."

She pushes her food around her plate and frowns. "They're really good."

I chuckle. "You don't look happy about that."

"I am." She tugs her bottom lip between her teeth. "I mean, I'm happy for Brinley. Everything she touches is magic over there, and she's worked hard for the kind of growth she's seeing."

"But . . .?"

Abbi sighs, pushing her food around on her plate. "But the longer I run The Patio, the more I'm sure that's not what I want to do for the rest of my life, and the better it does, the harder it is to leave."

"Wow." I lean back in my chair and fold my arms. "I had no idea. I thought you loved to cook."

"I do." She puts down her fork and scoops up her wine. "But the better things go over there, the less cooking I

actually do. And it's not just that, either. While I love cooking, I really, really love *baking*. That's my real passion, even
though I realize I'm being a diva if I want to leave a great
job with some baking in hopes of finding a career with a lot
of baking."

"You're not being a diva. I've had your stuff. You could
make a killing!"

She studies me for a long time then shakes her head.
"Don't tell Brinley we talked about this. It's all just fantasy."

"So what would you do?" I ask. "Imagine you left The
Patio for a career that centered more around your passions.
What would that look like?"

She sips her wine, and I can tell her hesitation is less
about not knowing the answer and more about not wanting
to say it out loud. "I'd like to open a bakery. Something
downtown, where people could run in and get a coffee and a
danish on their way to work. Maybe with a few tables in the
front. Customers could take meetings or coffee dates there
if they wanted. And I'd have a big glass display case by the
register and displays in the windows. I'd do wedding cakes
too, because those are the closest I ever get to being an
artist, and it's so much fun. And we'd do catering orders for
people who want coffee and snacks for their meetings or
parties." She's been picking up speed with each word but
suddenly cuts herself off. "Like I said. Pipe dream."

"Why? It sounds like you have a great plan."

"Eighty-five percent of bakeries fail in the first five
years, and a lot of those are run by people who actually
finished college." She takes a gulp of her wine. "I know how
to run a kitchen, but I don't know how to run a business."

"So you learn, and you contract out what you need to."
Leaning across the table to refill her wine, I give her a

gentle smile. "You might have some friends who know a thing or two about running a business."

She picks up her fork again and flashes me a smile. "You're sweet for believing in me, but I'm just not sure it's in the cards."

I don't want to push it, so I stand to clear the table and clean up.

"You really think I could help you?" she asks. "Stay away from Amy, I mean?"

It's certainly worked this week. "For sure."

"I think getting away from her would be good for you," she says. "I hope that doesn't make me sound catty."

"Nah. I get it. I agree, actually."

I don't like using my history with Amy as a way to talk Abbi into this, but it wasn't a lie. Staying away from Amy has never been easy for me. Not after we first slept together and I was trying to keep it as casual as she wanted, and not before then—when she and Kace had just split and she started with the heavy flirting. I knew then that giving in to that attraction was a bad idea. Of course, back then I was more worried about Kace and less about my heart. Now Kace is fine, but I'm the one who's a mess. The truth is that the last week of avoiding Amy has been the easiest since she first left Kace, and I know Abbi has everything to do with that. But I don't want her to do this just for me, either. Hell, I don't even want her to do this because she wants to be more confident in the bedroom. I want her to do it because she wants it—wants me. And the only way I can make sure that happens is if I take it slow.

She eats a few more bites of her dinner as I clean up, but gives up on her meal, pushing away her plate before she makes it halfway through her wrap. I don't think she touched her tots—which is sacrilege—but I let it pass, considering. I walk around the table and pull her from her seat. She stiffens when I press my mouth to hers.

"You can relax. I'm not going to fuck you tonight."

Something like disappointment crosses her face. "Oh. Okay. I wouldn't, uh—"

"And not because I don't want to," I add, grabbing her hips and pulling her body flush with mine so she can feel just how much I want her. "I'm not going to fuck you tonight because I want to focus on *other* things first." I tuck a soft lock of hair behind her ear. "Because waiting is its own kind of pleasure."

She coughs out a laugh. "Torture, you mean?"

I shift my hands down from her hips until I'm cupping her ass. She feels so damn good in my hands. "Definitely torture." I give her ass a little squeeze. "Even more so when I consider I have to leave for a meeting soon."

Sidestepping me, she turns to lean against the counter and cradles her wine in her hands. She watches me clear her plate and put her leftovers into the fridge. The wine's working on her—her shoulders have dropped from around her ears, and her flushed cheeks now frame a subtle smile.

"What?" I ask, quirking a brow.

"I had no idea you were so good in the kitchen." She shrugs, and the tip of her tongue grazes her bottom lip.

I smirk. "You like that?" I grab a rag and make a show of wiping down the counter, bending at the waist unnecessarily and shifting my hips from side to side, making a total fool of myself.

It's worth it when she bursts out laughing. "You're ridiculous."

"You're always the one in the kitchen when our friends

get together. I figured you deserved a chance to be the one relaxing."

She swallows. "That's sweet, but I actually don't mind being the cook. It makes me feel useful."

"Have you ever cooked for one of your dates?" I ask, unexpected jealousy snagging me by the throat. It's so easy to picture Abbi in the kitchen with some guy, her smile, her laugh as she chats with him over a cutting board of veggies.

"A couple of times. I don't actually date a lot."

Yeah, I guessed as much, since I haven't met a boyfriend of hers since she was in college. Cody. That dude was a tool. I realize I don't know how he treated her when they were alone, but when they hung out with me, Kace, and Stella, he acted like she wasn't there. He'd give her short, one-word answers to her questions and then gush about random, unimportant shit to Stella. The only reason I didn't demand Abbi dump his ass was because Kace told me to keep my mouth shut, told me I was just feeling protective because I saw Abbi as a sister. He was wrong about how I saw her, but he wasn't wrong that my feelings for her were coloring the way I saw her boyfriend. I wouldn't have liked any guy she brought home.

"Why *don't* you date more?" I ask, taking my seat again.

She huffs out a laugh. "I thought we already covered that."

"Sex," I say softly. Shit, that's crazy. Even people who don't *like* sex deserve good relationships. "Do you . . . I mean, is it because you have trouble finishing?"

She blinks at me, as if she's not sure what I mean. Then her eyes widen for a beat before she tucks her chin to avoid my gaze. "A lot of women can't, but depending on how things go, that's not exactly my problem. I know how to take care of myself if needed, so I don't really care about that either way."

Jesus. *I* do. I care *a lot.* "What about alone?" I ask, because I'm a fucking masochist.

Her cheeks are red now. She lifts her chin and looks me in the eye when she says, "I've got that covered."

I suddenly hate myself for my plans to go slow. I don't want slow. I want fast and reckless. I want her stripped bare on her bed and showing me just how well she's got that covered. I drag a hand over my mouth and groan.

"What?" she says. "You asked!"

"I know." I snag my wine glass off the table and drain it. I'd love to cancel my meeting and pour myself a second serving, but I won't. Not today. Today is for getting us both on the same page, for planting the seeds. "And now I'll be punished by thinking about it the rest of the day. That's a crazy-hot visual, champ."

She shakes her head and fights a smile. "*You're* crazy."

My phone buzzes on the counter, and a glance at the clock tells me it's a calendar reminder for my meeting with our newest client. "Not in the mood" is an understatement.

"Your meeting?" she asks.

Nodding, I stand and prowl to where she's still lounging against the counter. "I'm sorry I have to go so soon." I grab her hand and pull her close until her chest is a breath from mine. "Do me a favor tonight?"

Her lips part, and she levels her gaze on my mouth. "What's that?"

"When you touch yourself, think about me." She opens her mouth, and I can see the objection in her eyes, so I put a finger to her lips. "Please? Seems only fair, since I know I'll be thinking about you."

She closes her eyes and draws in a long, deep breath. "Okay." She nods. "I can do that."

"Good. I'm counting on it."

When she opens her eyes again, her pupils are dilated, making her brown eyes look even darker than usual. She's turned on, and walking away is pure hell.

CHAPTER NINE

ABBI

*M*onday is my day off, and the weather is beautiful, so I go on a long walk and then do a little yoga while my muscles are still warm. I'm sweaty, loose-limbed, and relaxed on my living room floor when my phone buzzes. When I see it's a text from Dean, my heart does a little squeeze-and-shimmy thing, like it's partnered up with my stomach in some ill-advised acrobatic swing dance.

> Dean: Did you think about me?

Think about him? Only four hundred times in the past hour. But that's not what he means, and my internal organs do a dance-off at the prospect of answering his question the way he means. I could put it off—take my shower and reply later—but I don't want to. I want to answer so he'll tell me if he thought of *me*. It's heady stuff, imagining Dean Jacob getting off to thoughts of me. If it were a weather forecast, it'd be in the zero to one percent range, but he said he would, didn't he? And he wouldn't be doing this if he weren't at least a little attracted to me, so . . .

I hold my breath as I type my reply.

> Abbi: I'm always true to my word.

I bite my lip as I imagine him reading my almost-coy response.

> Dean: . . . and?
> Abbi: And what?
> Dean: How was it?

I roll to my stomach and grin down at my phone, my cheeks burning as if we're having this conversation in public.

> Abbi: I know my way around pretty well at
> this point.
> Dean: Jesus. Serves me right for having this
> conversation right before a meeting.
> That's one hell of a mental picture, but
> that's not what I was asking.
> Abbi: No?
> Dean: How was the part where you thought
> about me?

Familiar. Way more familiar than I'll ever admit. He suggested it as if I'd never thought about him while touching myself before. In truth, I don't very often. I don't let myself. But I've been known to slip in my weaker moments.

> Abbi: Fantasy Dean had some skills. 10/10,
> would recommend.
> Dean: It might kill me to take this slow, you
> know that?

I swallow. I'm still not sure *why* we're taking it slow. I guess because we need to stretch it out if I'm going to help him get Amy out of his system. But more time doing this with Dean seems like more time to fall and fall hard. The problem is, if these last two days are any indication of what's to come, the promise of heartbreak wouldn't stop me. I'm clicking up the hill of the rollercoaster, and the signs are warning me that disaster is coming, but I want the stuff between here and there too much to stop the ride and climb out.

He texts again before I can figure out how to respond.

> Dean: I'm making plans for us. What day do
> you have off this week?

Plans? I hop off the floor in a panic.

> Abbi: Today and Thursday. But I have
> appointments today.

I don't have appointments today, but I promise myself I'll schedule some as soon as we get off the phone. I'm not ready.

Dean: I'm claiming Thursday, then. I'll do a
couple of things at the office first thing
and take the rest of the day off. Pick you
up at ten.

At ten? Isn't that a little early in the day for seduction
lessons? And to pick me up?

Abbi: Where are we going?
Dean: It's a surprise. Let's just say I think it
might be a good place for us to start.
Abbi: I don't think I like surprises.
Dean: Too bad. See you Thursday.
Abbi: I'm here for hints if you wanna drop
them!

He replies with a winky face, and I take in a deep breath
and dial The Orchid.

"Thank you for calling The Orchid, where peace and
relaxation are only an appointment away. This is Stella.
How can I help you today?"

Of course Stella answers. Because this kind of call isn't
awkward enough. I clear my throat. "Hey, Stell. This is
Abbi. I'm wondering if any of the girls can squeeze me in
for a Brazilian today?"

"Hi, Abbi! Let me see . . . June had a cancellation at
three. Would that work for you?"

I swallow. I have no idea what Dean has planned for
Thursday, but I refuse to be unprepared. "That's perfect.
Thanks."

"Of course. And would you care to add on a rejuvenating
facial with Wren right after?"

Why the hell not? My skin's pretty good, but I might as well flaunt my assets. "That would be great."

"Awesome. I have you booked. See you at three!"

"Thanks."

"You're welcome, boo."

"And Stella? Thanks for not making the whole Brazilian thing awkward."

She laughs. "That's literally my job, baby girl. See you later."

I look at the clock then race for the shower. I have a dozen things I want to do before my appointment—new underwear and a mani-pedi are at the top of the list.

TUESDAY AFTER THE LUNCH RUSH, I'm tucked away in my office when someone knocks on my office door, pulling my attention away from the order I'm placing for next week. "Come in," I call.

The door cracks, and Stella pokes her head inside. "I had to leave before you were done yesterday. How was the Brazilian?"

I huff out a laugh. "It hurt like hell. Everyone who ever said it's not that bad should have to undergo medical testing for the health of their nerve endings."

Stella grins, stepping inside my office and closing the door behind her. "I know. It's bad, but at least it gets better over time."

"If you say so."

She folds her arms and arches a brow. "That was your first, then?"

I nod. No escaping this conversation. In fact, I was

prepared. "Yeah. I'd done the bikini wax before, but this was a whole new level of torture. Poor June—I really thought I might kick her a couple of times."

Stella bites back a grin. "She's a pro. Definitely knows how to block those reflexive kicks."

I shake my head. "At least it wasn't as awkward as I expected."

"Yeah, she makes it feel totally normal." She studies me for a moment, and I do a mental countdown toward the question I've been waiting for since yesterday morning. "So . . . now that I'm talking to you as your friend and not a representative of The Orchid, I can ask . . . who was it for?"

There it is. "It was for me, of course."

She rolls her eyes. "Yeah? Because I don't know many women who put themselves through that when no one's going to be looking at their smooth hoo-ha."

I shrug. "I'm thinking about dating again."

She quirks a brow. "Dating or fucking?"

I turn up my palms as if to say, *There's a difference?*

"Well, get it, girl."

My phone buzzes on my desk, and when I flip it over, Dean's name flashes on the screen.

"You have work to do," Stella says, opening the door again. "I'll get out of your way." She points at me as she backs out. "But when you date again, I want to know all the details."

"Yes, ma'am."

I wait until she pulls the door closed behind her before I read the text.

Dean: I've given this more thought, and I

think we need to figure out what your
kinks are.

I bite my bottom lip.

Abbi: What if I don't have any kinks?
Dean: Everyone has kinks. Some are just
more taboo than others.

Outside my office door, I hear the hustle and bustle of
my staff preparing for the dinner rush. Doing this at work
feels scandalous in the best way.

Abbi: What are YOUR kinks?

I don't think I breathe in the time it takes him to reply.
The dots in the bubble bounce and then stop three times
before his reply comes through.

Dean: I like everything, honestly, but I have a
particular fondness for having sex in
places I shouldn't.

I swallow hard and try to think of the perfect reply. I
don't know why, but I don't want this conversation to
end yet.

Abbi: Like where?
Dean: So, here's the deal . . . I'm usually an
open book, and if you'd asked me that a
few weeks ago, I probably would've
rambled off a bunch of examples. But now

that you're not just my friend, I don't
want to talk about what I did with other
women.

Abbi: Not just your friend? What am I?

Dean: You're the woman I'm trying to get
naked. And instead of scaring you off with
my exploits, I'd much rather tell you what
I'd like to do with you.

I glance at my office door to make sure I'm alone then
muster all my courage to type just two little words.

Abbi: Tell me.

Dean: If I were in that office with you right
now, I'd have you sit on your desk and
spread your legs. I'd be really fucking
grateful that you wore a skirt to work
today, because it'd be easy for me to
stroke you through your panties. I'd play
with you until they were drenched and
you were begging in my ear.

I shift in my seat, suddenly a little achy and uncomfortable between my legs. This is crazy. Dean saying these
things to me is crazy. Me not shutting him down is crazy.
But dear Lord, *give me more crazy*.

Abbi: What if I didn't wear a skirt?

Dean: I can work with that. I know you won't
let me take off your clothes at work, so I'd
have to work you through your pants. But
you'd have to be quiet. There are people

on the other side of that door, and I know
you'd be embarrassed if they heard you
moaning.

Dean: I might whisper in your ear, tell you
how much I like feeling you squirm
against my hand, tell you that when I take
you out this weekend, I want you in a
skirt. Because if you were in a skirt right
now, I'd bend you over your desk and
fuck you.

I read that message at least five times. I like the picture
he's painting for me. I don't know if I'd be able to turn off
my rational brain enough in real life to ever let him do what
he's describing, but the words are hot all on their own.

Dean: You still with me?
Abbi: Yeah.
Dean: Am I scaring you?
Abbi: Not at all.
Dean: Are you wet?

My face is so hot. Then again, so is the rest of me. I feel
like my skin could combust. I know what I want to say—
how I want to reply—but it's just a matter of making my
fingers type the words I'd never say if we were on the
phone. I'd never have the courage. That realization is what
makes me reply the way I want to. I'm not doing this so I
can be the same person I was before. I'm doing this so I can
be better in bed . . . a better girlfriend all around.

Abbi: I don't want to answer that question,

but I wish you were here to find out for
   yourself.
Dean: Would you let me investigate? In your
   office, door closed?
Abbi: We'd have to be quiet, but I take
   meetings in here often enough that we
   could get away with it.

Those dots appear and bounce again and again before
his reply finally comes through.

Dean: I have a meeting in ten minutes, or I'd
   be on my way.

My stomach flips and twists. Texting hypothetical
fantasies is one thing, but the fact that a meeting is the only
thing standing between this moment and him acting out
what he just described? I'm pretty sure if he'd said he was
on his way, I'd be chickening out right now.
Thank goodness for afternoon meetings.

CHAPTER TEN

DEAN

*M*y brain is so foggy with lust that I don't think twice before heading in the main doors of The Orchid late Tuesday afternoon, but the second I see who's manning the receptionist's desk, I freeze in my tracks.

"Dean!" my sister calls out from her position behind the front desk. "What are you doing here?"

"I . . . I'm just . . ." I snap my jaw shut and smile, lowering my voice. "I thought I'd buy a gift certificate for Mom." *There.* That's a perfectly believable reason for me to come to The Orchid, and one that has nothing to do with wanting to feel up Abbi Matthews. Maybe my brain can work through lust after all.

"Oh. Sure. But . . . why?" She pulls a booklet out of a desk drawer and starts writing up the gift certificate.

"Just . . ." Shit. That's a good question. Mother's Day is

long gone, and her birthday isn't until March. "Getting my Christmas shopping done early."

Stella lifts her pen from the pad and drops it on the desk. "Oh, I'm sorry. Our gift certificates expire in ninety days, and that won't give her much time after you give it to her. Brinley's been meaning to get back to the numbers on that and see if we can justify a longer time frame, but it's a cashflow fail-safe leftover from the old owners."

"Oh. Right. Sure. No problem. I'll just . . ." I clear my throat, feeling like my true intentions are written all over my face. "I'll come back in December." I gaze toward the back hall—the one I was planning to take to Abbi's office.

"Sounds good. Can I do anything else for you?" She cocks her head to the side. "You look a little tense. Maybe I should schedule a massage for you."

I do enjoy a good massage, but the only hands I want on me right now are Abbi's, and I want them—

"Dean?"

I jerk my gaze back to my sister. "I'm sorry. What?"

"I said Wren just had a cancellation if you want a massage tonight."

I shake my head. "Nah. I'm not up for it tonight. I think I'll just run back to the kitchen and see if Abbi has any of her cookies lying around."

Stella grins and points to a table behind me. "Baked fresh every day."

I turn slowly, and sure enough, there's a whole fucking table with cookies, brownies, and coffee. "When did you start doing that?"

"It was Brinley's idea. It's good customer service to our spa guests but has also increased our carryout catering orders tenfold. Abbi's going to have to hire another baker to keep up."

"Shit," I mutter.

"It's no big deal," Stella says, totally misunderstanding my distress. "She works too much as it is. Brinley's been trying to get her to hire a second for months now."

"I guess I'll just go, then." I walk out the door, planning to swing around to the back entrance of The Patio, where the employees enter.

"Dean!" Stella calls from the door behind me.

I spin around and try not to snap at my kind and well-meaning but meddlesome-as-fuck sister. "What do you need?"

She frowns at me, as if she thinks I might be losing it. She might be right. She holds up a stack of cookies wrapped by a napkin on one side. "You forgot your cookies."

"Changed my mind," I say.

She steps onto the sidewalk, letting the door float closed behind her. Her expression grows serious as she studies my face. "Listen, I know you've been having a hard time lately. You've lost weight, and Kace said you work like crazy. I'm worried about you."

"Don't be." I accept the stack of cookies and take a bite out of the top one. The buttery, sugary goodness melts on my tongue, and the moan I release is one thousand percent sincere. "Sweet mother of God."

Stella laughs. "I know, right? That's the salted caramel with mocha chocolate chips. Abbi's a goddess in the kitchen, but she refuses to share the recipe with anyone. Said it's bad for business."

Just the sound of her name is enough to make my body remember why I'm here. This cookie is amazing, but I'm much more interested in the woman holding the recipe. "I bet I can talk her out of it," I say, winking at my sister. "Thanks for these." I walk away slowly, listening for the sounds of Stella returning to her post inside The Orchid so I can cut around the back.

"Dean," she calls again.

I paste on a smile as I force myself to turn. "Yeah?"

"Your car is that way," she says, pointing down the block in the opposite way I'm heading.

I don't let my smile waver. "I'm just going for a little walk."

She props her hands on her hips. "Are you really, though?"

No, Stell. I'm trying to sneak into the kitchen so I can fuck your friend in her office, and if I don't do it soon I'm gonna need to see my doctor, because I haven't had an erection that lasted this long since I was fifteen. "Really," I lie. "It's a nice night."

"You're not going to that dive bar to drink away your troubles?"

I follow her gaze and realize I'm headed in the direction of The Terminal. "I wasn't planning on it, but the more you annoy me about it, the more appealing it sounds."

"I'm your sister. It's my job to worry."

"Your job? I'm sorry to tell you that you're out of work. I closed that door, and now I'm doing a lot better." *So much better,* I realize. Thanks to Abbi. And it isn't just that she's distracting me, it's that she gives me something to look forward to. I didn't realize it before I started seeing Amy, but my life had become monotonous. The only thing I ever got excited about was work, and I was getting really lonely. When Amy dumped me, that loneliness came back with a

LEXI RYAN

vengeance. But now I have Abbi. At least for the time being.

"Okay." Stella sighs. "Enjoy your walk. I'll see you later." She turns to leave me, finally.

"Stella," I call out as she reaches for the door. "I do appreciate you, but I promise I'm fine. It was just a rough patch. I'm on the other side."

She stares at her shoes for a long time before lifting her gaze back up to meet mine. "She never deserved you," she says softly.

I shrug. Maybe she's right. Or maybe I never deserved Amy, or maybe that's not how any of this works. "I'm kind of moving on," I say, even though I shouldn't. "I've been seeing someone, and . . . she makes me really happy."

"You are? Who?"

I grin and back away. "I'm not talking about it yet."

"But she makes you happy? Would I like her?" She props her hands on her hips. "You can't marry a woman I wouldn't like. Our family isn't big enough for that."

"You don't need to worry. I promise."

Stella gives me her first real smile of the day. "I love this. Abbi said she's dating again too. It's awesome to see two of my favorite people putting themselves back out there." She heads back inside, and I stare after her.

Abbi's dating again too. Did Abbi tell her that? When Abbi told Stella that, was she talking about me or someone else?

If there is anyone else, I'm gonna make damn sure she's too busy thinking about me to give him a second thought.

I cut around the back of The Orchid, a man on a mission.

The back hallway is quiet, but I can hear people talking

110

and working in the kitchen. I make out Abbi's voice as she instructs the staff on their final tasks of the night. I love her voice. It's a little low and sultry, and I've spent most of my afternoon imagining that voice right in my ear, whispering, "See for yourself."

I pass the kitchen and swing into her office, claiming the chair behind the desk. Tonight might not be the night for propping her up in front of me and putting my mouth between her legs. At least not here. Her desk is small, and there isn't much flat surface that isn't occupied. But I'm sure as hell gonna touch her.

Leaning back in the chair, I grab my phone and tap out a quick text.

> Dean: Meet me in your office, please? I have some things I'd like to discuss with you.

Her response comes so quickly that I almost laugh.

> Abbi: What? You're here?

Before I can reply, she appears in the doorway and stares at me in her chair. "What are you doing here?"

God, she's cute. How have I managed to shut off the part of my brain that notices for so long? Tonight, her long hair is piled into a bun on top of her head, and she's already taken off the long-sleeved white chef's coat she wears when she's cooking, leaving her in only black leggings and a loose T-shirt that advertises The Patio on the left breast. She looks completely comfortable in every way except the blush on her cheeks and the lip between her teeth.

"Come in and shut the door."

She obeys, but tentatively. "My staff is still here."

"I know." Rolling the chair back away from the desk, I depress the buttons under the arms to lower them down and out of the way. "Come here."

Again, she does as I ask, walking around the desk and stopping in front of me.

"Closer," I say, leaning forward to take her by the hips. I guide her to straddle my lap. Her breath catches and she stiffens. "What's wrong? Talk to me."

She swallows. "I can't sit on your lap."

"Why not?"

She looks at the floor. "I'm not a small girl."

Well, fuck. Why do I keep forgetting that everything comes back to this for her? Some guys would lie and tell a woman in this moment that she's not big, even if, objectively speaking, she's bigger than his past girlfriends. A pretty lie isn't going to help her feel better. I could tell her she's not as big as she thinks, but while that might be true, the sentiment makes me uncomfortable. It lends power to the idea that there's something *wrong* with being bigger. So I stick with the simple truth. "I can handle it."

This time when I tug on her hips, she straddles me and lowers herself onto my lap. I can feel her trying to keep some of the weight on her toes, but she's too short and has to put all her weight on me. And *fuck*, I love it.

I groan at the feel of her pressing against my erection. *So good.* And yet in the way the smell of dinner is good when you're starving, it's not enough.

"You okay?" she asks.

I squeeze her ass and tug her even closer against me. "I'm horny as hell. Someone got me all worked up with her text messages earlier."

That earns me a smile. She loops her arms behind my neck. Abbi's so much shorter than me, but when she's sitting on me like this, we're face to face. I like her this close. I'd like her even closer. No clothes. No pretenses. Just skin and desire and pleasure. "I think you're the one responsible for that," she says.

I press my lips to the spot just beneath her ear then trail down to the crook of her neck and suck lightly. Her barely audible gasp is the hottest sound I've heard all day. I graze my teeth lightly along the column up her neck, back up to her ear. "Tell me I wasn't the only one suffering today."

I cup her breast, finding her pebbled nipple through her shirt and bra and squeezing it between my thumb and forefinger. There's no cleavage showing in this shirt, which is a damn shame. Abbi would look fucking fantastic in a shirt that dipped low in the front, something that showed the swell of her full breasts. But I like this too. More than I ever could've guessed I might. I like knowing I've seen something hardly anyone else gets to see. I like knowing that she might hide herself from the world, but she doesn't hide from me.

"Tell me you've been walking around as turned on and aching as I have."

"So much," she says. Then she shifts the angle of her hips and rocks against me. Just barely. Just enough to show me what she wants. What she needs.

"Will they need you out there anytime soon?" I ask. If I'm going to have to let her walk away in two minutes, I need to brace myself for it now.

She shakes her head. "They're wrapping things up. I was supposed to be going home."

"Home sounds good," I say, cupping her other breast.

"Home means a bed and a chance to get these clothes off you."

She stiffens. So . . . she's not ready for that. *Got it.*

I change course. "But this. Here. This means I don't have to wait to feel you, and I've already waited all fucking day. I don't want to wait anymore."

"Me neither," she says, and I can tell the admission is a leap of faith for her.

"Turn around. Stay on my lap and keep your legs straddling mine, but face the desk."

She holds my gaze for a long time before nodding.

When she's faced away from me, her legs spread wide, she glances over her shoulder as if to say, *Now what?*

I slide both hands around her, flatten one against her stomach, and bring the other up to her breast. "Relax. Lean back." She reclines slightly, resting her head on my shoulder. "Like this."

Fuck yes. Her mouth is right there, and if I slide my hand down—

Her breath leaves her in a rush as I cup her between her legs. I can feel the heat of her through her leggings, and my dick pulses in greedy anticipation. He'll have to wait. This is about her. And I need to touch her even more than I need to find my own release.

I stroke her gently at first and then with more pressure as I experiment with what she likes. I'd rather have her bare, have her slickness on my fingers and her sensitive skin right there, but that'll have to wait too. Her back arches and she presses her head into my shoulder.

I snake my hand up under her shirt, finding the waistband of her leggings, then slide it down and inside the cotton underwear beneath, desperate to feel her.

The moment my fingers connect with her slick heat, she moans my name, and I feel like a fucking superhero.

"I've been thinking about this all day, and it's even better than I imagined," I murmur in her ear. I slide a finger inside her, and she gasps, squeezing tight around me. She's more than ready, ready enough that I slide a second finger inside. "I could pull out my cock right now." If she's this wet from my texts, I know she likes the words. "I could peel these pants off and drive into you."

She clenches around my fingers, lips parted, eyes closed as she loses herself to the pleasure. "Maybe you should," she rasps.

The invitation is so fucking tempting. But this'll have to do. The way she squeezes my fingers as she grinds her ass against my cock will have to do. "Someday you're going to wear that skirt for me. Someday you're going to find me in here and you're going to get wet just knowing what's coming."

"Tell me," she begs, arching her back and rocking into my hand.

I love that she wants to hear. Love that she needs the words. "You ever been fucked fully clothed? We'd have to be so quiet, but I'd drop my jeans, just enough to pull out my cock—and I'd be so hard for you. I'd bend you over this desk and pull your panties to the side then drive into you from behind." Her pussy clenches hard and tight around my fingers, and I give her neck a hard suck. "You'd make these little moaning sounds just like you are right now, and I'd have to use my hand to muffle them. You'd bite my palm to keep yourself from screaming out as I use my other hand to make you come."

She's so close. I feel it in the way she squeezes my fingers and the way she squirms against my cock.

"I want that," she says. "I want that now."

I suck her earlobe between my teeth and let it pop out. "Not today." Because as much as she might want it right now, I know she's not ready, and when I'm finally inside her, I want her to want me with every piece of herself. "You feel so good. Just fuck my hand a little harder and let yourself go."

She writhes in my arms, body winding even tighter. She turns her face toward me, mouth seeking mine, and I press my mouth to hers right as her orgasm rolls through her. Her kiss is messy and desperate and hungry. It's teeth and tongue and gasps, and *fuck*, I want a thousand more kisses like this, moments like this. I want to make her come over and over.

I don't know how long this arrangement will last, but I already know it's not enough.

It'll never be enough.

CHAPTER ELEVEN

ABBI

*F*ake it till you make it.

That's my plan when Dean comes to my door, looking absolutely edible in his faded jeans and fitted T-shirt.

Today is the day of the Big Surprise. Okay, that's not what he's calling it, but Dean's been dodging me all week about the specifics of our plans. The week went both too quickly and too slowly. After his little visit to my office on Tuesday, I've been dying to see him again and hardly been able to think of anything else. But I've also been nervous. If what we did in my office was his idea of taking it slow, I'm not sure what I should expect today. I'm determined to face whatever plans he made for me with confidence.

He slowly drags his gaze over my off-shoulder T-shirt and jeans, all the way down to my sandals. "Damn."

I laugh. I went with my typical wardrobe for today—deciding that each and every one of the other fifteen outfits I tried on made it look like I was trying too hard. "There is literally nothing special about this outfit."

"I mean, I would've rather had you greet me in a skirt, but—"

I clear my throat, feeling my cheeks heat. "Sorry to disappoint you."

Reaching out, he skims his thumb over my bare shoulder. "I like this nonetheless." His tongue darts out to touch his bottom lip just before he lifts his gaze to mine. "Ready?"

"Depends. What are we doing?"

He winks at me and heads to his truck, jingling his keys in his hand the whole way.

Dean's truck isn't just an aesthetic choice. This truck takes a beating with his work, and he looks damn good driving it. I have to bite my lip and try not to stare as he makes his way down the road and turns on Main, parallel-parking in a busy area.

"You ready?" he asks, shutting off the engine.

"Ready as a girl can be when she has no idea what's happening."

"Trust me. You'll like this."

Dean hops out of his side and is at my door to help me before I get my door open. He helps me out of the truck before heading down the block, leaving me to scan the area and wonder where we're going. We're only a block from Smithy's, but I'm pretty sure we would've just parked in the back if we were going there. There's a Hispanic grocery store a couple of doors down—could he want to buy ingredients for us to make lunch together? Or there's a wine-tasting bar for a local winery, and that doesn't sound too bad either, but ten a.m. on a Thursday seems a little early for that.

My gaze flicks past the gym and to Bella's Café. He would've told me if this was a brunch date, but—

It's at the gym that Dean stops and pushes the door open for me.

I stop dead in my tracks. "Dean."

He grins. "It'll be fun—come on."

Shit. I should've seen this coming. You let a beautiful, fit, sculpted guy know that you don't have much self-confidence and that you want to feel more confident in the bedroom, and *hello, personal trainer.*

If I didn't think Dean would be the type to do this—if I didn't believe he'd push me into a workout plan or have me sign up for some diet? Well, that's my fault, isn't it? This whole world thinks we should aspire to be gym rats striving for a daily calorie deficit.

That's just not who I am. Not that I haven't tried before. The problem is I've tried so many times, and I've found I control my weight better when I'm *not* trying all the time. Nothing like a plan to start a diet on Monday to inspire a binge.

I shake my head. "I'm sorry." My face is so hot. I'm so *embarrassed.*

Releasing the door and letting it fall closed, he folds his arms and cocks his head to the side. "You've never done this before?" Jesus, he's *smirking.*

"I work out *a lot*, actually," I say, sounding as defensive as I feel. Now my cheeks are hot and I'm straight-up offended. "I like yoga—*at home*—and I have friends I walk with

119

several times every week. I don't think people *realize*, but fat girls can be fit too, even if we don't like to go to the gym to—"

"Abbi." Dean's eyes are so wide that you'd think he just saw the Easter Bunny in the flesh. He glances at the door behind him and shakes his head. "We're not here for the gym. Jesus, if I wanted to work out with you, I would've had you wear workout clothes." He steps closer and lowers his voice. "And I'd probably want to do it in my home gym so I wouldn't have to keep my hands off you."

"Oh." I swallow. *So I wouldn't have to keep my hands off you.* Well, suddenly working out with Dean doesn't sound so bad. "Then what are we here for?"

He lifts a hand and taps the logo on the door—the one just *below* the name of the gym. *Inner Peace Massage.*

My eyes fly to his. "We're here for a *massage?*"

"Yeah," he says, looking me over. "I mean, I'd enjoy giving you one myself, but Rachel is the best in town. She used to work as a massage therapist for the Atlanta Falcons. She knows what's up." He steps closer, gripping my shoulders and squeezing. "You work so damn hard. You're on your feet all day, and I thought it would be good for you to get some body work done."

"Shit," I say.

"I wanted it to be a surprise because I figured you'd object to the cost and me picking up the tab."

"I'm such an idiot."

"Stop that. You're not. I just didn't think this through. It never occurred to me that you'd think I'd bring you to the *gym.*"

I study a crack in the sidewalk. A bunch of weeds grow there in a vivid green. I wonder how long they'll last before someone comes and sprays them. "I'm sorry. It's just . . . you need to understand how frequently people try to fix me—try to help me lose weight, or get into shape the way they think I should be in shape, but . . ." I shrug. "I've been like this my whole life, and I'm tired of fighting it. Getting skinny isn't part of the plan this time."

I feel his fingers under my chin, and then he lifts my face until I'm looking him in the eye. I feel like he can see every insecurity written on my soul. "I don't want to change you. If you remember, my whole point when we started this was that there's nothing wrong with you. You don't need to learn to be good in bed, because you already are."

"But this is different. This is—"

"It's really not. There's nothing wrong with you, Abbi. I'm not trying to change you. That's not what I'm after here." Those searching eyes settle on my lips and stay.

"Everything okay?"

Dean drops his hand and jumps back, as if I sparked on fire. "Kace! Hey." He nods toward the entrance. "We're heading in for massages. What are you doing here?"

"You *both* have massages today?" Kace asks.

"Yeah." I bite my lip and turn to face my brother. "Crazy coincidence, huh?"

Kace's shrug says he doesn't *actually* care. "Cool. I'm gonna squeeze in a workout before meeting Stella for lunch."

"Nice," Dean says.

"Don't worry," Kace says, grinning. "I promise I'm still treating your sister like the goddess she is."

"I know." Dean coughs. "Seriously, we're way past that. It's fine. I . . . I hope you two have a nice lunch."

DEAN

When Kace disappears inside the gym, I let out a long breath.

In truth, if anyone should be cool about his best friend dating his sister, it'd have to be Kace. He didn't tell me when he and Stella first started hooking up—which was probably for the best, considering it wasn't even a relationship back then. But ultimately, I decided to trust him with Stella. I'd like to think he'd trust me with Abbi, but he's pretty damn protective. I can't blame him for that. That's the way he's made.

The thing is, no one needs to protect Abbi from me. If anything, the reverse might be true.

"Ready?" I ask.

She blows out a breath. "Sure. I haven't actually had a massage in . . ." She shakes her head and laughs. "You'd think working in a spa, I'd be the person who gets them all the time, but somehow it never works out." She frowns. "Why didn't you schedule these at The Orchid? Brinley would beat your ass if she realized you were supporting the competition."

I chuckle. She's not wrong. "I considered it, but then I realized it'd be easier to keep this thing between us *between us* if we didn't roll into the place your best friends work for a couples massage."

She shrugs as if to say, *You have a point there.* But there's something else in her expression too, and I can't help but feel like I've disappointed her somehow. Does she think I *want* to sneak around? She's the one who insisted we not tell anyone. Even though my rational brain agrees with her reasoning, a bigger part of me wishes I didn't have to hide a thing.

"Besides, I got a great deal on this."

"I hope so. I don't want you to feel like you have to spend money on me."

"It's just money." I shrug. I could tell her that I like an excuse to spoil her a little, but I'm not sure that would put her at ease.

She worries her bottom lip between her teeth until it's red and swollen. I want to taste it. "How does a couples massage work, anyway?" she asks, pulling my thoughts back to safer territory.

I shake my head. "No idea. I've never had one before." I push open the door. "Let's go find out."

After we check in at the front desk, they send us up the stairs to the massage area. The place is run through the gym, but the second floor has its own atmosphere. Soft music plays in the background, and the air smells subtly of citrus and lavender. I'm already relaxing just from stepping into this space.

Rachel's waiting for us behind a small receptionist desk. "Hi! Dean, it's good to see you again."

"Hey, Rach. This is my friend Abbi."

"We're just friends," Abbi blurts. "I just . . . thought doing this together would be more fun."

Rach frowns for a beat before smoothing out her expression. "Sure! No problem. I think we've met at Smithy's. You're friends with Brinley, right?"

"Yes, I remember." Abbi smiles, but the way she shifts tells me she's nervous about this.

Rachel stands and waves for us to follow her. "Come

back here, and I'll show you the room. I'll have you undress to your comfort level, and then you'll each take your place on one of the massage tables."

"Will you be going back and forth between us?" I ask. "Or how does this work?"

Rachel grins and shakes her head. "No, no. That wouldn't be very enjoyable, I'm afraid. My other therapist will be joining me. Hudson's young, but he's excellent. Good hands, good intuition."

"Hudson?" Abbi asks, eyes wide.

Rachel opens the door to a dimly lit room and gestures us inside. There are two beds—or tables, I guess—and candles flicker in their sconces on the far wall. A small fountain gurgles in the corner and low, relaxing music plays in the background. "Do you know him?"

Abbi clears her throat. "Yeah, you know, small town," she says with a forced smile.

My stomach drops. I'm missing something here for sure. Did Abbi and Hudson date? Do they have some sort of history? Jealousy makes my back teeth clang together.

"For sure." Rachel looks back and forth between us. "Do you two have a preference of who works on whom?"

I lock eyes with Abbi and make a quick decision. "I want you to work on Abbi, Rach. I'm sure this Hudson guy is great, but Abs is on her feet constantly and needs the special Rachel experience."

Rachel nods. "No problem at all. I'll just step out and let you two undress. We'll go ahead and start facedown."

I wait until she pulls the door shut behind her before I turn to Abbi. "Who's Hudson?"

She blinks at me. "He's your massage therapist—I

thought we just covered that." She folds her arms. "I'm proud of you, by the way. You wouldn't believe the number of men who are afraid to let another man give them a massage. They can barely keep the male massage therapists in work at The Orchid. Men prefer women and women prefer women."

In truth, I prefer a woman too. It's just a comfort thing but not a deal breaker, but I'm happy to take any sort of praise from Abbi, so I shrug. "It's no big deal. But you had a definite reaction when she named the other massage therapist. Who is he? Do you two date?"

Abbi huffs. "No."

"Then what?"

She shrugs. "Nothing. Hudson works downstairs at the fitness center, and anytime he sees me at Smithy's, he tries to get me to schedule a personal training appointment with him."

"Oh." I blow out a breath. "Good."

She frowns. "Good?"

"I don't exactly want the girl I'm seducing to be naked in the same room as some guy she sees sometimes."

She bites her bottom lip, eyes crinkling in the corners. "The girl you're seducing, huh?"

I close the distance between us and slide a hand into her hair, twisting it around my fist so I can tug and tilt her face up. "What would you call this?"

She stares at my mouth with parted lips. "I don't know. I can't figure that out."

I didn't plan to kiss her in here, but I can't resist, so I lower my mouth to hers and suck her bottom lip between my teeth. The sound she releases is half moan, half sigh, and

LEXI RYAN

it makes my dick half hard, so I back away. "I didn't think that through." I walk to the other side of the room and strip off my shirt. The distance does very little to change the direction of my pumping blood.

Abbi touches her fingers to her mouth. "What just happened?"

I quirk a brow. "I kissed you." I pop the button on my jeans, and her gaze drops to my hands. *Hell.*

"No, I mean . . . why'd you run?"

I chuckle. "Because I don't want to be sporting a semi during my massage."

Her face splits into a grin. "Got it."

I shove my jeans down my hips, and she continues watching me as I step out of them, leaving myself in nothing but my boxer briefs. "You're staring."

Her cheeks flame red. "Sorry."

"I wouldn't complain, but again, massage etiquette and hard-ons don't go hand in hand."

She snorts. "Seems like there's a dirty joke somewhere in there."

No doubt.

I usually get massages in the nude, but given the circumstances, I decide to keep my briefs on. I fold my clothes into a neat pile then turn to Abbi, who hasn't removed a stitch of clothing. "Everything okay?"

"Sure. Why?" She's wringing her hands.

I look her over. "Because you're not undressing?"

"Right." She glances down. "Could you . . ." She twirls her finger in the air. "Face the wall?"

I open my mouth to object—to list all the reasons she doesn't need to worry about stripping in front of me—then think better of it and give her my back. "Just tell me when you're ready."

"Don't hold your breath," she mutters, and I grin at the wall.

CHAPTER TWELVE

ABBI

I am total goo. Any muscles I had were completely melted and obliterated by Rachel's magical hands. It's a wonder I was able to dress myself after, let alone walk to the car.

Dean asked if he could take me on a picnic, and since it's another beautiful day with the slightly cooler autumn temps I live for, I said yes. But other than that, he's been quiet since we left the spa, cutting looks to me from time to time but mostly keeping to himself.

I figure he's reveling in the post-massage Zen state too, but there's something about his expression that finally makes me speak up. "What's on your mind, porcupine?"

He scoffs out a laugh and shifts his gaze back to the road. "I've never heard anyone but your mom say that," he says, smiling.

I shrug and tuck one leg under me. "Can't hear it every

day through your teen years without it becoming part of your vernacular." I laugh. "But oh man, I hated it back then."

The corner of his mouth twitches. "I remember. Kace used to say it just to piss you off."

I shrug. "I was a moody teen—what can I say?" I wait a beat. "But you didn't answer my question."

He squeezes the steering wheel. "You'd tell me if there was something between you and Hudson?"

"That's really what you've been stewing about? If I'm dating a fresh-out-of-college dude-bro?"

"I wouldn't say I'm stewing, but . . . Well?"

I shake my head. "No. I'm not dating Hudson. Never have dated Hudson, have no plans to date Hudson. Why?"

"So when you told Stella you were dating again . . .?"

I gasp. "She told you that?" Did she tell him I got a Brazilian? It shouldn't matter. After Tuesday, he's well acquainted with the state of things between my legs, but it's a little embarrassing to admit I did that just for him.

He cuts his gaze to me again. "Was it supposed to be a secret?"

"No, but . . ." I shift in my seat. "I just didn't realize the two of you talked about me."

"It's not like that." He reaches out and squeezes my thigh. His hand is warm and strong, and when he leaves it there instead of pulling it away, all my attention goes to those fingers and the heat seeping through my jeans. "Hudson's massage was okay, but he spent most of the time looking over at you. I just didn't know if there was a reason beyond him having a crush or something."

I roll my eyes. "You and Layla."

"What about me and Layla?"

"She thinks he's into me too. Trust me. He's not. But it doesn't matter. I'm not into him."

He nods. "Okay. I just wanted to know."

I place my hand on top of his and thread our fingers together. After what we did in my office on Tuesday, it's crazy that holding hands should feel so intimate. But it does, and my heart races with anticipation until he gives my hand a reassuring squeeze in return. "So your massage wasn't as good as mine then, huh?"

"Who knows?" He turns down Park toward the lake and his house. "Hudson wasn't the only one distracted by you. Did you know you make these soft little porno sounds when you're getting a massage?"

I gape at him. "I do not!"

"Oh, but you do. They're not quite sighs and not quite moans, and it's a damn good thing Hudson wasn't the one responsible for those noises or I would've jumped off the table and yanked his hands off you."

"But you're fine with a *woman* making me moan?" He flashes me a lascivious grin, and I pinch the back of his hand. "That's ridiculous."

He shrugs. "I'm sorry for being a hypocritical, double-standard-holding, patriarchal jackass. It shouldn't matter. They're professionals, and I'm as aware as any regular that there's nothing sexual about massage. But I would've been jealous as fuck if Hudson had been the one touching you. Give me some credit for being self-aware."

I can't hold back my chuckle. "Well, at least there's that."

He turns into his driveway and shuts off the engine. "I'm just gonna run in to let Trixie out and grab our food, and then I'll be back."

"Oh, I haven't seen Trixie in forever!" I unbuckle. "Let's have our picnic on the deck so we can hang with her."

He stares at me for a beat before leaning across the console and pressing a firm kiss to my lips. "Don't change."

❦

LUNCH WAS AMAZING. Chicken salad sandwiches on focaccia with butternut squash soup and fresh strawberries. This is the second time Dean's fed me. I don't think I've ever dated anyone who cooked for me or brought me food. Food has always been my territory, and I was expected to deliver. As much as I enjoy cooking, I can't deny it's nice to be taken care of once in a while.

I'm happily full and stretched out on a chaise on his deck, petting Trixie and letting the afternoon sun warm my skin.

I love Dean's house. Not only is it bigger than my place, but it also features an incredible view of Lake Blackledge and is shiny and updated in ways my Pinterest boards have only ever dreamed of. Perks of owning a home renovation business, I suppose.

I'm not sure what feeding me and letting me snuggle with his dog have to do with seduction, but I'm not complaining. This is the best day I've had in a long time, and I'm grateful for Dean's determination to take this slow. I never would've been able to enjoy an afternoon like this if I thought we were leading up to naked time.

"Want some coffee?" Dean asks, standing from his own chaise.

"I either need caffeine or to surrender to a nap."

131

He grins. "I'd let you nap here. Not to brag, but I have the best bedding in the world."

Laughing, I roll my eyes. "Does that line really work? 'Come nap in my bed, baby. My sheets are super comfy.'"

He grabs my hand and pulls me out of the chaise until I'm standing in front of him, smiling up at his warm brown eyes. "It's true," he says, gaze on my mouth. "And it'd be a good lesson for you too. Letting me hold you." He cups my jaw in his big hand and skims his thumb across my bottom lip. "And I know all the secrets to help you fall asleep."

"A massage, lunch, and an orgasm?" I grin. "I don't think you're teaching me to be better in bed. I think you're spoiling me for all other men."

Something flashes in his eyes. Before I can get a read on his expression, he lowers his head and sweeps his lips across mine. "Is that a yes?"

I've been unexpectedly at ease all afternoon, but this question on the tail of his offer makes my stomach shimmy. "I might need to test out this bedding before committing to anything."

Grinning, he takes me by the hand and leads me into the house, Trixie trotting along behind us. When we enter his massive bedroom, we don't make it to the bed before he spins around and pins me against the wall. Mouth on mine, hands in my hair, his body hot and hard against mine.

I release a little moan into his mouth, and he smiles against my lips. "That sound right there. I wanna hear it over and over again."

"I'm pretty quiet in the bedroom, actually." I don't want to talk about this. I don't want to think about it. I just want to *feel*. But I also need to prepare him for what's coming. Disappointment.

"Not with me." He trails his mouth down my neck, licking and sucking.

My nerve endings go on high alert, and I gasp. I melt under each touch of his tongue, each scrape of his teeth.

"You're so sensual," he says. He slides his hand beneath my shirt and up to cup my breast, and I can't help but arch into it. His big hands feel like they were made to touch me. "And I'll use every trick I have if it means making you moan."

Another desperate, breathy sound slips from my lips, and then I groan when I realize what I've done. "You're determined to make a liar out of me."

"I'm determined to make you moan my name," he murmurs, pinching my nipple. "Tell me what you imagined me doing when you were touching yourself."

"No fair. You made me tell you if I thought about you, but you never said if you thought about me."

He buries his face in my neck and chuckles. "What do you think?"

"I think you made me say it, and double standards suck."

He pulls back and grins down at me. "I thought about you." He scans my face, his expression going serious. "I think about you all the time. Now tell me."

His face is serious, his eyes dark and penetrating. I gather all my courage. "You were over me. Touching me. Watching your fingers slide over me."

His nostrils flare. "That can be arranged."

"What about your fantasy? What was I doing when you thought about me?"

"What *weren't* you doing?" His teeth scrape over my earlobe.

This time the sound that slips past my lips is a whimper, but it's muffled by the phone ringing in Dean's pocket.

He ignores it and shifts his stance to position a thigh between my legs. I rock into the pressure, and he growls against my neck. "Fuck yes."

His phone stops ringing and immediately starts again. Reluctantly, I press at his shoulders. "You should check that."

Sighing and licking his lips in a way that just *does* something to me, he tugs his phone from his pocket, frowns at the screen, then answers. "What's wrong?"

I can't hear the person on the other line, but Dean takes a step back. Physically, it's less than a foot. Figuratively, it's miles.

I swallow back my disappointment, already sure our fun is going to come to a premature end.

"Nothing. I'm at home."

Nothing. As in, an answer to *what are you doing?*

My disappointment is crushing and completely hypocritical. I'm the one who insisted this had to be a secret. It's not fair to think he's lying about me because he's ashamed.

"No. It's fine," he says. "I'm glad you called." His gaze flicks to mine. "I can be there in ten. Just hang tight . . . Yep. Not a problem. See you soon." He ends the call and blows out a breath as he returns his phone to his pocket. "I'm sorry."

"It's fine." I force myself to shrug, but I feel heavy with doubt. "I mean, you own a business. I don't expect to have you all to myself in the middle of the week."

He shakes his head. "It's not work, but I have to go. If you want to stay, you can. I'll be back in an hour, maybe two." He drags a hand through his hair and mutters a curse. "I'm so sorry."

Who was on the phone?

I could ask. I trust that he'd tell me the truth. But I know as well as anyone that you shouldn't ask a question if you don't want to hear the answer. And what right do I have to demand to know how he spends his time? On the other hand, I don't know if I can do this if we aren't transparent with each other.

"Are you sure going is a good idea?" I ask. Because it doesn't matter what Amy's reason is for calling him, and it doesn't matter why he feels responsible for helping her, but —what happens next? That matters. And not just to me. Not just because it hurts to know he'll drop me and run to her the second she calls. But because I'm supposed to be helping him get past her.

He shakes his head. "Her parents are out of town and her best friend is at work. She doesn't have anybody else right now."

That's such bullshit. I bite my tongue and hold back the words.

He cocks his head to the side and studies me. "Hey." He grazes his thumb along my cheek. "She's vomiting with a nasty migraine. This isn't a booty call. I'm picking up meds and Gatorade at the pharmacy and keeping her company until the worst passes."

My throat feels tight. "You're a good guy." I'm afraid my pain leaks through my words.

Dean grabs my hips and tugs me toward him. "I wish you'd wait for me, but I understand if you don't want to."

Wait for him for an hour. Maybe a few. Maybe most of

the night. Tears sting the back of my eyes. "It's better if I don't."

He nods. "When can I see you again? This weekend? You have a short day on Sunday, right? I could steal your afternoon."

"I have plans with Layla." I force a smile. He wants to see me. He wants to make plans. There's no reason I should feel like going home to cry. "Shopping."

"After?" he asks.

I nod, trying to convince myself he'll still want that Sunday, that he won't be busy with Amy again. "I can text when I'm done."

"It's a plan." He lowers his mouth to mine and kisses me so long and deep that I wonder if he isn't trying to convince himself too.

&

DEAN

It's late when I finally get back home, and I'm glad Abbi didn't wait for me.

Amy's migraine was a wicked one. She didn't want me to leave, and I didn't want to be the guy who left. If someone needs you, you stick around. If I learned nothing else from my father, it was how much it screws with you when someone who said they care doesn't show up when you need them.

I know what it's like to be alone. Hell, I'm pretty fucking good at it at this point, but Amy's not. She had Kace taking care of her for years, and she gets panicked when she gets sick and no one's around.

I helped because that's the kind of man I want to be, but that didn't make it easy, and it doesn't change the look on Abbi's face when she realized where I was going.

At least being around Amy tonight didn't fuck with my head. Two weeks ago, it would've done a number on me. Especially since she needed me for something other than sex or drunken fun. Especially since she thanked me a hundred times and told me she didn't know what she'd do without me.

She wanted me to stay the night. She wanted me to hold her. And somehow I wasn't even tempted. All I wanted was to get home and text Abbi—to see her again so I could stop remembering that disappointment on her face. So as soon as Amy fell asleep, I got the hell out of there.

I whistle for Trixie and go out back with her, plunking myself into a chaise in the dark and pulling out my phone to text Abbi.

Dean: Finally home. How was your evening?

I watch the dots bounce for a long time. Long enough that I know she's rewriting or at least rethinking what she's trying to say.

Abbi: Fine. Took a long bath and read a new book.

I'm sure she's censoring her thoughts, but that's not a terrible mental picture.

Dean: Bubbles? Wine? Orgasms?
Abbi: Two out of three's not bad.

Dean: I guess that depends which two.

I hold my breath, hoping she'll let me flirt a little, that we can get back to where we were before my phone rang.

Abbi: How's Amy?

Apparently not. I squeeze my eyes shut. I don't want to talk about Amy. But I owe her something.

Dean: She's better. Her doc called her in
    some meds for the nausea—that's what I
    picked up—so she was doing a lot better
    once those kicked in.
Abbi: I can't decide if I failed you as your
    Sober Sponsor or if you're just that nice.
Dean: You didn't fail anything. And I'm sorry
    our afternoon was ruined. How can I
    make it up to you?

Those dots start their bounce-and-disappear dance again. And when I'm finally ready to give it up and let her be for the night, another text comes through.

Abbi: You don't have to make anything up to
    me. I remember Amy's migraines and
    have been the one to run to the pharmacy
    a couple of times myself when she and
    Kace were still together. She's lucky you're
    such a good friend.

A heady mix of gratitude and affection warm my chest.

Because *damn*. I'm not sure I deserve to get off the hook that easily.

> Dean: Are we still on for Sunday?
> Abbi: If you're still interested.
> Dean: As if there's any doubt.

CHAPTER THIRTEEN

DEAN

I've taken to spending Friday afternoons at the office doing paperwork—writing up quotes, replying to emails, and doing my part to keep up with the mind-numbing administrative tasks that come with running a business. It's never my favorite part of the workweek, but it makes it a little easier to enjoy my weekend, so I make myself do it anyway.

This Friday *drags*. All I can think about is seeing Abbi again. Sunday night seems way too far away. I give in to the temptation I've been feeling all day and text her.

> Dean: I want to take you out on Sunday.
> What sounds better to you—a chill night
> at Smithy's, or a slightly fancier dinner?

She's at work, so I'm not surprised when it takes her a while to get back to me.

>Abbi: Don't you think people might ask
>questions if they see us out together—just
>the two of us?

Disappointment floods me. She's right. They might, but that doesn't really bother me. Unfortunately, it seems to bother her.

>Dean: I suppose we could handle that in one
>of two ways. We could just tell them we're
>(gasp!) dating. Or we could pretend we're
>just hanging out as friends. And, yes,
>Abbi, it'd be pretend, because I don't do
>the things to my friends that I intend to
>do to you.

There. That's the best way I can say "This is more than a friendly favor" without risking her running scared if I say what I really want. I can't change my past or my family, but maybe with time she'll change how she feels about it.

>Abbi: Both of those options result in people
>gossiping about us.
>Dean: Let them gossip. IDGAF.
>Abbi: I'm not sure you're thinking this
>through. Imagine what would happen if
>we told Kace and Stella we were dating.
>Dean: Well, I'd hope they'd just be happy for

us as we are for them and mind their own
business.

As if she summoned him, I look up from my phone to
see Kace take two steps into my office.

He gets one look at my face and back-pedals toward the
door. "Want me to come back at a better time?"

I glance at the clock. "This is fine. Didn't we plan to
meet now?"

He folds his arms. "Yeah, but you look . . . pissed."

Oh, shit. I guess I am scowling. That's what happens
when you realize you've once again fallen for someone who
doesn't want anyone to know she's dating you. Or fucking
you. Or whatever the hell it is we're doing. This is what
happens when you're me and make the same fucking
mistake over and over. It's not like I didn't know the rules
when we started this.

I blow out a breath. "Sorry. Not work-related. I'm fine."

My phone buzzes, and I can't help but look.

> Abbi: Listen, I know this might not be a big
> deal for us once it ends, but I don't think
> it's fair to expect our friends to
> understand the limits of our relationship.
> I just don't want to make drama where
> there doesn't need to be drama.

Right. Why should I expect my friends to accept this is
temporary when even I can't?

Kace pulls one of my guest chairs away from the wall
and closer to my desk. "Let me guess," he says. "Amy?"

I shake my head. "No. Not Amy."

Kace arches a brow. "You're not just saying that?"

"I've moved on. Seriously, you were all right, and I needed to let that ship sail. This is . . ." I blow out a breath. "This is someone new." I hate it, I realize. The secrets, the sneaking around. Yeah, it's fun to fuck around in public places, fun to have to be quick and quiet so no one knows what we're doing, but that's just a sexual turn-on. It's not life. I don't want to live my life like this.

"Stella said you mentioned something about someone new. When do we get to meet her?"

I lean my head side to side, stretching out my neck. "You already know her, and go ahead and stop your questions there, because I can't say anything else."

"Another secret affair?" he asks, but there's no bitterness in his voice—none of the resentment he's entitled to. My sister did that for him. She helped him move on from Amy when no one thought he ever would. And Abbi did it for me.

The difference is that Stella wanted Kace, and Abbi . . . hell, I guess I don't know what Abbi wants from me, if there's any chance she might want more than some confidence in the bedroom. That's probably something we should figure out. But maybe not yet. Maybe first I need to finish giving her exactly what we started this for. Even if the idea of seeing her with another guy one day down the road kills me.

"Secret for now," I finally reply. "You know how this town is." It's the best excuse I can muster. I can tell Kace isn't buying it, but he's a good friend and doesn't push the issue.

My thoughts snag on the night in Kace's backyard when Smithy said Abbi and I couldn't stop staring at each other, and I wonder why he's not the least bit suspicious. Then he saw us together outside the gym, and we fed him that bullshit about how it was a big coincidence that we were both there for massages at the same time. Is it that hard for him to imagine Abbi might give me a chance?

I shove the thoughts away. I'm pretty sure I'm overthinking this.

"Mom's been nagging me about bringing you to Sunday dinner," Kace says. "Get your ass there soon so I don't have to hear any more of it, okay?"

"I have plans this Sunday."

"With the girl?"

"Yeah." I hold his gaze and wonder what he'd think if he knew "the girl" was his sister. Does he want his sister to end up with someone with my history? My shit father sure didn't seem to be an issue for him with Stella, but maybe there's a double standard there. I blow out a breath and try to bring my thought spiral to a halt. "Anyway, I've been avoiding dinner with your folks for a reason."

Kace narrows his eyes. "And what would that be?"

I clear my throat and for the thousandth time realize I was such a fucking idiot with Amy. I should've never messed around with her to begin with. "I mean, the thing with Amy . . ."

Kace shakes his head. "Mom and Dad don't know anything about that."

My shoulders sag. Until this moment, I hadn't realized how heavily that was weighing on me. "Thank you for that."

Kace smacks me between my shoulder blades. "Don't mention it." He flashes a grim smile. "But seriously, don't mention it. You don't want to wake Mama Bear Matthews."

I grin. "Trust me. I remember."

"I respect your time with your girl, but get over there soon."

Nodding, I grab my phone and type out a quick reply to Abbi. There's no reason for me to get all butthurt about her not wanting to go out with me. That was never our agreement.

Dean: I get it. Your place, then?

I guess I should be grateful that the nature of text messaging hides the disappointment I know Kace can see in my face.

❦

STELLA WOBBLES under the weight of the sledgehammer and teeters in her heels.

I cringe. "This is a terrible idea."

"Shut up," she growls. "I'm not a weakling. I can do this."

It's Saturday, and since Abbi has to work all day, I agreed to help Kace start his latest project by gutting his old master bath.

"Ignore him," Kace says. "Just keep a good grip on it and swing."

Stella adjusts her grip and lifts the sledgehammer over her shoulder before swinging it down toward the shower wall. She cracks a single tile, and her eyes light up. "I did it!" She rushes into Kace's arms, and he wraps her in a hug, pulling her into his chest.

My sister has carried a torch for my best friend since we were teens, but I never imagined they'd actually end up together. Now that they have, I wonder why I never saw it coming. Kace is the rock my flighty sister needs in her life, and she's the carefree fun Kace desperately needed in his. They work, and I love seeing them both so happy.

"Here you go," Stella says, handing the sledgehammer back to Kace.

"You're done?" he asks, laughing.

She wrinkles her nose. "I mean, unless you need me?"

Kace kisses her forehead. "Dean and I can take it from here."

"Well, have fun. I hope it goes smoothly. Don't forget we have plans tonight."

He settles the hammer on the floor and grabs her before she can get too far. "How could I forget?" When he lowers his mouth to hers, I look away. I'm stoked they're happy, but I could do without the constant PDA.

"Dean, do you have plans tomorrow night?" Stella asks, pulling my attention back to them.

"Sort of." I'm planning to talk Abbi out of her clothes, but I keep that information to myself.

Stella grins. "*Sort of* isn't good enough. You should come with us. We're going to that new brewery just south of here after dinner with Kace's parents. They have firepits out back by the lake. I reserved one for us, but it'll be more fun with company."

"Thanks for the invite, sis, but I'd rather not spend my Sunday night as a third wheel."

"Then we'll bring Abbi too. Come on, it'll be like a double date."

I open my mouth to say Abbi's working late, but I'm cut off by Kace's grunt.

"No offense, Freckles, but that's a terrible idea."

I bristle, and my sister pulls out of Kace's arms and glares at him. "Why would you say that? You don't think Abbi knows how to hang out and have fun?"

"No, but she's busy tomorrow. She already said she won't be at Mom's for dinner because she has something going on."

I relax a bit.

"And anyway," Kace says, "I don't think Abbi should go on a date with Dean." His gaze skips to me for a beat before going back to Stella. "No offense, dude."

No offense? I clench my jaw, and my molars ache.

"Why not?" Stella asks, folding her arms.

Normally, this is when I'd excuse myself from the conversation. Stella and Kace are great together, but they're both strong-willed. When they butt heads, I make myself as scarce as possible. But this time I stay. Because I want to know too.

Kace glances at me again, and at least this time he grimaces like the conversation makes him uncomfortable. "It doesn't matter. We're talking about your brother and my sister. That only happens in the movies."

Stella's gaze shifts to meet mine, and I see it. This isn't a random idea on Stella's part. She *knows* something. Or at the very least, she suspects. And more shockingly, she hasn't told Kace. "Abbi needs a little fun in her life," Stella says, holding my gaze.

"Abbi needs someone who'll be gentle with her," Kace says. He shifts his weight from one foot to another. "Come on, you're going to be late for work. I'll walk you out."

Stella flashes me a final apologetic glance before following Kace out of the bathroom. Their voices grow muffled for a bit, but the moment they step outside, I can hear them again through the open window.

"I'm all for fixing her up," Kace says, "but she doesn't see dating the way Dean does."

"What do you mean by that?" Stella asks.

"Listen, I know he's your brother and you feel protective toward him, but he's also a *player*. If he were even interested in dating Abbi—and *that* is another conversation entirely—they'd end up fooling around, and she'd get attached."

I close my eyes. *She'd get attached? Joke's on you, bud.*

"I don't want her hurt," Kace says.

"He wasn't a player with Amy."

The silence stretches so long that I'm not sure if they're out there having an epic stare-down or if they started whispering.

"I can't help but be protective of her," Kace says. His voice is so low that I can barely hear him. "She's been hurt before."

I can hear Stella giving a sharp reply, but I can't make out the words over the sharp sting of disappointment in my chest. This thing with Abbi is temporary, and I need to remember that.

ABBI

"Yes, girl! Yes!" Layla says, clapping her hands.

I turn side to side, trying to get a better view of myself in the short black dress. Other than the fact that it only goes down to my mid-thighs, I like it. The waistline is higher, and the skirt flares, camouflaging my tummy pouch and hips. "I'm afraid it's the magic of dressing room lighting," I finally say.

Layla glances up at the canned lights of the dressing room. "What about it?"

"You know, when you try something on at the store and you love it, but at home it's all wrong. Like the lighting made you lose your mind for a minute."

She folds her arms and walks a slow circle around me. "Nah. Nope. Not this one. It's hot. And *you* are hot in it."

I glance down at the abundance of cleavage visible in the low-cut top. I can't deny that I want to be the kind of girl who feels confident in a dress like this. Layla would, and I'd be the first to cheer her on. But me? Yikes.

Nobody said change was easy, did they? "Okay. I'll get it."

Layla beams. "Awesome. Go change, and we'll check out and run to the shoe store across the way."

"I have shoes."

She arches a brow. "Do you? For *that* dress?"

"Sure."

"Tell me about them."

"Black ballet flats. *Classic*."

She frowns. "Do you ever wear heels?"

"Not unless you count boots."

"But you wear heeled boots? So if I put heels on your feet, you'll be comfortable walking in them?"

I shrug. "I guess."

"Good. Because that dress begs for some sexy heels."

I smile, giddiness fluttering around in my chest. Layla's enthusiasm is contagious, and today has been so much fun.

I have new jeans and a half-dozen new shirts. And this will be the *second* dress I've splurged on today.

And dresses make me think of Dean and his promises of what he'd do if I ever wore a skirt to work. My stomach shimmies with anticipation—silly when I don't plan on wearing this to work *ever*, but something about buying it just feels courageous and a little naughty.

I haven't seen him since I left his house on Thursday afternoon, but we've texted a little bit. Though none of his messages have been super racy, and he definitely hasn't surprised me with any appearances in my office. Which is . . . good, I guess?

After I change back into my jeans and T-shirt, I check out, and Layla and I head to the shoe store. Layla makes a beeline toward a pair of peep-toe strappy heels that could double as deadly weapons.

"Yes?" she asks. "I think yes."

I nod, take a seat, and try them on. I actually like my feet. They're cute, and I always keep up with my pedicures, so they're even soft. Today my toenails are a light pink that matches my T-shirt, but I think I'd paint them red for these shoes.

Layla is distracted by a pair of red, sky-high stilettos, so I give in to impulse, snap a picture, and send it to Dean.

> Abbi: Splurging a little today. What else
> should I get?

I'm slipping my Converse back on when he replies.

> Dean: With those? Black lace panties and a
> matching bra.

"I can't believe you!"

My head snaps up at the sound of Stella's voice. *Shit.* I plop my phone back in my purse. "Huh?" My cheeks are burning. She's standing right in front of me. Did she see whom I was texting? What we were talking about? I didn't want my friends finding out about this, but this has the potential to be more embarrassing than what I imagined.

"You never go shopping with me!" She folds her arms across her chest and sticks out her bottom lip. "I feel betrayed."

Relief is like a cool breeze across my hot cheeks. "Oh, I'm sorry."

Layla spins around, still holding a red stiletto. "Stella! Hi! What do you think of this shoe? Does it say, *I do what I want?*"

Stella grins. "I'm pretty sure you deliver that message no matter what you're wearing."

Layla laughs. "True." She looks back and forth between us. "If you're shopping, why don't you hang with us? We still need to get lingerie and . . . maybe a piercing."

"A piercing?" I ask, genuinely curious. Sexy panties don't scare me. I might be the only one who sees them, but I like to feel good about what I'm wearing beneath my clothes. "What kind of piercing?"

Layla cocks her head to the side and looks me over. "Nose or navel. You choose."

Stella gapes at her then at me. "*You're* going to get a piercing?"

I already have my navel pierced. It was a crazy, impulsive college thing I did after Cody told me he thought navel piercings were hot. When I surprised him with it, though, he just shrugged and said it was "okay" but maybe I should get rid of it so people didn't think I was trying too hard.

Keeping my navel ring was the most rebellious thing I ever did in that relationship, and every time I've thought about taking it out for good, I don't out of sheer spite for the guy who broke my heart. *Real mature.*

Layla puts down the shoe and nods. "She wants a makeover, and in my experience, not much makes a girl feel hotter and in control of her body than a new piercing or a new tattoo."

I shake my head. "I'm not a tattoo girl."

"That's what I thought," Layla says.

"A makeover?" Stella's gaping at me again, and I feel like I'm seconds away from blurting out everything.

Yes, I wanted a makeover so I could be more confident when Frankie moved to town, but now your brother's working on the root of my insecurities and I hope Frankie never gets here because I don't want my time with Dean to end.

Gah. I'm a mess.

"Spill," Stella says. "Is this all about you dating again?"

I look to Layla, desperate for help.

Layla shakes her head. "Hey, I'm not going to spill your secrets. That's on you."

"You remember Frankie Perez?"

Stella's eyes go round as saucers. "The wine guy? Are you *finally* going out with him?"

"Yes— No . . . I don't know." *I'm kind of too busy lusting after your brother to give another guy much thought.* "He's moving to the OV, and I wanted to be prepared. In case something happens."

"He totally gave her his number and said he wants to get

together when he moves to town," Layla says. "The boy has it *bad*."

I shoot her a look. "What happened to not telling my secrets?"

"Sorry, I thought we were sharing." Layla shrugs.

Stella claps her hands. "I'm so excited. And a little shocked."

I huff. "Thanks a lot."

She swats my arm. "Not that he wants to go out with you, goober." She wrinkles her nose. "I think I guessed all wrong about what you meant when you said you were dating again, but I'm proud of you."

"We've officially spent way more time talking about this than I wanted to. Please change the subject."

"Okay, okay," she says, bouncing on her heels. "I'm just so excited."

Layla returns to her inspection of the red heels, and Stella joins her. I slide my phone from my purse to see another text.

> Dean: Scratch that. On you, I want those shoes, black lace panties, and no bra. On my bed. Nothing else . . . except maybe a glass of wine in your hand.

My stomach flip-flops. I glance at the girls to confirm they're still distracted before typing out a reply.

> Abbi: If you can get me comfortable with being like that in your bed, then your work will be done.

Dean: Oh, hell no. If you're like that in my
     bed, my work has only just begun.

"So, a navel piercing?" Layla says, pulling my attention away from my phone.

I shake my head. "I already have one, but I'd be up for buying a new piece of jewelry for it."

"Deal," Layla says.

Stella gapes. "What *else* don't I know about you?"

I cough and force a smile. "Hard to say."

CHAPTER FOURTEEN

DEAN

*J*t's good to have a drink with my buddies, but I can't deny I'm distracted. Distracted by Abbi and our plans for later. Distracted by memories of the sounds she made while I touched her, the perfect way her lips parted when she came. Distracted by everything we didn't get to do on Thursday. If I worried one afternoon playing nursemaid to Amy was going to send me spiraling into my unrequited feelings again, I needn't have. My brain and libido only care about Abbi.

Smithy, Kace, and Marston are all sipping beers, their attention on the football game on one of Smithy's big-screen TVs, and I keep looking at my phone. I'm not even a third of the way through my beer when I cave and text her again.

Dean: Can't. Stop. Thinking. About. You.

Abbi: The feeling is mutual. Out of curiosity .
. . what are your thoughts on navel
piercings?
Dean: On you? HOT.
Abbi: You don't think it's weird for a girl who
will never—never, ever, ever—wear a
bikini to get her belly button pierced?
Dean: But you know it's there, right? I think
it'd be cute.

The TV cuts to a commercial break and the guys turn
back to the table, so I flip my phone over, images of a glit-
tering navel ring dancing in my head.

"Where are your ladies this afternoon?" Smithy asks.

Because I'm a fucking idiot, I actually open my mouth
to answer.

Thankfully, Kace beats me to it before I realize my mistake.
"Stella was working this morning, and then she needed to run
to the mall before we head to Mom and Dad's for dinner."

Marston nods. "Brinley had to work today too. I think
she and Stella were planning a staff retreat or something."

Smithy grins. "Think they'll do each other's hair? Model
lingerie?"

Kace cocks his head to the side and narrows his eyes at
our goofball friend. "Did your mom drop you on your head
when you were a baby? What do *you* do at staff meetings?"

"My staff isn't as hot as Brinley's," Smithy says.

"I heard that!" Nathan the bartender calls from behind
the bar.

"Except for you!" Smithy calls back to the burly middle-
aged biker.

"Hey, speaking of the girls," Marston says, "Brinley and I are inviting everyone over for dinner at the house next Sunday. The last of the renovations are done thanks to you guys"—he nods toward me, then Kace—"and we're ready to enjoy it with our friends."

"Sounds good to me," Kace says. "Amy has Hope next weekend. I'll talk with Stella and make sure she's free."

"I'll be there," Smithy says.

I nod. "Same."

My phone buzzes, and I have to wait until the guys shift their attention back to the TV, but once they do, I have zero chill as I grab it to see the latest from Abbi.

> Abbi: Yeah? Because if you'd gotten my shirt
> off on Thursday, you might've discovered
> something about me . . .
> Dean: Seriously?
> Abbi: Yeah. Crazy, huh?
> Dean: Who is this new Abbi, and how do I
> keep her in my life for good?

As soon as I send the message, I want to yank it back. *Not so subtle, Dean.* Hell, maybe she should know that I'd be up for something more than a temporary fling, but I don't want to scare her away either. Not when I'm not the kind of guy she's looking to build a life with.

> Abbi: Haha. I always figured I could take it
> out if I wanted . . . but for whatever
> reason, I never have.

I can't decide if I'm frustrated or relieved that she didn't take me seriously. A little of both, I suppose.

"Another beer?" Nathan asks me, grabbing our empties from the table.

I shake my head. With any luck, Abbi will be headed home soon, and even though I can walk there from here, I don't want to risk being buzzed. "I'm good."

The guys place their orders for another round, and I give my attention back to my phone.

> Abbi: Wrapping this up earlier than I
> thought. Should be home in thirty. I have
> chicken noodle soup in the Crock-Pot and
> I'm making homemade biscuits for dinner
> if you wanna come sooner than we
> planned.
> Dean: You had me at COME.

She responds with an eye-roll emoji, and I chuckle, sliding my phone into my pocket. The guys are all focused on the TV again.

"I'm gonna head out."

Kace glances at me. "Cool. See you in the morning."

"See ya. Thanks for the company." I scoot my chair back, and Smithy jumps out of his.

"Let me walk you out. I need to ask you something."

Shit. "Sure." I frown at Smithy, but he just nods to the exit, so I head to my car with a sigh, and he follows.

Once we're outside and out of view of the bar, he grabs my arm, stopping me. "Let me see your phone."

"What?"

"You were texting someone right before you decided to

leave. You've been texting all damn afternoon. I want to know who." He extends a hand, palm up.

"I'm not giving you my phone."

Smithy crosses his arms and rocks back on his heels. "That's what I was afraid of." He shakes his head. "Fucking magical pussy."

"Excuse me?"

"I know you're going to see Amy, and I'm not okay with that. You're doing better. You're happy and looking less like death warmed over. Going back for a quick fuck now makes you the addict who thinks he can handle one bump of blow without fucking his life up again."

"Wow. You don't have any strong opinions about my sex life, do you?"

He arches a brow. "Do you deny it?"

"I'm not going to see Amy, if that's what you're asking."

"Prove it."

I can tell by the tense line of his jaw that he's not just going to let this go. And, hell, I should be grateful he's being such a good friend. Amy *was* bad for me, and I *was* making trash decisions where she was concerned. Sighing, I pull up my texts with Abbi but just as quickly shove my phone back into my pocket. *That shit's private.*

"Fuck," he mutters. "I wanted to be wrong."

"It's not that." I tuck my hands into my pockets. "I'm not going to see Amy. My plans are with someone else, and I don't want to show you my texts with her because they're private."

He doesn't budge. Just waits, brow raised. "Who?"

I look away. I don't want to betray Abbi's trust, but I also don't like keeping this a secret. "I'm not supposed to say, but I can tell you I've been spending time with . . . a friend. And honestly, since we started hanging out, I've all but forgotten why I was so hung up on Amy."

"A friend."

I nod.

He shakes his head. "I want to believe you, but the only friend you have who you'd be willing to ditch Amy for is . . ." His eyes go wide. "Well, shit. Tell me you're not banging Kace's baby sister."

I cringe. "First of all, she's not a kid anymore, and she can make her own decisions. And second of—"

"You are. Holy fuck. For real? You're playing a little lust-and-thrust with Abbi?"

"Would you lower your fucking voice?" I growl, looking around. "I'm not, actually, not that it's your business."

"But you're messing around." He smacks his hand over his mouth. "Holy flaming testicles. You finally did it."

I hold up a finger. "Stop making assumptions. You don't know what you're talking about."

"I was there on her twenty-first. Do you forget? Everyone else might be blind to it, but I've known how you felt about her all this time." He grins. "And you finally made it happen. Good for you."

"It's not like that, Smith."

"Then what's it like?" He's still smiling, though I'm feeling a little ill with the mention of Abbi's twenty-first.

I shrug. "She just needs a little confidence, so I'm helping her with that."

Smithy fists his hands at his sides and thrusts his hips forward. "I bet you are."

I stamp down my irritation. He doesn't mean to be crude. He just . . . *is*. "Don't ever thrust your hips in the context of Abbi again. She'd knock you out."

Smithy holds up both hands, face going solemn. "Got it. But for real . . ." He glances around as if he's afraid someone might be listening. "I always thought it was just the booze talking that night. She didn't mean the shit she was spouting off about. It was like a defense machination or whatever."

"You mean a defense *mechanism*?"

"If you say so. Are you two serious?"

I swallow the lump in my throat. Everything she said that night made perfect sense to me. Everything she wanted in a guy. All the things that mattered most to her. All the ways I could never fit the bill. "No. It's not like that. She just wanted . . ." Seduction lessons? No. I can't say those words to Smithy. *No way.* "It's temporary, and she doesn't want anyone knowing about it."

His lips press into a thin line. "I don't like the sound of that."

Me neither, but the whole damn thing was my idea, so I don't exactly feel like I'm in a position to complain. And honestly? At least this time I know where I stand with Abbi. "It'll be fine."

"Be careful. Your heart's still a mess from Amy."

I shrug. "I know what I'm doing."

He smacks me on the shoulder and gives me an awkward little salute, and I walk to my car, trying to shove thoughts of Abbi's twenty-first birthday from my mind.

∾

ABBI

Dean is on his way over and I'm feeling uncharacteristically confident, so naturally my uterus decided this was the perfect time to do its monthly thing.

Maybe I wouldn't care—would've been relieved, even—if I hadn't been picturing the scene Dean painted for me. It's not so much that I'm dying to be in bed in nothing but heels and a pair of lacy panties, but the idea of him imagining it is a serious turn-on, and I might've bought the perfect panties to finish the scene. Panties that are definitely *not* period friendly.

When the doorbell rings, I'm anything but the seductress he described. I'm barefoot in the jeans and T-shirt I wore shopping, my hair tied up in a sloppy bun on top of my head because I just made biscuits, and cooking with your hair down is gross.

I swing open the door, and his gaze rakes over me like a hungry caress. "Hey."

"Hey."

He pushes into my foyer, kicks the door shut behind him, and grabs my hips as his mouth finds mine. It blows my mind that it feels so natural to slide my hands into his hair and kiss him back. He tastes faintly of beer, and his mouth is warm and hungry over mine.

He breaks the kiss and grins down at me. "I've been thinking about that all day."

"Yeah?" I ask, my voice shaking a little.

"Oh, yeah. Haven't you?"

I nod. "But I have bad news. I just started my period—like, *minutes ago*. My body hates me."

He chuckles. "So the pants stay on tonight. I can handle

that." He slides one hand behind my head, lacing his fingers into my hair and making several strands fall. "You look beautiful."

I laugh. "I'm wearing jeans and a T-shirt."

He shrugs. "Looks good on you. I've never been the kind of guy who gets off on seeing a woman dressed in something that's *supposed to be* sexy."

"Liar." I shake my head, but just having him this close makes me smile.

"Don't get me wrong—a woman in lacy lingerie is hot as fuck, but only if she wore it for me. Seeing a girl wandering around my house barefoot and in one of my old T-shirts is more my style." His eyes sweep over me, as if he's imagining it. "You'd look hot in anything. And if you wore it just for me, that'd be an even bigger turn-on."

"You don't actually have to pretend I'm something I'm not."

He cocks his head to the side. "I don't follow."

My smile falls away. This is where things get awkward, but I don't want pretty lies. Not from Dean. "I know we're on a mission here, and that you want to build my confidence, but you don't have to say things that aren't true. That'll just come back to bite me later."

He lets his hands fall to his sides. "What have I said that you don't think is true?"

"You say things as if I'm thin and beautiful, and I don't think pretending is going to—"

"I haven't."

"What?"

He steps back and folds his arms. "I've said you're beautiful because you are, but I haven't said shit about your size."

I flinch and bow my head. "Right. I guess I misunderstood."

Dean blows out a breath. "Abbi, I don't get you. You're so beautiful and so confident, and you'd be the first person in line to knock someone on their ass who made assumptions about a girl because of her size. But you have a double standard when it comes to yourself. I'm not going to pretend you're thin because—why should I?" He must see me tense, because he adds, "I don't say that to hurt you, though I can see it does."

I shake my head. "No, I know I'm not."

Dean puts two fingers under my chin and tilts my face up until I meet his eyes. I'm afraid he can see every inch of my insecurities in mine. "I say it because it's important you understand that I *see* you," he says. "You're not thin. *And* you're fucking beautiful. Not *but*. Not *despite*. Both are true. You're the one who's convinced one has anything to do with the other."

I feel completely exposed. This is my biggest secret. My shameful truth. "I don't think it's true for everyone, but . . ."

"When you thought I was taking you to the gym for a workout, you were upset."

I nod. "Yeah. Having you push me into some workout routine would've crushed me."

"So you don't have any plans of changing your size as we go through this?" he asks.

I blow out a breath. "I'm just sick of trying. I've lost weight before—ten or twenty pounds here and there—but I always gain it back, and it makes me miserable. My whole life revolves around food, and I get obsessive and can't enjoy normal things." I hate explaining this to anyone, but I especially hate explaining it to Dean. "Maybe I should try again, but—"

"That's not why I'm asking," he says, expression soft. "My point is there's part of you that's accepted that you're bigger than your friends, part of you that would rather focus on being healthy at this size than chase something your body resists."

I nod, but this conversation makes me miserable.

"I think that's awesome." He reaches out and brushes a hand down my arm. "It's way healthier—emotionally and physically—than these crazy diets I see people going on, but you're missing one piece."

I hold his gaze for a long time before finding the courage to ask, "What's that?"

"This is you. This is who you are. Now you need to see what I see—a big girl who's fucking hot, who fills my mind with dirty ideas and turns me on, and who's as worthy of the same lust, love, passion, and fulfillment as everyone else."

My vision goes blurry with unshed tears. "You are possibly the best guy I've ever—" I scoff and tip my face to the ceiling. "I was going to say dated, but I guess that's not what we're doing. I mean, I know what this is and what it isn't."

He doesn't respond, and when I have it together enough to look at him again, he's just staring at me.

"Good talk," I whisper. I've screwed this all up.

He swallows audibly. His expression is so severe that I think he's about to go with something serious when he says, "It smells amazing. Should we go eat?"

CHAPTER FIFTEEN

DEAN

*T*he text message on my screen makes the delicious dinner Abbi just fed me churn in my gut.

> Sandy: You have every right to be angry, but don't make decisions today that you'll regret in the future. You only have one father.

I close out the messaging app and darken my screen. I have a whole evening with Abbi, and I won't let my dad's wife ruin my mood.

Dinner was delicious, as expected, but instead of letting me clean up, Abbi sent me to her living room with a beer, insisting I'd done all the work the last couple of times we ate together, so she wanted me to relax this time.

I use the opportunity to watch her move around the

kitchen. She exudes such confidence in that space. She owns it, and it's hot as hell. The perfect distraction from the reality waiting for me on my phone.

When she finally joins me in the living room, I set my beer on the end table and grab her around the waist before she can sit. I scoot to the edge of my seat and guide her to stand between my knees.

"Hi," she says. "How are you?"

"I'm good now." I slip a hand under her shirt and brush my thumb over her navel—over the jewel waiting there. I pull in a shuddering breath over the evidence of her sexy little secret. "Does it hurt to touch it?"

She shakes her head. "I've had it since college. It was tender that first six months or so while it healed, but it's no different than my pierced ears now." She tugs on an earring to demonstrate.

"Good." With both hands, I shove her shirt up to just beneath her breasts, exposing her soft stomach and the blue jewels sitting just above and just inside her navel. I flick my gaze up to hers and hold it as I lean forward and suck the top stud into my mouth.

Abbi draws in a ragged breath and sways toward me. "Whoa." Her hands slide into my hair as I kiss the skin around the piercing—licking and nipping and sucking until she's unsteady and the hands in my hair are the only thing keeping her upright.

Standing, I tug her shirt off over her head and toss it onto the couch. I see the moment she tenses, see her hold her breath as if waiting for me to deliver the verdict on her shirtless-ness. So I give it. "Fucking beautiful," I murmur. She's wearing a simple black bra, and her full breasts swell over the cups.

I want to bury my face in them, to feel them fill my hands, to see if I can get her off with nothing but my tongue and fingers on her nipples.

"Bedroom," I say, but the word comes out like a growl.

Abbi bites her bottom lip but backs toward her bedroom door. "I thought we were keeping our clothes on tonight."

"*Pants*." I take a step forward and smack her ass. "I made no promises about tops or bras, and I'm dying to get my mouth on those perfect tits of yours."

Her cheeks blaze red, but she backs toward the bedroom then inside it, eyes glued to me as I prowl toward her, step for step. The back of her thighs hit the bed, and she stops.

I close the distance between us and snake my arms around her to the clasp on her bra. She shuts her eyes and holds her breath. I stop myself. "Breathe, precious. You're safe. Right here, right now, with me, there's nothing you need to worry about."

"I know." She opens her mouth as if she's going to explain but then closes it again as she steps out of my arms. She wraps her arms around herself, and that signal of insecurity, of defensiveness, breaks my heart.

"Tell me what you're thinking." She's quiet for a long time, and I wait, channeling my thoughts. *You can trust me. I promise I won't hurt you.* When she still doesn't say anything, I ask, "Do you want me to leave?"

She turns to me again and shakes her head. "No. I just . . . When you came to my office and we fooled around? That was one of the hottest experiences of my life."

"Same." I step closer and stroke her sides with my thumbs.

"I liked it like that because there was no reason to rush."

I cough out a laugh. "You mean you like the rush?" Because if she thinks that was me taking my time, she's going to be shocked when I finally do get her naked. "It's hot sometimes, but a slow weekend in bed is good too." I kiss her neck. "I want to do things to you that I need *hours* for."

She shivers in my arms. "I mean, you won't feel like you need to rush if it's the under-clothes sneaking around."

I frown, still not following, and pull back to study her face. "I don't understand what you mean."

The tits on a Barbie are more natural than her smile. "Nothing. It's nothing. Forget I said anything."

"Abbi . . ."

She sways toward me, her soft breasts pressing against my chest. "Please?"

I swallow and nod. I'm not sure I could say no to anything when she says *please* like that. "Okay. For now."

"Thanks," she says, then her smile turns real. "Now can I take your shirt off too?" She's already grabbing the hem, and I lift my arms overhead to help her peel it off.

After she tosses it on the floor, I cup her breasts and dip my head to skim a kiss over the swell of each one. She trembles in my arms. "Sensitive?" I graze her nipples through the fabric.

She shivers. "Yeah."

I flick each with my tongue, tasting satin when I'm craving her skin. "Too sensitive?"

She arches her back. "It's good." Taking my hands, she backs onto the bed and guides me to follow.

I straddle her hips and bend to kiss her deeply. Her hands stray down my chest and over my stomach. She finds the bulge of my erection through my jeans and strokes me. I straighten to give her better access and thrust gently into her hand. "You feel that? I fucking *want* you."

"I love it," she says, her gaze bold as she strokes me. She pops the button on my jeans, and I'm aching so badly that I groan.

"I thought we were keeping pants on."

She slips her hand into my boxers and pulls my dick free.

Holy hell, the feel of her hand on my cock about makes me lose it right there. "Abbi," I say. It's not a warning or a question. It's more like a prayer. A desperate plea for this aching need. "Shit, that feels good."

She slides her hands around to my ass, tugging. "Come here."

"I'm right here." I want her hand back on my dick. I want all of her.

"Up here," she says, tugging again.

I realize what she means and pull back so I can see her face. "Yeah?"

"If you want me to feel safe, if you want my fear to go away, let me." Her expression is so damn earnest that I'd have to obey even if I weren't dying to get that mouth on my cock.

I slide up her body, and she guides me until my dick is brushing her lips. She licks the bead of moisture from the tip, and I nearly lose it right then.

"Closer," she murmurs, and her lips brush my cock.

I grip the top of the headboard and let her pull me into her mouth. She looks up at me with those big brown eyes as she takes me between those soft pink lips. It's the hottest fucking thing I've ever seen. I can't look away. She leads my hips back and forth, urging me to fuck her mouth. Her nails curl into my glutes, and I fucking love the contrast of the sharp sting against the velvety softness of her tongue.

Her eyes water as she takes me deep. I pull back, but she groans and urges me forward again. Then she sucks and —*fuck*, I lose it. All control. Every effort to be gentle and slow is out the window as she sucks me deep and moans around my cock. I fuck her mouth, gripping the headboard for dear life. Every time I try to pull back, she pulls me deeper, until I'm lost to everything but the sight of her mouth on me and the feel of her lips and tongue wrapped around the root of my cock.

"Abbi," I rasp. "Fuck, Abbi. I'm gonna come."

Her moan of approval vibrates against my balls, and I let go.

※

ABBI

I can't believe that just happened.

Only, I can. Because it was the perfect way to ensure no more of my clothes came off. And because now Dean is next to me, barely holding on to consciousness, his hand running lazy circles on my stomach. And because I can still taste him on my tongue. Still remember the look of pure lust in his eyes as I took him into my mouth.

"I think I've been punked," he mutters, wrapping his arm around me and tugging me closer.

I laugh. "How so?"

He cracks open one eye. "You tell me you're bad in bed and then you do that?" He closes his eye again and nuzzles my neck. "In case there's any question, you should know you just rocked my world."

"Oh, I noticed."

He pinches my side, and I squirm away before he tugs me back again.

I've had a *lot* of practice, though I'm sure Dean doesn't want to hear about that. That last year I was with Cody, he asked for blow jobs all the time. I just didn't realize then that he found it easier to get off if my clothes stayed on. "Giving head isn't one of my insecurities," I say.

"Nor should it be." His words are low. Sleepy. "I didn't mean for that to happen tonight, though."

"I liked it. It was hot. No apologies."

"No," he whispers. His body goes lax, as if he's drifting off to sleep. "No apologies. Only endless fantasies of returning the favor."

I bite back my smile, even though he can't see it. Then I lie there wide awake, reveling in the feel of his strong arm wrapped around me as he sleeps.

CHAPTER SIXTEEN

DEAN

F riday night, I'm home alone when I get a text from Abbi.

> Abbi: I know we've both been busy this week,
> but this is your gentle reminder that we
> are friends first and this stops the second
> you want it to. If what happened on
> Sunday freaked you out, we can move on
> and never speak of it again.

Sunday *did* freak me out, but not in the way she thinks. I stare at the message for a long time while I try to figure out how to reply. I haven't seen her once in the five days since she took me into her bedroom and put her mouth on me.

Five days of straight-up avoidance, and she's calling me on it.

I never nap, but on Sunday I napped in Abbi's bed for a couple of hours. When I woke up, it was dark out. I reached for her, thinking to steal a make-out session in the dark before I left. But she wasn't there. She was in the kitchen baking cookies for the residents of one of the local nursing homes.

"They love homemade baked goods," she said when I asked her about it. "The stuff they get from their cafeteria is okay, but it's not made fresh. I just like to make them smile."

She shrugged as if it was nothing, but her smile told me just how much *she* loves to do it, and I felt that familiar tug pulling me under. It's never just been physical attraction for me with Abbi. It's who she is. The things she does and cares about. The way she makes me and everyone else around her feel. "You're fucking amazing—you know that?"

She flashed me the sweetest smile over her shoulder. "I was raised by good people. I'd probably be a selfish shit if they hadn't taught me to think of others first."

That was when I panicked, memories of her twenty-first flooding back.

"You deserve a good guy."

"Someday." She looked up at the starry night sky and her face twisted as she tried to fight her grimace into a smile. "Someday I'm going to fall in love with a guy who knows how to treat a woman. One who has a good family—a father who taught him how to be a man and take responsibility for his actions. Someday."

I said goodnight and got the fuck out of there. Because it's one thing to mess around. It's one thing to help her out while fulfilling some fantasies of my own.

It's quite another to fall in love.

I've avoided her all week—which wasn't too hard, since our schedules are so at odds. Most days by the time I get home from work, the busiest part of her shift has just begun. She invited me to meet up at her place after work on Wednesday, and I made up an excuse about an early meeting the next day. Other than that, we exchanged polite texts, but I kept it pretty surface as I try to grapple with my feelings.

I thought I was being stealthy about my avoidance until now, when she's texting me from work and giving me an out. I've been avoiding her, and she knows it.

Even if I end this now, I'm already too deep. I've been too deep for Abbi since she came home from college and started helping me and Kace stage the houses we were flipping. I loved being around her—her grins, the sass she only shows to people she trusts, her big heart.

I was twenty-five and she was twenty, and I told myself I'd wait until her twenty-first birthday to make my move. So I did, and that night I found out exactly why I needed to keep my real feelings to myself. Abbi doesn't want a guy like me. Not for the long term. And I can't even blame her, so I backed off and put myself back in the friend zone, where I belong.

I'm not sure those feelings ever went away completely, but anything that was buried has been brought to the surface with our recent time together. Cutting it off now won't change that, but it might screw with her confidence even more.

Dean: I don't want to stop. In fact, I very much want to keep going. You?

Her reply comes so quickly that I know she's carrying her phone around with her at work.

> Abbi: So much. It's dirty thoughts central
>   over here.
> Dean: Yeah?
> Abbi: For real. Aside from the moments I
>   worried I scared you off, I've been
>   fantasizing about you visiting my office
>   again. I can't even sit in that chair without
>   feeling turned on. It's a problem.

I laugh and adjust myself in my sweats. She's not the only one who can't think about an office visit without getting turned on, but the topic reminds me of what she said when we were in her bedroom on Sunday.

> Dean: Tell me what you meant on Sunday—
>   when you said we didn't have to rush
>   when we weren't in private.

Her reply is a long time coming.

> Abbi: It doesn't matter.
> Dean: It matters to me. I hope to get you
>   alone and naked soon. I feel like I should
>   know your expectations . . . and any way
>   guys let you down in the past.
> Abbi: It wasn't their fault. And it's not the
>   ALONE part that's the problem.
> Dean: Naked?
> Abbi: Yeah.

Dean: . . . ???

Right. This doesn't surprise me, given all her self-esteem issues related to her appearance and size, but the pieces still aren't matching up for me.

> Abbi: You're going to make me spell it out,
> aren't you?
> Dean: I promise I'm not being dense on
> purpose.
> Abbi: I don't look like a supermodel, okay? I
> mean, obviously, but it's even more
> obvious when I'm naked. So . . . it's fun to
> mess around when our clothes are on,
> because there's no rush.
> Dean: Don't worry. I'm not going to let you
> rush me when I finally get you naked.
> Abbi: Ha! I was never the one doing the
> rushing.
> Dean: Again, not trying to be dense, just
> want to make sure I'm following—you're
> saying some guy rushed through things if
> you were naked.
> Abbi: The majority did.

I'm still trying to process this when she texts again.

> Abbi: Can we stop talking about this now?

I don't know all the guys Abbi's dated in the past, and I wouldn't know where to find the ones I could name. But that's suddenly a very good thing, because if I had a list, I'd have to hunt down every single one of them and give them a piece of my mind. It wouldn't end well.

> Dean: Never tell me where I can find your
>   exes.
> Abbi: Why?
> Dean: I don't want to go to jail.

❧

ABBI

Our schedules were at odds all week, and Dean and I never ended up getting together. I'm not sure what we would've done if we'd managed. Had coffee and discussed why I froze up like a maniac when he tried to take off my bra?

I ended up closing at The Patio every night, and Saturday I've worked all day prepping for and pulling off our biggest full-dinner wedding reception yet. It's exciting to watch the catering side of the business grow like it is, but it's also reaffirming all my suspicions that this isn't my dream job. I want to be the woman who came in to set up the elaborately decorated wedding cake, the one creating the cupcake tower centerpieces, not the one instructing the staff how to serve the pre-plated steak dinner.

Despite being completely exhausted after we wrap up the reception, I invite Layla out for a drink. Dean and I have agreed to go to his place tomorrow night, and it doesn't take a mind reader to know he plans to get me naked. I really, really don't want to screw it up.

So here I am, sitting at Smithy's in my work clothes,

sipping a lemon drop martini and preparing to pour my heart out to a girl I don't actually know all that well. Not that Layla seems to mind. She's one of those people who lights up in social situations, and after midnight at Smithy's is no different.

"You said you needed some advice," she says, rubbing her hands together. "Lay it on me."

I blow out a breath. "I'm a disaster in bed."

Coughing on the sip of martini she just took, Layla puts her glass down and nudges it away from herself. "You want *sex* advice?"

I shake my head. "I want *confidence* advice." I bite my bottom lip. "Okay, so I'm going to tell you something no one else knows, but you have to promise it stays between you and me."

Her brow furrows. "Of course. I'm loud, but I know how to keep a secret."

"My friend Dean—Stella's brother—he agreed to teach me how to be . . . good in bed."

She cackles, and the people at the next booth turn and stare. She gives them a pointed look until they turn away again. "How selfless of him." She chuckles again. "Jesus, I didn't think that happened in real life."

I fold my arms. "Don't mock me."

She holds up both hands. "I would never. Though, come on, you can't pretend this is a purely practical endeavor on your part. You're not blind. Dean's *hot*."

"So hot." I press my hands to my cheeks. "And not just hot. He's a freaking awesome guy. He's been best friends with my brother for years, and I've always known he was the real deal, but over the past few weeks, I feel like I've really gotten to know him. He's . . ." I shake my head. "I like him a *lot*. I think we're going to have sex soon, and I don't want to screw it up with my issues."

"Whew, boy." She grabs her martini and takes a big gulp. "So Dean's supposed to be teaching you how to be good in bed, but you've caught feelings and are hoping I can *tell* you how to be good in bed before then so it's not some traumatic, regrettable experience for both of you?"

I grimace. "I mean . . . pretty much?"

"But you said yourself that your issue is confidence, right?"

I nod. "I've had some really bad experiences. Guys who liked my curves, but when they got me naked seemed shocked to find out you don't get to have a butt and boobs like this and still have a thigh gap."

She grunts. "Preach."

"I've just never been with someone who's really into me physically, but I think Dean might be, and I don't want to ruin it with my epic lack of confidence once I get naked."

"So, tell me about the exes," Layla says. "No, tell me about the first guy who ever made you feel self-conscious about your body."

I snort. "I didn't need a guy to do that. I grew up a chubby girl in twenty-first-century America."

She frowns. "I hear you, but I think there's more." She leans forward. "You can't ask me to fix you like some high-priced shrink and then hold out on me."

I shift in my chair. "I guess I'm carrying some baggage from my first—and only—serious relationship." Every time Cody comes up in conversation, I just want to disappear. "Well, he and I were together in college—before I dropped out." I *hate* that this is my college story, that I was that girl who was cruising right along but couldn't cope anymore once her boyfriend broke up with her. I failed out of every class but one that last semester, and I had to decide if I wanted to retake those classes to get my GPA back up or if I just wanted to go *home*.

At that point, the idea of seeing Cody on campus with other girls sounded miserable. I was homesick and questioning everything about myself, and I didn't want to be there anymore.

"We were together a couple of years," I say. "I really thought we'd end up married, you know? I was so madly in love with him, and—" I swallow, feeling the tears pricking the back of my eyes.

"And he broke your heart," she says.

"Not exactly a unique story, is it?"

"Not on the most basic level. But every story has its nuances, and I feel like there's more to yours?"

I nod. "He didn't just break up with me. He cheated on me."

"Asshole."

I smile, appreciating her solidarity whether I deserve it or not. "I found out from a friend, and when I confronted him about it, instead of being contrite, he was defensive. He felt like I should be able to forgive him the occasional transgression, as he put it, because he was out of my league."

"The *fuck*?"

I bow my head. "And he was. He was kind of a heavier guy when we started dating, and pretty shy, but a few months into our relationship, he started lifting weights and eating this really regimented diet, and he got . . ." I laugh. "I always thought he was cute, but his new muscles gave him confidence—*swagger*—and the girls on campus noticed. He noticed them noticing."

"That hardly made him out of your league," Layla says.

I shrug. I never tell this story. One, because I don't particularly like reliving it. But also because my friends are all so thin and beautiful, and I don't think they have any idea what it's like to have your appearance be the reason your relationships fall apart. "After I found out he was cheating, he told me he loved me, that he cared about me, but he wasn't attracted to me and never had been. As much as he liked spending time with me, he had this other part of himself that needed . . . release."

"What an ass. So he laid it all on you?"

"Me and his dad. Everything was his dad's fault in his mind."

"Abusive?" she asks.

I shake my head. "No, just absent. He didn't have a male role model and used that as an excuse for so much." I roll my eyes. "He said he'd only started dating me because he didn't think he could do any better, and then by the time he realized he could, he didn't want to hurt me by breaking up. He had this whole speech about how physical attraction is instinctive and guys just can't *make* themselves lust after girls like me."

"Oh, Abbi," she says, cringing. "That's *awful*. That's why you assumed your date bailing had something to do with your appearance."

I shrug. "It stands to reason."

She shakes her head. "He messed you up *good*. How have you never told anyone this?"

"My brother knows the gist of it," I say. "I poured my heart out to him when I dropped out of school. It was the only way he'd shut up about me needing to go back."

She laughs. "And what did he say?"

My eyes feel hot when I think about Kace's reaction to what Cody said to me. I've never seen him so angry. "After I convinced him not to go after Cody, he gave me this really awkward speech about how I *am* pretty and someday I'd find a guy who sees me as I am and doesn't want to change a thing about me." I shrug. "It was sweet, but he's my brother, so I didn't put too much stock in it."

She hums thoughtfully. "Too bad, since he was right. What about your other friends? Do they know?"

I shake my head. "I can't talk about this with them. Obviously I'm more comfortable talking about this with you."

She frowns, and I snap my mouth shut. "Why is it easier to talk to me than friends you've had for years?"

"I just mean they don't understand what it's like to be a big girl. What it's like living with that every day."

Leaning back in the booth, she folds her arms and studies me. "It's obvious this is a sore point for you, but Abbi, don't stick me in a box. Don't stick yourself in a box, either. We're both big girls, and as a big girl, I think you should know that a lot of what you're dealing with has nothing to do with your size. I bet your friends will understand it better than you think."

"What do you mean it has nothing to do with my size?" I shake my head. I thought she was a good listener, but maybe I was wrong. "Cody straight-up said—"

"He may have told you he wasn't attracted to you, but it was just an excuse. He was caught being a douche—a cheater and a user. And instead of owning up to his mistakes, he hit you where it hurt. He knew exactly what he was doing. All he had to do was allude to your weight, and you instantly believed the end of the relationship was your fault."

I want to accept what she's saying, I do, but it feels like the easy way out. "I've always prided myself in seeing things as they are. I don't sugarcoat anything—not for anyone else, and definitely not for myself."

"I've had guys bring up my weight before," she says. "And you know what? It didn't get them anywhere but straight out the door. If someone has an issue with my size, that's about *them*. It's not about me. Do I wish people didn't make assumptions about me based on my appearance? Sure, but we all do it. You're doing it to your friends by refusing to share your pain with them just because the number on their clothes is smaller."

Her words hit me like a blow. I want to defend myself, to back-pedal and prove that I'm not doing that, and yet I can't. She's right. "I'm really sorry," I say. "I didn't mean to hurt you or—"

"You didn't hurt me. I just want you to understand what I see. You walk around wanting everyone to believe your worth isn't determined by the scale, but you're the one who decided it is. You're the one who decides that every day. *You're* the one giving your size so much"—she laughs softly —"well, *weight*, for lack of a better word."

"It's hard not to."

Her expression softens. "I know. I get it. And there are dicks out there who'll make everything about your body, who don't respect you just because you wear a double-digit clothing size, but they don't get to give that kind of power every day. Most of what you're feeling is coming from you. Especially when it comes to Dean. Has he ever given you a reason to think he's *not* attracted to you?"

I rub my thumb along the rim of my martini glass. Tiny sugar crystals scatter onto the tabletop. "I know he's attracted to me, but I just don't see why he'd be as attracted to me as he is to someone like Amy—the woman I'm supposed to be helping him get over."

"Your attractiveness, your appearance, they're *your* issues. Don't saddle him with that."

I swallow hard. "I know what you're saying, but it's . . ."

"You know what I said the first time Brock asked me out?" she asks.

I arch a brow. "What?"

"I looked him over and *really* liked what I saw." She grins. "Then I looked him in the eye and asked if he had a job to go with that pretty face."

I laugh so suddenly that it comes out as a snort.

"It's true. Because I've been with guys before who believed that since I'm a big girl, somehow that might translate to me *owing* them for being with me. They'd try to make me believe I had to take care of them to keep them." She shakes her head. "But I don't need to buy love, and I'm not interested in anyone who expects me to."

"I love that about you."

"You don't need to, either. You don't need to buy it or earn it or prove you're worthy of it by losing weight."

I huff out a laugh. "Well, don't worry about that. I gave up on losing weight a long time ago."

Layla doesn't laugh with me. "Listen, I'm not good at sugarcoating shit, so I'm just gonna say it as I see it."

"Why stop now?" I ask, grimacing.

"You have this part of you that's so damn hardened." She smiles softly, but it's like someone saying *no offense* after they insult you. "That hardened part of you? She's defensive and insecure, and she hides herself from anyone who gives a shit. Fuck, we can't blame her. Not really. And it's okay to have ugly parts. Personally, I have many. But instead of letting that part come along for the ride, you're letting her drive the damn bus. You're allowed to shield yourself. You're allowed to be insecure, but you need to understand you're giving all the power to that part of you when there are so many other parts that show the world who you truly are. That hardened part of you decided a long time ago that every guy after Cody felt the same way he did, and that assumption is what's killing you. You're breaking your own damn heart over and over again."

I bite my bottom lip, and the backs of my eyes burn. She's right. I can't even deny it. "I wish I could be more like you. I'd love to have that kind of confidence. You're so beautiful and—"

"So are you, Abs. You're gorgeous. Obviously, Dean thinks so too."

"I want this to be good."

Layla grins. "So show him every inch of you and don't stop him when he falls to his knees in *devotion*."

CHAPTER SEVENTEEN

ABBI

As excited as I am to spend a night with all my friends on Sunday, I'm even more excited about going home with Dean after. Well, fifty percent excited, thirty-five percent nervous, and ten percent giddy. The other five percent is a colorful smorgasbord of feelings I try to avoid analyzing. Any time I do, I'm reminded of what I felt when Cody admitted he wasn't attracted to me. When *those* feelings surface, I want to run far and fast.

I focused on giddy and excited as I dressed for tonight, but by the time I pull up to Brinley's, I'm already questioning my wardrobe decisions. I feel awkward, and the last thing I want is for everyone to stare at me. The hair and makeup are okay, though I kept looking in the mirror and thinking I looked like a kid playing dress-up, but the dress is more revealing than anything I've worn in public since I quit dance class at twelve.

It falls just below my knees and shows off the best part of my legs—calves that are strong and sculpted from lots of walking and yoga—but even that is more than I normally show. The cut is a flattering A-line, and the soft lace sleeves cover my arms, which was probably why I let Layla talk me into buying it, but the neckline . . . the neckline shows enough cleavage that I'm practically bracing myself for Smithy to, at best, make a comment and tuck a single between my boobs.

I intentionally didn't let myself bring a sweater. First, I'll roast alive if I put a sweater on top of these sleeves, but mostly because I knew if I let myself even put one in the car, I'd end up with it buttoned up to my neck all night long.

Of all the places to test out my new look, this is my safest option. Brinley gave me the perfect excuse when she asked us to get "gussied up," and these are my friends. If I make a total fool of myself, it'll be okay.

That doesn't make it any easier to climb out of the car.

Stella and Kace beat me here, and I watch from the safety of my car as they're greeted by Brinley at the door and ushered into the house. I take a long, deep breath. *It's just a dress and a little makeup. These are my friends. There's nothing to be afraid of.*

Mustering more courage than this should require, I reach for the handle, but before I can, Dean's opening my door from the outside. "Are you okay in there?" he asks, then his gaze sweeps over me and his jaw unhinges.

There it is. Evidence that I look like a fool and the first sign that people will be staring at me all night.

"Jesus," he murmurs.

My cheeks heat. "Layla picked it out," I blurt. Because

I'm an adult who can't take responsibility for her own stupid decisions, apparently.

"Remind me to thank her." He takes my hand and leads me from the car before looking me over again. When he lifts his gaze back to mine, his eyes are dark, and I recognize the heat in them. "Are you trying to kill me?"

I bite my bottom lip. "You don't think I look ridiculous?"

He coughs—half laugh, half horror. "I think you look *delicious*." He glances toward the house and the empty front porch before stepping close and dropping his mouth to my ear. "You look so good that I'm not going to be able to focus on a damn thing. But did you forget the plans I had for you when I finally caught you in a skirt?"

My cheeks flame. I did *not* forget, but I thought he might. If my memories of those words sent little thrills through me as I got dressed tonight, I figured that was something I'd need to keep to myself, but the look in his eyes tells me he'd like to know. "I remember," I say, lifting my chin.

He releases a low growl. "They're watching, but I really want to kiss you right now." Stepping closer, he draws in a long, deep breath. "Let's get up there before I decide to do it anyway."

I'm practically floating as we walk up the drive, side by side. Dean looks gorgeous as always dressed in dark jeans and a soft white button-up shirt he has rolled up to his elbows. It'll take a feat of superhuman strength not to stare at those forearms all night.

"I missed you this week," he says softly.

I swallow. "We texted."

"If you opened that bakery instead of running The Patio, I could see you more."

That thought had crossed my mind too, but since this is only temporary, that seems like a pretty terrible argument for leaving a steady job I enjoy, working with people I love. Even if I might love a bakery of my own more. "Shh," I say, climbing the steps. "No talking about that tonight. I still haven't decided."

"My lips are sealed."

Brinley opens the door before we have a chance to ring the bell, and we say our hellos to her and Marston and Kace and Stella. Behind us, Savvy, Smithy, and Layla are heading up the drive.

Everyone slowly trickles into the foyer, chatting and catching up as if most of us don't work together all week long.

I turn to Layla, who's checking her phone. "Is your boyfriend coming tonight?"

Sighing, she puts her phone away and nods. "When I talked to him half an hour ago, he said traffic was making him run a little behind, but he should be here soon."

"Knock, knock!" someone singsongs at the open front door.

We all swing around to the stranger waiting there as Layla runs to him. "You found us!" she says, wrapping her arms around him.

"I told you I would." He nuzzles her neck for a beat then whispers something in her ear. When they pull apart, he gives her a wink that's somehow both suggestive and completely adorable.

We all stare. Layla's boyfriend is, in a word, *hot*. I shouldn't be surprised. In fact, I'm a little annoyed with myself for my surprise. Layla is beautiful, and better than that, she's an awesome person—funny and smart and caring. She's as worthy of a hot boyfriend as the next girl. Not all guys are hung up on size. I mean, look at Dean. He hasn't let it stop him. Layla's boyfriend has that country-boy look with sandy-blond hair and dreamy brown eyes. He's in faded jeans and a long-sleeve thermal shirt that hugs a very muscular chest.

"Everyone, this is my boyfriend, Brock Ford. Brock, these are my new friends—most of whom work with me." She laughs awkwardly then goes around the circle, introducing everyone.

"Brock Ford, like the country music YouTube sensation Brock Ford?" Stella asks, gaping.

"Yes, ma'am," he says.

"I love your music," Brinley says. "It's so good. You're just amazing."

"Oh, now, I'm not all that," he says, smiling.

"Don't gush," Layla says. "You'll give him a big head."

"I promise," Brinley says, palm to her chest. "No more gushing."

They all laugh, but I stay silent. I just got a good look at part of myself, and don't like what I saw. I was shocked that someone like Layla, even as beautiful and amazing as she is, could land a guy as Hollywood-hot as Brock. When my friends were stunned to silence, I assumed they felt the same way, but that wasn't it at all. They were shocked to find an up-and-coming country music star in their midst. *I* was the one who thought they were a surprising couple because of her size relative to his hotness.

Layla was right. This is my issue, and I assume everyone else fixates on it as much as I do. It's not a nice thing to recognize about yourself, and it's not easy to swallow. I take a deep breath and hold on to the thought. It'd be so much easier to dismiss this realization or to tell myself I *wasn't* thinking that, but I don't want to let myself get away with that kind of crap. At least I see it so now I can work on it.

"Come on." Marston waves us deeper into the house. "Let's show you all around."

⚜

THE HOUSE IS AMAZING. Marston bought this place back when he first returned to Orchid Valley. He said it was an investment property, but anyone paying attention knew he never intended to give up on Brinley. She was his first love, and from what I can tell, the most important part of his life —even during his years away.

Brinley's cute as she shows us around. She's a little bashful about showing us the updates they made. I'd expect someone who grew up in a house as grand as Brinley's to be comfortable having money—to take it for granted, even. She doesn't, and I know it makes her feel a little awkward for us to see how they live. Marston worked hard for it, though. He was a homeless teen when the courts sent him to Orchid Valley to live with his aunt. He had to fight the odds, to scratch and claw to get where he is. Now he runs one of the most respected consultation companies in the country.

Brinley shows us the refinished deck overlooking Lake Blackledge, and the newly furnished living room done in a subtle French country style that makes the space look warm and inviting but not overdone. Upstairs, we get to see Cami's room, which they've painted in the palest lavender.

Cami's new loft bed has a desk beneath it with fairy lights twinkling overhead.

The master suite isn't part of the tour, but we're all nosy so we peek inside anyway, swooning at the wall of windows that overlook the lake.

The tour circles back downstairs and to the front of the house and ends in the dining room.

"And here's where we'll have dinner," Brinley says, a little breathless.

The dining room has vaulted ceilings and more large windows, these overlooking the expansive front yard. A long walnut table with a live edge sits in the center of the room, upholstered chairs at each of the ten spots.

Each of the place settings is labeled with one of our names.

Dean finds his and grins at me. "Looks like it's my lucky night. I'm right next to you, Abbi."

My cheeks heat. It's not that I'm ashamed of what's happening between me and Dean, but if our friends find out, they'll make something more of it than it is. The last thing Dean needs is Stella coming after him for leading me on.

I don't know if she'd understand that I can handle what's happening between me and Dean. I can handle the inevitable end of it too. I'll have to. He never promised me more.

"Your home is beautiful. Thank you for having us over," I say, giving Brinley a quick squeeze before skirting around the table to find my seat.

"You're welcome anytime," Brinley says.

"It's amazing," Stella says, eyeing the beams on the

vaulted ceiling. "Kace, when are you going to fix me up a place like this?"

"Would you move in with me if I did?" he asks with an arched brow.

Stella shrugs. "I don't know. Depends how well you do."

Kace grabs her sides, tickling her, and she folds over, giggling.

Marston clears his throat uncomfortably. "I second what Brinley says. You're all welcome anytime. We're grateful for your friendship."

"Hear, hear!" Smithy says, hoisting a glass of amber liquid in the air. Bourbon, if I had to guess.

Dean cocks his head and frowns at him. "Where did you get that?"

Smithy shrugs as he takes a sip. "There was a bourbon bar in the library. I assumed the happy couple wanted us to make ourselves at home."

"We didn't even show you the library," Brinley says. "How did you end up in there?"

"I saw the bourbon," Smithy says, as if this explains everything.

Everyone laughs and finds their spots at the table, and Marston fills our glasses with a Pinot Noir he says pairs well with the duck we're having for dinner. He admits that Brinley prepared our meal herself, and we all gape at her in disbelief. To say that Brinley isn't the cook of the group is an understatement.

"I'm learning a few things in the kitchen," she says.

"I could've cooked, Brinley," I say. "I don't mind."

She waves a hand in my direction. "It's your evening off. I'm not going to put you to work."

"Abbi's just worried we're about to eat something that tastes more like roadkill than gourmet," Stella says.

I elbow her in the side. "I am not."

"I promise I followed the directions," Brinley says, flashing me a smile before disappearing into the kitchen.

Marston and Brinley work together to serve everyone their pre-plated meal, and someone starts passing rolls around the table, everyone chattering happily as we dig into our meal.

The duck actually *is* incredible. "I'm so impressed, Brin," I say, taking the last bite of mine not long later. "That was so good."

"You mean it?" she asks, beaming. "I was so nervous what you'd think. I bought the duck because the guy at the butcher said you can't dry it out, but when I was researching recipes online, I kept seeing all these warnings about how you have to score it correctly, and since I didn't think they meant on a scale of one to ten, I realized I was in over my head." She goes on, rambling a bit about how she prepared the meal, but I barely hear a word.

Under the table, Dean's hand has found my thigh. He's stroking subtly, slowly inching upward.

I always fantasized about what it'd be like to be the kind of girl who was so beautiful that her guy could never take his hands off her. To be so attractive that your boyfriend would find any moment possible to touch you and kiss you.

Any heartache that's coming my way—and let's be honest, it surely is—will be worth it. I'll get to know what it was like to be *wanted*. To be *desired*. I always imagined this, but never thought I'd get to experience it for myself. I might not understand it, but Dean wants me. Maybe it's just the secrecy, the *forbidden*, that turns him on. My brother is his business partner and best friend. We're messing around right under our friends' noses.

Whatever the reason, I relish these moments. His attention. The hot look in his eyes when I catch him watching me. Heat floods my veins as he strokes the outside of my thigh, and is ignited as he strokes higher.

God bless Layla for making me buy this dress and whatever courage I found to wear it tonight. I love the feel of his warm, callused hands on my bare skin.

As all our friends discuss their lives, my attention is all *right there*. Under the tablecloth, under my skirt.

"Don't you think so, Dean?" Kace asks, leaning forward to look down the table.

Dean's eyebrows shoot up into his hairline. "What's that?"

"The Dennisons. Don't you think they'll sell rather than move in there themselves?"

The Dennisons are a local family. Their matriarch owned one of the biggest houses in town before she passed away. It isn't as big as this one or as ostentatious as the one Brinley grew up in, but it's still bigger than anything the rest of us can imagine living in.

"I can't wait to get in there," Kace says.

Dean hums in approval, his hand drifting higher.

My breath catches as his pinkie skims the edge of my underwear.

"Absolutely. Can't take my eyes off her," he says, flashing me a grin.

I give him a pointed look, though it takes everything in me to make it stern and not desperate. He said he likes messing around in public places. Maybe that's why he's touching me like this now. But it makes me burn for a room with a lock on the door and hours—*days*—with only the two of us inside.

Dean uses the conversation at the other end of the table as an excuse to turn in his seat and lean toward them. Toward me. As he does, he keeps his hand on my thigh—hot, stroking, forbidden.

I train my expression and try to appear interested in the conversation when all I want is to drag Dean to one of the guest rooms upstairs and beg him to make good on his skirt-related promises.

When Brinley comes around with dessert, Dean pulls back. He straightens in his chair and faces forward, hands in his own lap, and I'm not sure if I'm relieved or disappointed.

She sets the plates of lemon tart in front of us and returns to the other side of the table to take her seat next to Marston.

Forks clatter on plates as the guests take their first bites of dessert.

Dean pulls his phone from his pocket and frowns at the dark screen. "Sorry, everyone. I need to take this. It's my mom."

Stella perks up at the mention of their mother. "Is she okay?"

Dean waves her off. "Everything's fine, but I sent that HVAC guy over there today, and she was supposed to call if she needed me to talk to him."

"Oh." Stella nods. "Thanks for taking care of that, Dean." She turns her attention back to Savvy, who's in the middle of a story about one of her more colorful personal training clients.

The conversation continues around the table as Dean

disappears down the hall. I take a small bite of my lemon tart. It's delicious, but I'm too worked up to have an appetite.

I know Dean's mom didn't just call him. Was he trying to get me away from the table? Does he want me to meet him somewhere?

When my own phone buzzes in my purse, I somehow know without looking that it's Dean. I grab my purse off the back of my chair and drape it over my shoulder, pushing back from the table. "Excuse me. I need to use the restroom. Where was it again, Brinley?"

Brinley points down the hall. "Second door on the right."

"Thanks."

Once I'm out of view of the dining room, I pull my phone from my purse, and sure enough, there's a message waiting from Dean.

Powder room. Second door on the right. Don't make me wait.

Those words light fire in my blood. My hand's shaking as I pull open the partially ajar bathroom door to find Dean, lounging against the counter, arms crossed over his chest.

He looks me over slowly—from my face, stalling on my lips, down to my breasts and the flare of my hips, down to the legs he was just touching—and there's so much heat in his eyes that I'm half convinced this is a dream. But no. Even in my dreams, Dean doesn't give me looks that hot.

"Close the door," he says, voice husky. "Lock it."

CHAPTER EIGHTEEN

ABBI

I do as I'm told but don't have a chance to turn around before Dean takes me by the hips, spins me, and pushes me back against the counter, his mouth on my neck.

"Are you sure you don't want our friends to know about us?" His teeth scrape the skin at the juncture of my shoulder and neck, and I can barely think straight. "Because you look so damn fuckable in that dress that I'm not sure how I'm supposed to hide what I have planned for you."

"It's . . . just a dress." I lean my head to the side, because I love the lightly sucking kisses he's placing against my neck. *So good. So damn good.*

"It could be just a dress," he says. "Or it could be something you wore for me. Something you wanted me to see. Something you wanted me to *do*. Which is it, Abbi?"

"I . . ." I swallow hard. I can hardly find words right now. "I wore it for you."

"I love that," he growls. "If I put my hand between your legs now, am I gonna find you wet?"

"Yes," I say.

He doesn't make me wait. His hand is already up my skirt and between my legs, his fingers stroking the thin cotton of my underwear against my clit.

I'm already on the edge. Every stroke on my thigh under that table wound me so tight that now I could come with the lightest touch.

Grabbing me by the hips, he hoists me onto the counter. I gasp, shocked, and he presses his mouth to mine, quieting me. I melt into him, into this kiss and his hot body as he parts my thighs and steps between them.

He trails his mouth to my ear. "You have to be quiet. Can you do that for me? Tell me you can."

"Yes," I say, because one of his hands has already found its way back between my legs and he's stroking me with a featherlight touch. "Please."

"Please what?"

More pressure, more touching, more kissing, more of *him*. "Dean . . . Just . . . Please."

He pulls back to look me in the eye. "Tell me what you want," he says, his touch going even lighter.

I rock my hips forward, seeking his delicious teasing.

"Or do you not want to say it?"

"I want you." And I mean it. I want *everything*. His hands, his cock, his mouth, *anything*. "Do you have a condom?"

He chuckles in my ear. "Oh, hell no. Not now."

I curl my nails into his shoulder blades in frustration. "Then why are we in here?"

"Because you're wearing this dress, and because you're so wet I had to touch you." His nostrils flare. "As much as I want to give you my cock right now, I'm going to need a whole lot more space and a whole lot more time. But for now . . ." In one smooth motion, he drops to his knees and tugs my panties down my hips and to the floor. His head disappears beneath my skirt as his big hands press my thighs wide and he devours me with his mouth.

I almost cry out but bite my lip at the last moment, silencing myself.

He's relentless between my thighs—tongue flicking, searching, seeking, teasing, and demanding in equal measure. He sucks my clit into his mouth until it's almost too much, then he retreats and teases me with the gentlest flicks of his tongue.

All I can do is brace myself on the counter, fingers curling into the granite as if I might fall off the edge. The cool stone against my fingertips is the only thing keeping me grounded in reality, the only thing reminding me that I can't scream out in pleasure.

He strokes my thighs, sliding around to cup my ass so he can pull me forward, closer to the edge of the counter and closer to his face. Instinct has me bucking against his mouth, against the added pressure, and he growls low.

He teases me, circling my entrance, making me want to scream. And just when I think I might anyway, he slides two fingers inside me, plunging them deep twice before I lose what little hold I had on my control. I disintegrate.

He stays put, licking and sucking, taking me all the way over the edge and back to the ground.

When he stands, his hair is mussed and his lips are swollen. I know without looking that his scruff has left marks on my inner thighs, and I can't wait to see the evidence of what Dean Jacob just did to me—and judging by the look on his face, he *enjoyed it*.

There's a knock on the door and my eyes go wide.

"Everything okay in there, Abs?"

It's Brinley. If I had to choose between her and Stella, it's a no-brainer. Brinley will bring way fewer complications. But still. Did she hear me? *Excuse me while I hide. Be back never.*

"I'm fine," I say, shocked I can even manage the words.

"Hmm. Well, I'm going to take the others out back, so you two just take your time." Dean coughs out a laugh into his fist, and Brinley whispers, "I don't think they know. I won't say a word, but you and I are talking later."

"Mm-hmm," I say, biting back a laugh.

We stay quiet as we listen to the sounds of her steps retreating down the hall, then Dean leads me off the counter by the hand and helps smooth my dress.

"You go out first," he says. "I'll meet you out there soon." I reach for the knob, but he stops me with his hand on mine. "You're okay?"

I nod. "More than okay."

He drags a hand over his beard then lifts his head to stare at the ceiling. "I might've gotten a little carried away."

I take his face in both hands and kiss him firmly. I taste myself on his lips, and more warmth pools in my gut at the realization. "I liked it. Don't apologize."

He smiles against my mouth. "No regrets?"

"Not a single one."

"You're a fucking wet dream, Abigail Matthews."

"Thanks." I suddenly feel ridiculously shy. "For, you know, all of it."

He winks at me. "Anytime."

And apparently *anyplace*. I scurry from the bathroom to find our friends, smiling the whole way.

DEAN

I think what guys like about seeing a woman dressed up is knowing she did it for him. The *idea* that sexy underwear on a date could mean *I was hoping you'd see this*. Or a low-cut dress could mean *I want you to look at me*. It's probably not always that simple. There are as many reasons for a woman to choose sexy clothes as there are women, but the male ego likes to imagine it's all about *him*. At least, mine does.

So today when Abbi showed up in that dress, her lips pink and glossy, her hair curled before she pulled it up off her neck? Yeah. That did it for me. If only because I like to think she made those little efforts for me—that she wanted me to look at her lips or notice the smooth skin of her neck. That she wanted me to think of the things I could do to her in that dress.

We're all lounging on Marston and Brinley's deck, enjoying the nice evening. Most of the girls are sipping wine, but the guys have switched to bourbon. I took a very short pour for myself, but I've barely touched it. My recent indifference to alcohol has made me realize just how hard I was leaning on it when things were bad with Amy. My friends were right to worry about me. I didn't like who I was becoming. But now? Now I feel damn good, and I'm starting to wonder if maybe this doesn't have to be temporary. Maybe Abbi's changed how she feels about guys like me. Maybe the fact that I was raised with a piece of shit for a father isn't a deal breaker for her anymore.

Abbi and Brinley are having a hushed conversation at the far end of the deck. I wonder what Abbi's telling her. The truth? That we're messing around because she has a ridiculous idea that she's bad in bed? Or something more? Maybe she's talking to Brinley about the same thing I've been thinking myself—that it was supposed to be physical, but she's feeling something more now.

I want to punch myself in the face for being so damn hopeful, but I can't help it.

"She looks amazing, doesn't she?" Stella asks, and I jerk my gaze off Abbi.

"What?"

Stella gives me a crooked smile and nods to where Brinley and Abbi are standing. "Abbi. Everything she's doing to be more confident is working. You can even see it in the way she presents herself at work."

I swallow. What does Stella know about it? "What do you mean?"

Her smile grows and she leans toward me. "There's this guy—Frankie something—and he was her wine supplier for a long time, but a few weeks ago, he told her he was leaving that position and training to open a wine-tasting room. *In Orchid Valley.*"

I frown. "I don't understand."

Stella rolls her eyes. "She has a massive crush on him, and he wants to take her out when he moves to town, so she's decided to make some changes to, you know, set that relationship up for success."

I'm gonna be sick. "She really likes this guy?"

"Really, really. And frankly, it doesn't even matter to me if it works out between them. I'm just glad to see her happy and loving herself a little more."

"Right. Understandable." I push out of my chair. If I have to listen to any more, I might actually get sick.

I wander away from the group and prop my forearms on the deck railing, breathing in the cool night air and trying to shake the sick feeling in my stomach.

I wait until I see Abbi head into the house to use the restroom and follow shortly after. I wait in the dark hall, and when she emerges, I pin her against the wall and lower my mouth to hers, kissing her. Hard.

She moans against my lips and opens under me, feeding my hunger for her more. I love the way she responds to me, the way she sounds when she moans, the way she lifts on her toes and arches into me, pressing her breasts into my chest as she loops her arms behind my neck.

Our friends could catch us so easily here.

"Tell me you want me," I growl into her mouth.

"I do." I feel her smile against my lips. "So much."

"Tell me you're mine tonight."

"I'm yours."

I don't know what's gotten into me. Except maybe I do. The idea of this all being for some other guy isn't sitting right. The idea of being her dirty secret riles me. I've been there before with Amy, and I never meant to find myself here again. So I just kiss her again and again until lust roars so hot and fast through my blood that there's no room for frustration or irritation.

When I tear my mouth away, we're both breathing hard.

"What was that for?" she asks. Her lips are swollen from

the assault of my kisses, reminding me all too much of the way she looked in bed after she took my dick into her mouth, the way those lips parted earlier tonight when I slid my hand between her legs, reminding me of other things I want to do with her—things that have *nothing* to do with wanting to teach her skills for some other asshole.

"You're beautiful. You know that?" I ask.

Her cheeks, already flushed from our kisses, glow brighter. "I don't," she says, "but I almost believe it when you say it."

I brush the back of my hand across her cheek, then down, letting my knuckles graze the side of her neck before gliding over the front of her dress, across the mound of her breasts. "Come home with me," I say, watching her face, her brown eyes.

She glances toward the door for a beat then smiles. "I could make up an excuse to get out of here." She trails her hand up and down my arm, her fingertips lingering on the ridge of every muscle. I don't even think she realizes she does it, but I fucking love that she can't keep her hands off me. Is this just physical for her? Am I just a means to an end? The thought makes me crazy, wakes up some caveman instinct that tells me to take her home and make her come over and over again until she forgets all about him. "Brinley will know what's up if we both leave early, but she won't tell anyone."

I frown. "Would it be the worst thing if she did?"

She cocks her head to the side. "I mean, it's just gonna make this awkward for everyone if—when it ends."

"Abbi." I kiss the side of her neck then down to the juncture of her neck and shoulder. I nuzzle her there, breathing in the smell of her, and groan. "You make me crazy."

She laughs. "Why?"

"Because I don't like thinking of this as something with a firm expiration date." Though it has one, I realize now. Whenever Frankie moves to town, I'll be kicked to the curb. I bet Frankie comes from a nice nuclear family. Probably played ball in the yard with his dad growing up. No cheater in his DNA.

"But this isn't . . ." Abbi clears her throat. "I mean, we're not . . ."

Right, so I'm not the only one struggling to define the changes in our relationship.

"This isn't real," she says, and even though I know she doesn't mean for the words to be a blow, they are. They hit me square in the chest, and they fucking hurt.

Abbi has no way of knowing Amy said the same thing, that she said what we had wasn't real but "just unattached fun," as if that was supposed to change the fact that I'd fallen for her.

"I call bullshit." I brush my lips across hers to soften my words and to remind her just how *real* this feels. "It doesn't feel *fake*," I say softly, and her breath catches. Her expression shifts, her eyes tightening in the corners as worry creeps in, and when she draws in the breath of a woman preparing herself to let the guy down easy, I don't want to hear it. "I know," I say before she can speak. "I know this is just temporary. Just an . . . arrangement. But I knew even before that first time I kissed you that it'd be good. That once I touched you, I wouldn't want to stop. I was right. So let's fucking enjoy it rather than focusing on what might happen in the future."

She forces a smile, but she can't hide the confusion on her face. "Okay. I can do that."

"Are you seeing anyone else?"

She coughs out a laugh, as if this is a ridiculous question.

"I mean it. I want to know."

"Are you?" she asks me.

I hold her gaze. I need her to look at me when I say this. "I'm not interested in anyone else, and I don't want anyone else. I'm yours for as long as you'll let this last." Whatever *this* is. "I can't be with you one night and plan to be with someone else the next. That's not who I am." God, I need her to believe me. I need her to *trust* me. "Your turn."

"I'm not seeing anyone, Dean. Have you forgotten why we started this to begin with? I don't exactly have guys lining up—this milkshake's not bringing the boys to the yard."

I still think she's wrong about that, but I have another concern at the moment. "But there's someone that you want. Or someone you wanted before we started this."

She swallows. "Right now I don't want anyone but you."

That's what I needed. Maybe it won't be enough tomorrow, but today it's a start.

Claiming her mouth in a fierce kiss, I pour all of my need and hope and jealousy into the sweep of my tongue and the scrape of my teeth over her lips. I slip my hand down the front of her dress and inside her bra, cupping her breast. I graze my thumb across her taut nipple. "I want this in my mouth," I say. I cup her face with my other hand and trace her lips with my thumb. "And I want these on my cock again. I'll never fucking get enough of that."

Her cheeks flush darker. *God,* she's beautiful. "Go ahead and go home," she says. "I'll meet you there."

"I've heard that before," I say, giving her a pointed look and then softening it with a smile. "If you're not ready—"

"No. It's not that." She swallows. "Better yet, I'll go home first and you can meet me there. That way if I chicken out, I'll still have to face you."

"I just need to run home and let Trixie out first."

Her eyes light up. "Bring her. I don't want to feel guilty about taking you away from her all night. And she'll distract me if I'm too nervous."

I hold her gaze for a long time. "I promise you have nothing to be afraid of."

"I don't want to disappoint you."

"Never." I brush my lips against hers.

"What are you guys doing in the dark?"

The hallway lights blaze to life and then suddenly I'm standing there in front of Stella with my hand down Abbi's dress.

Abbi shoves me away, but it's too late.

Stella's eyes are wide. She knows what she saw. "What— When— How . . .?"

My heart races as I stare at Stella, waiting for her to deny it somehow.

"Holy shit," Stella says, gaze bouncing back and forth between us before landing on me. "Kace said I was imagining things."

Abbi's cheeks are bright red as she meets Stella's eyes. "Sorry about the secrecy. We're just . . ." She cuts her gaze to meet mine for a beat. "It's not what you think."

Stella blinks at her. "What is it, then?"

I close my eyes, not ready to hear the truth from Abbi's lips.

"I don't want to put a label on it, Stell," Abbi says. "Please?"

When I open my eyes, Abbi's staring at me, as if she's nervous about my reaction to this request. In truth, I'm relieved. If Abbi's willing to do what she's asking Stella to let us do—to feel it out before we put any labels or limits on it—I couldn't ask for anything more. It's not enough, but it's a start.

Stella gives me one last worried look before nodding to Abbi. "Okay. I . . . No problem."

When she's gone, I turn back to Abbi. "You okay?" Two of her friends know now, I realize. Our secret isn't so secret anymore, and I desperately want her to be okay with that.

"I think so." She shrugs. "I should've known we couldn't keep a secret for long."

She flashes a tentative smile, and I kiss it away to keep myself from asking any more questions—to keep myself from saying anything she's not ready to hear. "Go home. Drive safely. I'll see you soon."

CHAPTER NINETEEN

ABBI

I'm grateful for my new, insatiable lust. It's the only thing keeping me from calling Dean and telling him I changed my mind. I want him, and I trust him, and I know it'll be different with him, but I also know he won't let me get away with my old tricks.

I haven't been with a guy with the lights on in three years. The last time I was, I thought it'd be okay because that guy said he loved my curves, but then he spent the whole time he was inside me closing his eyes because, as he told me after when he suggested I "do a little toning," "only tits and ass should jiggle."

The last guy I was with didn't care that I wanted the lights off. He just wanted to get off. To be fair, so did I. We were both buzzed, and lonely and orgasms don't require a clear view. It was over way too quickly. He rolled over and started snoring like a freight train, and I was so turned off by his lack of effort toward my own pleasure that I didn't even bother taking matters into my own hands.

The times between those were various degrees of unsatisfying, but I can accept the blame for a lot of that. Sex makes me feel exposed, and experience has taught me that even guys who think I'm hot when my clothes are on change their mind when they come off. Things get awkward.

I'm shaking with nerves, but this is Dean. He doesn't pretend to be attracted to me. He really wants me.

All I need are his hot eyes and magic hands on me, and I'll forget everything else. Or at least I hope I will.

While I wait for Dean, I pour myself a glass of wine and change out of my dress and into a silky slip I bought last Monday. I was feeling so confident and sexy after my evening with Dean that I splurged. It's light pink and short, with spaghetti straps and matching lace panties. The last time I had the courage to wear something like this was in front of Cody, and considering how that ended, I haven't bothered with lingerie since.

For Dean, I'll face all my fears.

When my doorbell rings, I'm armed with the pink slip, sexy music, and a glass of wine, and I'm still not prepared for the look on his face when I open the door. Trixie pushes past me into the house and begins sniffing all the furniture and corners, but my attention is entirely on the man on the other side of the threshold.

"Jesus." He pushes into the house and shuts the door behind him. The only time his eyes leave me is when they flick to my wine glass.

"Do you like it?" I shouldn't ask. I should just fake confidence. As if it's completely normal for me to greet a man at the door while wearing something so slinky.

"That depends. Are you wearing it for me?"

I chuckle. "Of course."

"When did you buy it?"

I frown. He's acting . . . different. "Monday."

"Why?"

I swallow. "Why did I buy it?"

"Yeah." His voice is rough, as intense as his dark gaze. "What made you buy it? Were you thinking of me or just—"

"You. *This*."

"Then I love it." His gaze flicks to the wine again. "Tell me you're sober."

"So sober."

He takes the glass from my hand. "Let's keep it that way." With his other hand, he leads me into my own apartment, depositing my wine glass on a living room end table before pulling me toward the bedroom.

Stopping at the bed, he turns to me as he unbuttons his shirt and tosses it on the floor. When he peels off his undershirt, exposing his strong, sculpted chest, my insides quiver in anticipation. He's gorgeous. I've always thought so, but any attraction I felt to him before is amplified by the intimacy we've shared over the last few weeks.

"We're not playing pretend right now." Stepping close, he fingers the thin strap of my negligee then slides it from my shoulder. "This is one hundred percent real."

I cock my head to the side, studying him. "I didn't mean to upset you when I said that. I just don't want you to worry I'll get clingy or something."

Gently lacing his fingers around both my wrists, he places my hands to his warm, hard chest. "By all means. Cling. I think I'd enjoy a little of that. Or a lot."

I grin up at him. I don't think he understands exactly what I'm saying, but it doesn't matter. He knows just what to say to put my worries at ease, and tonight I'm grateful for that above all else. I skim my fingers down his chest, over his stomach, and along the waistband of his jeans. "You're gorgeous."

His nostrils flare, eyes darkening. "And you're beautiful." His tongue darts out to touch his bottom lip as he sweeps the strap off the other shoulder. "I like this."

"Me too," I admit.

"I bet you hoped I'd fuck you in it," he murmurs, and my breath catches at the rough language. "I bet you imagined me pushing you onto that bed and driving inside you without bothering to take it off."

Heat pools between my legs. "The possibility may have crossed my mind."

"Tempting." He slides a hand beneath each strap, guiding them down my arms. The satin slides over my skin, and I gasp as I realize he's taking it off, letting it slide down my body instead of over my head.

My breasts are bare, then my stomach. His eyes are on mine, not on my body, though he's too close to see all of me anyway. When the slip falls to the floor in a pool of satin around my feet, my heart races.

"Tonight, I need to see all of you," he says.

I'm in nothing but lacy underwear, and I've never wanted someone to find me sexy as much as I want Dean to right now. I've never wanted anything to be real as much as

I want *this* to be real. This night between us. This connection. This hunger he feels for me. I gobble up every bit of it.

❧

DEAN

Abbi's practically vibrating with nerves as I peel her panties from her hips and let them drop to the floor. I press my mouth to her neck and palm her breast in my hand. "I've got you," I murmur in her ear. "I promise you don't have to do a damn thing."

"I want to," she says, stepping back. She tugs her bottom lip between her teeth. "I don't want to be afraid. I want this. I like it when you touch me. I like . . ." She swallows. "This should be no different, right?" When she takes another step back, I realize what she's doing. She's giving me a view. Letting me *look*.

And as much as I've been dying to see these curves of hers uncovered, as much as I've ached to get her bare beneath me, I recognize this moment for what it is. My chest feels too damn tight because I know this is huge for her. She's trusting me with her body when others have used it to hurt her.

She takes a third step back, lifting her chin as she does, and a hungry moan slips from my lips as I drag my gaze over her naked curves.

I can't breathe. I ache to close the distance. To return my hands to her full breasts, to drop to my knees and press my mouth to the soft curve of her stomach. I want to strip out of my jeans and feel her skin against mine. But I don't rush it. I don't let myself. Because she's beautiful. Because I need to take in every inch of her. And because, I realize, she needs this in a way I wouldn't have understood before we started this . . . whatever *this* is. She needs to let me look and know that seeing her only makes me want her more.

"Say something," she whispers.

"You're so fucking beautiful."

"I want to be. For you."

"You are." My voice sounds so husky, as if my need wrapped itself around my throat and squeezed. "Lie on the bed."

She sits on the edge of the bed, then slowly lowers herself back, her head on the pillow. "Like this?" Her chest rises and falls with her uneven breaths, and I can tell by the flush of her skin that she's as turned on as I am right now. I can't wait to feel the evidence of that between her legs.

"Hold on to the headboard," I say, and she obeys, gripping the white slats of her bed so tightly her knuckles turn white. I slide my gaze down her body again, slower this time, and even slower on the way back up, but when I meet her eyes, there's something there that looks too much like fear. I sit on the edge of the bed and stroke her cheek. "Hey, what is it?"

She forces a smile. "I'm nervous. My insides are shaking."

"Do you want to stop? We don't have to—"

"No." She shakes her head, still clutching the rails. "I like the way you're looking at me. I like . . . everything. It just doesn't feel real, and I'm afraid I'm gonna screw it up. Or worse, wake up and find out none of it was real."

Killing me. She's killing me. I dip my head and sweep my lips across hers. It's killing me that I'm not holding her right now, and I have to fight every instinct not to climb into this bed and pull her into my arms. But I'll go slow for her. I'll take all fucking day if that's what she needs. "Tell me what you're afraid of. Tell me how I can make you feel safe."

There's nothing but raw trust in her eyes as she says, "I'm afraid it'll change after tonight. Afraid that now that you've really seen me . . . I know I'm not like your girl-friends or—"

"Hey." This girl is going to fucking destroy me. "I do see you. I see all of you, and I *love* what I see." I open my mouth, thinking it might be time to explain my hunch about her past experiences with guys "rushing" once she's naked, but then snap it shut again. There'll be time for that later. Time to explain that everyone's got insecurities and they probably sensed her freezing up and thought it was about them. Or maybe they were all assholes. I doubt it, but either way, it's their loss.

We don't need to go over any of that tonight, though. This—right now—is about us. Fuck the rest of them. "You know you turn me on."

For that, I get a crooked grin. "Yeah."

"And you know how much it's killing me to not be buried inside you right now, touching every inch of you."

She swallows. "Is it? Really?"

Standing, I rid myself of my shoes and socks, then shuck my jeans and boxers in one smooth motion and kick them to the other side of the room. When I turn back to her, some of the worry has left her expression, replaced with hot lust as she looks me over. I love the way she looks at me, love that she likes what she sees. I just wish she would believe it goes both ways.

I take one of her hands from the headboard and hold it in mine as I climb onto the bed to straddle her hips. I wrap her fingers around my cock.

She bites her lip as she immediately starts stroking me.

"Any questions?" I ask. She licks her lips and begins to pump in earnest, and I throw my head back and groan. "Fuck that's good, but you need to stop."

"Why?"

I pull her hand away. "I recall promising you I wouldn't be rushed, but with your hands on me, with the sight of you bare beneath me?" I shake my head and cup her breasts in both hands. Her hard nipples pebble tighter beneath my thumbs. "I've wanted this too long, and I only have so much control."

She arches into my touch. "I like that."

"That's the idea."

"No," she says. "I mean, yes, that too, but I like the idea of making you lose it a little."

I lift my head. "Good. Because I might need a couple of rounds to prove myself." I lower my mouth to one peaked nipple, flicking it with my tongue, then switch to the other side.

She moans and releases the headboard with one hand to stroke down my back.

Fuck. I'm going to embarrass myself. "Headboard, precious. If you touch me, I can't make good on my promises." Hell, her sounds alone could make me come. It's a wonder I didn't in Marston's bathroom when she was squirming all over my face.

"But I want to touch you," she says. She's already obeying, though, placing the straying hand next to her other and gripping the headboard tight.

"You'll get your turn." I grin up at her as I kiss my way down her stomach and suck on her navel ring. "But right now, I wanna play."

ABBI

Dean's mouth and hands cover every inch of me—every inch, that is, except for the space between my legs that's aching for those fingers or lips, that tongue. Hell, right now I'd take a well-placed thigh.

I'm squirming, forcing myself to hold on to the headboard as he worships my body. When his fingers finally slide down past my navel to investigate the slickness between my legs, I think I might come from the first touch. My hips buck off the bed, and a desperate cry slips from my lips.

"Is this what you need, baby?"

"Yes."

He slides two fingers over my clit, circling. "Tell me."

"I want to come."

He dips his fingers lower, circling my entrance now. "I love making you come," he says, but he still doesn't give me what I need. "Do you want my fingers, or are you ready for more?"

My brain is so foggy with lust that, for a minute, I don't understand why he's hesitating. His fingers, yes, but also more. Of course I want more. But then I see he's pulled back and is watching me. "I'm not scared of having sex with you."

"I brought a condom, but if you have your own that you'd prefer to use . . ." His fingers circle again as he says this, and my hips lift off the bed, chasing.

"Just hurry."

He grins at me. "Got it."

I almost close my eyes out of old habit. Cody said it weirded him out when I watched him put on a condom, so I trained myself to look away, but when I watch Dean, I regret nothing. He stands beside my bed, forearms flexing as he slides the latex over his impressive length. "That could be its own kind of porn."

Dean winks before crawling back on the bed and over me, settling his weight onto his elbows and his hips between my thighs. "You're okay?"

"No," I say, grinning. "I'm *dying here.*"

Chuckling, he shifts his hips to slowly slide into me, and the smile falls from his face. "Christ, you feel good." He dips his head to sweep his lips over mine, and I kiss him back with hunger and need and a tenderness that takes me by surprise.

This man—the way he handles my body, my heart—I wasn't ready for him, and now he's here, inside me, looking at me like I'm something exquisite as he slowly moves in and out of me.

I don't know how long we stay like that—staring into each other's eyes and moving together so slowly that I could never call it anything but making love—but when he sneaks a hand between our bodies and finds my clit with his thumb, I'm already on the edge. He strokes and strokes, and I feel like something he's building from the ground up, stretching taller and taller, higher and higher, until finally I find release. My sex pulses around him as the orgasm rolls through me. I open my eyes just in time to see him surrender, eyes closed, neck straining as he thrusts his hips hard—once, twice—before collapsing onto me.

He buries his face in my neck. "Trixie and I are staying tonight."

I smile, noting that he's telling me, not asking. "I'd like that."

CHAPTER TWENTY

DEAN

I don't want to move. I'm afraid she'll disappear. Or worse, start spiraling into a flurry of regrets. I can handle a lot of things, but if Abbi regretted this, it might break me.

She doesn't seem in any hurry either, but I force myself to get up and take care of the condom. I bring back a warm washcloth, and love how soft her eyes are as I clean her up.

After I toss the washcloth back into the bathroom, I return to the bedroom to find she's pulled the pink nightie back on. I still think it's hot as fuck, but I scowl at it anyway. "Seriously?"

"What?"

I press my palm to my heart. "I've been working so hard to get you naked, and you're going to cut me off so soon?"

She bites back a smile. "You'll live, Dean."

"Will I, though?"

"It's not like I'm fully clothed."

"True." I climb into bed and slide my hand between her legs, pushing the satin up as I go. "I certainly don't mind the easy access, but . . ." I slide back down into bed as I move my hand up her further, to her waist and then her breasts. "All of this is covered."

She laughs and rolls toward me. "I suppose you'll argue that I should spend time naked because that's going to increase my confidence in bed?"

I would've argued that a few weeks ago, but our arrangement hasn't even crossed my mind tonight. We're together because we wanted to be, and I don't want to remember there's another purpose behind all this. But I push that from my mind and give her the answer she expects. "It's true, isn't it?" I roll on top of her, straddling her hips, and finish pulling up the slip until I'm tugging it off over her head. "That's better."

She glances down at herself and smiles. "How do you do that?" she asks as I flop to the bed beside her. "How do you make me see myself so differently?"

"I don't make you see anything. You are beautiful." I touch my index finger to her lips, then trail it down her chin, her neck, between her breasts and over her stomach. "I love this body." *I love you*, I think. But I don't say it. I know better, and after the reminder that this is just an arrangement to her, I can't. Not yet.

She rolls to her side to face me, and we just lie there for a long time, looking into each other's eyes. "Thank you," she whispers.

"For giving you confidence?"

She shrugs. "Yeah. You make me feel beautiful—make me believe I am. I needed that. But also for seeing me and for being my friend."

I dip my head and scrape my teeth across the swell of her breast, sucking briefly before looking her in the eye again. She's gone all hazy-eyed. I love that. "I like being *more* than your friend, if you hadn't noticed." I sweep my mouth across hers. "A lot."

She snags my bottom lip between her teeth and sucks, and I groan as my cock responds enthusiastically. "I've never done this before," she says. "I've never lain in bed naked with someone after making love and just . . . talked."

"Hmm, well, you've been missing out. Naked time is the best."

Her smile is so bright for a beat, but then it falls away. "Sometimes I wonder if I would've been different if my first time had been with someone like you. Maybe I wouldn't have been so screwed up."

"Well, depending on how old you were, I probably would've volunteered, but then Kace would've beaten the crap out of me and busted up this pretty face, so . . ."

She laughs. "I was eighteen. Freshman year of college."

It could've been me, I think, but lucky for me and my face, it wasn't. "So . . . Cody?" I ask, and she nods. She brought him home with her a couple of times that following year, and I hated him on the spot. He acted like he was too good for Abbi. "You two were together so long, he probably set the tone for a lot of things."

"In some ways." She shrugs. "What about you?"

I cringe. "Do I have to answer that?"

She pokes me in my sides, tickling me. "Yes."

Grabbing her hands, I roll over onto her and pin them over her head. "I was sixteen. It happened at a party with a girl from school."

"Who?" Abbi demands, because this is a small town and chances are she'll know her.

"Addison Clairmont."

She rolls her eyes. "Of course. Blond, cheerleader, brilliant. Did she rock your world?"

I release her hands and prop myself on my elbows, taking some of my weight off her. "I mean, I was sixteen and it was sex, so . . . pretty much?" We laugh, and I love that there's no real jealousy in her eyes. There shouldn't be. "But back then, I had no idea how good it could be. Hell, I'd never been in love. I guess at least you had that with Cody, even if he was completely unworthy of you in every other way."

She scoffs. "Nice of you to say, but I'm pretty sure that's not true."

"Oh, it's completely true. I knew it the first time I met him and he—" Shit. No need to rub salt in that wound.

"He what?"

I shake my head. "Never mind."

She shoves my chest gently with her palms. "Don't do that."

"He was your boyfriend, but that time you brought him home over the summer and we all hung out at the lake, he wouldn't stop checking out Stella."

All the playfulness leaves her face.

"See? I should've kept my mouth shut."

She shakes her head. "No. I already knew that. He actually made a move on her that visit."

At first I'm outraged that Stella didn't tell me, but it doesn't take long for me to piece together why. It wouldn't have been pretty. And it was Abbi's business, not mine, so Stella told the only person who needed to know. "What a fucking dick."

"Yeah. I guess he was, but in my defense, our first year together was really good. What about you? Who was your first love?"

"Do you remember Grace Lettinghouse?"

"Ah, yes, the first girl *you* brought home from college. I remember thinking she'd end up modeling."

"She did. For a while, at least. Now I think she's an acting coach in L.A."

She searches my face. "You wonder why I'm so insecure when you've dated all of these beautiful women."

"You can't hold that against me," I say. "I like beautiful women." I drop a kiss on her lips, then her neck, then kiss my way down to her breasts. "As is evidenced by the fact that I'm in bed with you." I flick my tongue over her nipple. "Tell me something else I don't know about you."

She arches under me. "Like what?"

"First kiss?"

"Eighth grade. Spin the bottle. It was awful. He spun his tongue around in my mouth like it was a propeller." She shudders under me. "You?"

"Ninth grade. After a cross-country meet. Not awful, but not great. I remember thinking she smelled a little and that she probably needed to use a better deodorant."

She laughs, making her breasts shake under my lips, and I swear I'd tell her all my most embarrassing stories if it meant hearing that laugh.

"First crush?" I ask.

This time when she smacks my chest with her palms, she does it with so much force that I roll off her.

"Are you okay? What's wrong?"

She grabs a pillow and smashes it over her face. When she speaks, her words are muffled. "You can't ask me that. It's not a fair question."

For a moment, I struggle to remember what I asked, but then it clicks and I grin. "First crush?" I pull the pillow away, and she reaches for it, but I toss it onto the floor. "Why don't you want me asking about your first crush?"

She squeezes her eyes shut and groans. "It's so clichéd it's obvious, and I can't believe your ego is so desperate for attention that you're going to make me say it."

My grin grows. "Clichéd to have a crush on your big brother's best friend?" I ask, grabbing her by the hip and turning her body toward mine. "It's not a terrible cliché. So how old were you when you realized I was irresistible?"

"I take back every nice thing I ever said about you. You're the worst."

I press my smile to her lips. "Is that a nice thing to say to your first crush?"

She softens against me, and her hand tangles in my hair as she kisses me back.

She wasn't my first crush. She was just a kid when I started really caring about girls, and I definitely had an eye for the more *mature* girls. But if she thinks she's the only one in this relationship who had to deal with unrequited feelings, she's got it all wrong.

"I love that we're here now," I say against her mouth. I kiss her, gently but deeply. It's a promise of everything she is to me, and everything I want this to be. I can't tell her, not with words, not yet, so I tell her with my kiss. I slip my hand between her legs, and she gasps. "I was an idiot for ever giving up."

"Giving . . .?"

I slide two fingers inside her, and her question is lost on a gasp as I show her the first of a long list of reasons she should love this too.

ABBI

Two more orgasms and another condom later, I'm curled in bed beside Dean, the blankets pulled over us.

"You good?" I ask, because he's been lying here staring at me for a long time.

He nods and then presses a gentle kiss to my mouth. I've never been with anyone who likes kissing as much as Dean does. I'm not sure I ever liked it this much with anyone else. "You?"

"I feel . . ." A laugh slips out of me.

"What?"

"You'll think I'm pathetic."

"I really doubt that."

I haven't been this vulnerable with a person in a long time, but it's been good. So why stop now? Here, naked in my bed with my head on his chest and the steady beat of his heart in my ear, I'm being vulnerable, but I don't *feel* vulnerable. What I feel is less alone than I have in a long time. Maybe ever. I can't help but wonder if he feels a little of that too. "I feel reborn. Like I'm still me but . . . better." I sound like a nut. "Don't you dare laugh."

He grins. "I *like* making you feel good." He reaches down and strokes my hip then up my side to my breast. "There's nothing funny about that."

"I'm rather fond of it myself," I say, nuzzling his neck. The clock on my nightstand says it's almost midnight. I know Dean has to work tomorrow, but I don't want this night to end. I don't want this *connection* to end. "Tell me about Amy."

He grunts. "You want me to tell you about your ex-sister-in-law? What do you think I know that you don't?"

I bite my bottom lip. Maybe I should let it go, but . . . "Tell me about *you* and Amy. How did that happen?"

"Booze, mostly."

I peel myself off his chest, propping up on one elbow to look at him. "That's a deflection."

Closing his eyes, he takes a deep breath. "I'm embarrassed that it happened at all. Embarrassed that after it happened, I let my feelings get away from me and let her string me on for so long. Embarrassed that I let her screw me up that way." He shakes his head. "Not my proudest moments."

"I'm not judging. I mean, I did at first. Absolutely." He flashes me a mock scowl, and I laugh. "I'm sincerely curious."

"I care about her," he says. "So maybe that was the reason I let it happen. Or maybe it was because of what she and Kace had? Before she left him? I was . . . envious of that."

"Their marriage may have looked perfect from the outside, but it wasn't. No one's is."

He reaches up and hooks a lock of my hair with one finger before wrapping it around his hand. "I know that. Intellectually, at least."

"And if you wanted marriage and a family so badly, why have you always been Mr. Commitment Is Overrated?"

"That's not who I am."

"It's who you were. You went for the party girls—women who just wanted a good time and nothing more."

He groans and rubs his palms against his eyes. "I don't think it's a bad thing to have casual relationships with people who only want casual relationships."

"Well, sure, but that doesn't explain what happened with Amy."

He pinches my side. "The only explanation I have for that is temporary insanity."

Or loneliness, I think, but I don't say it. What if loneliness is the only reason he's found himself here with me? Would that be so bad if we both get something good out of it? All night, hope's been surging in my chest—that we can make this something more, that maybe this doesn't have to be temporary—and now it's tangling with doubt. He never promised me anything and never claimed to want more than I offered. I paste on a serious expression and say, "Maybe it's not that. Smithy says Amy has a unicorn pussy, so maybe that's it?"

"Fucking Smithy," he mutters, but he's smiling now. "I promise her pussy had nothing to do with it."

I scoff. "Okay, *sure.*"

"I mean it. I'm not going to pretend the sex was bad, but . . ." He rolls us so he's on top of me, his knees straddling my hips. He slides a hand down my body and between my legs. "If we want to talk about a pussy I can't stop obsessing over, I have a lot to say."

I'm a little tender from earlier, but that doesn't stop me from rocking into his hand. "Why talk when you can put your mouth to better use?"

"That's what I thought," he mumbles, already disappearing beneath the sheets.

CHAPTER TWENTY-ONE

DEAN

I don't know why I'm surprised to see my sister waiting for me when I get to my office on Monday morning. I should've expected this from the moment she saw me in the hall with Abbi.

"At least now I know why you looked so frazzled when I told you about Frankie last night," she says by way of greeting.

I blow out a breath. "Good morning, sis."

"She didn't tell you she's planning to date this guy when he moves to town." She pouts so hard her bottom lip juts out, just like it would as a kid. "*Is* she still planning on dating him? Because that's screwed up."

"I don't know," I mutter, putting my laptop case on my desk. "I didn't know the name Frankie until last night. I just knew Abbi wanted a little more confidence in"—*fuck* —"with dating and stuff. I offered to help."

"You're hoping she'll catch feelings," Stella says, hands on her hips. "Admit it."

I shrug. I can't deny it. This morning when she asked if she could cook for me tonight, I gave Abbi a key to my place so she wouldn't have to wait around until I got home. Warning bells clanged in my brain, telling me the key wasn't just about convenience but about what I *want* our relationship to be. I did the same thing with Amy months ago, but neither woman used the gesture to crack into my psyche—for better or worse. "Am I supposed to apologize for that?"

My little sister can be fierce, and I brace myself for her lecture. Instead, she sighs and shakes her head. "No. I don't want you apologizing. I'm just afraid you'll end up hurt."

Nodding, I study my shoes. "I've thought about that, but I think . . ." I swallow hard. "I think there might be a chance for us."

"Have you told her how you feel?"

I shake my head. I can't go into this with Stella. The things Abbi said the night of her twenty-first would hurt Stella as badly as they hurt me, and I don't see any reason to do that to my sister. "She knows it's not just a game to me." The worry on her face makes me want to crawl under a rock. "Please don't look at me like that."

"You know, I like Abbi. She's sweet and fun, but she can also be . . ." She swallows. "I tried to talk to Kace about her last night—"

"You did what?" I stiffen.

"I didn't tell him anything. I just asked why she doesn't date more, and he said she's been hurt. That asshole she dated in college—the one who hit on me that summer?—he really did a number on her."

I sink into my office chair and lean my head back. "I know."

"So sometimes when people have been hurt, it can make them put up defenses. Nasty ones."

"I know what I'm dealing with." I don't love Stella talking about Abbi like she's some wounded animal, but I can't deny that I need Abbi to trust me a little more. Need her to believe she *can* trust me.

"And when will you tell Kace?" Stella asks.

"As soon as Abbi is okay with it. This isn't just my secret."

She stares at me so long that I feel like I'm ten again and in the principal's office for putting gum in Meredith Ralston's hair. "What?"

"You know why I didn't like you with Amy," she says.

I scoff. "Yeah."

"This is different. With Amy, you were up against her selfishness and her . . . loose relationship with the truth."

I arch a brow. Most people would've just gone with *lies*, but Stella is trying so hard to have a decent relationship with Kace's ex. I've gotta respect the amount of maturity she's showing with the whole thing.

"With Abbi, though," she continues, "you're up against some pretty thick walls she's built around herself."

I squeeze the back of my neck. "I do renovations for a living. Taking down walls is a specialty of mine."

"I hope so." She hoists her purse onto her shoulder and heads for the door. She stops in the doorframe and turns back to me. "I should probably also tell you that Dad—"

"Stop."

She heaves an exasperated sigh. "Dean, I'm headed over there tomorrow. He's—"

"No." The word snaps in the air. A warning shot. "You know how I feel."

"Okay." She nods. "But I'm here if you ever want to talk about it."

WHEN I GET HOME from work on Monday night, my house smells amazing. Like garlic and onion and . . . I close my eyes and draw in a deep breath.

Chocolate and Abbi.

I follow my nose to the kitchen and find Abbi at the stove, stirring whatever deliciousness she has going on the burner as she shakes her hips to a beat I can't hear. She's wearing jeans and a loose T-shirt, and her hair is pulled up into a sloppy bun. Her phone is sticking out of her back pocket, and she has in earbuds.

Folding my arms, I lean against the opposite counter and watch her, knowing she'll stop dancing the second she realizes I'm here. Sexed-up Abbi is sweet and cute and seductive in a way I never expected. If I need to take it upon myself to keep her this way for a very long time, I'm game.

When she opens the oven, the smell of rich chocolate fills the kitchen. My mouth waters, but I honestly don't know if it's because of the brownies or the sight of the woman bending over in front of me. Dear Lord. *That ass.*

Images from last night flash through my mind, answering my question. Definitely Abbi.

She pulls the brownies from the oven and plops them onto a cooling rack before returning her attention to the stove. Only when I'm sure she's not at risk of startling and hurting herself do I clear my throat.

"It smells amazing," I say, stepping toward her.

She flashes me a smile over her shoulder and tugs her earbuds from her ears. She tucks them in her pocket as she turns to me. "I told you I'd take over your kitchen. Hope you don't mind."

I drag my gaze over her. Big T-shirt, fitted jeans, bare feet. She looks comfortable, and that does more for me than the meal she's cooking—which is saying something, given the smells happening in here. "Mind? I'm pretty sure I'm the luckiest guy in town tonight."

She grins. "You say that now, but once you taste my chicken piccata, there'll be no room for doubt."

A few weeks ago, the only compliments Abbi knew how to take were ones about her cooking. But tonight? I grab her by the hips and pull her forward until our bodies are flush. "What if I wasn't talking about the food?"

She looks up at me with big, hungry eyes. "Then I'd wonder when you might kiss me," she says softly, surprising me as she slides a hand into my hair.

Groaning, I lower my mouth to hers, sucking her bottom lip between my teeth. Images of last night flash through my mind—Abbi all flushed and needy beneath me, the way she moved against my mouth. Goddamn, I could barely focus on my work today because I was so distracted by the memories and my plans for her tonight.

When she breaks the kiss, we're both breathless, and my body has forgotten all about its need for food. Right now, all that matters is my need for *her*.

"Will that be okay on the stove for a while?" I ask, kissing my way down her neck.

"Hmm?" She tilts her head to the side, giving me better access to all her most sensitive spots.

"I haven't stopped thinking about you all day, and I don't know if I can make it through dinner without getting my mouth on you again first."

"You . . . already have your . . . mouth on me," she says, as if piecing the sentence together takes all her effort.

"I do," I say, flicking my tongue against her earlobe, "but I'm craving . . . other parts." I tug up her shirt and slide a hand between her legs, stroking gently.

"I can't think when you do that."

I fucking love that I scramble her mind like that. I want her so turned on that she forgets all her worries and all her insecurities. So turned on that she forgets this Frankie guy. I only want her thinking about me. "That was the idea."

She shakes her head and steps out of my reach. "Get over there." She points to the opposite side of the kitchen. "Seriously. If you stay next to me, dinner will be burned."

I smirk. "I think I might like you bossy." But I obey, watching her finish our dinner. We eat, and it *is* incredible, but I'm impatient and have her naked and moaning my name before we make it to dessert.

ॐ

ABBI

Tuesday morning comes too soon. I make myself get out of bed when Dean gets up to get ready for work. Only seems fair, since I was the reason he didn't get much sleep.

I didn't intend to stay the night, but when it was time for me to go, Dean pinned me down on the bed and kissed me until I forgot why I needed to sleep alone. Not that I tried too hard to remember.

We ate brownies naked on the bedroom floor, and he "accidentally" smeared frosting across my chest and feigned insult when I suggested we take a shower to clean it off.

He promised he could do a better job than a shower-head and proved himself. Then we took the shower anyway, and he did some seriously wicked things to me with his removable showerhead before hooking one of my legs over his hip and driving into me, the cold tile against my back.

After that, we both collapsed in bed and slept hard, spent, sated, and exhausted. But that didn't keep him from pulling me close when the alarm went off this morning. He rolled me to my stomach and slid into me from behind, trailing kisses across my back and shoulders as he tortured me with deep, slow thrusts of his hips.

When he headed to the shower, it would've been so easy to roll over and fall back to sleep for a few hours, but I don't. The least I can do is make him some coffee before he goes to work. And anyway, I like this—the sleepovers, the morning coffee, and the way he looks at me. It makes that hope surge. Hope that maybe this can be more, that maybe this feels like a real relationship because it is and not only because I want it to be. I know I need to find the courage to have a conversation about it, but I don't want to rush it either. Our relationship feels like a blooming flower that might fall apart if it's examined too carelessly.

I dress in my clothes from yesterday then head to the kitchen. I'm surprised to hear a knock on the door. I hesitate in the kitchen, not sure if I should risk answering in case it's one of our friends. It's just after seven, so I'm not sure who else it would be. On the other hand, if it's Kace or

Smithy, they'll just let themselves in anyway. I'm not sure I want to sneak around to the degree that I'm hiding in closets.

I'm being ridiculous. Dean and I are friends, and I'm fully clothed. There's no reason my presence should make them suspicious. It's not like anyone would suspect we'd be a real couple, anyway.

With that decided, I head to the door and pull it open to see a young man I've never met before. He backs up a step when he sees me. "Oh." He clears his throat. "Sorry. I . . . Is Dean around?" There's something familiar about this guy. He has reddish-blond hair and a patchy beard that makes him look like a kid trying to appear older than he is.

"Can I tell him who's asking?"

"Yeah. Name's Milo. I'm . . . Uh. His brother?"

Oh. That's when I see it—the resemblance. This kid's eyes turn down in the corners the same way Dean's do, and he has the same strong jaw. He must be a half-brother from Dean's father, who left when he was a kid. "Sure. Um, come on in." I pull the door the rest of the way open and wave him inside. "Make yourself at home. I'll be right back."

The kid follows me in, his expression filled with awe as he glances around Dean's small but impressive place. I wave him toward the living room before cutting across to the bedroom. I close the door behind me and find Dean in front of the mirror, combing his hair. He's shirtless and in jeans that are unbuttoned at the top. He's still a little dewy from the shower, and I have to stifle the urge to lick a bead of water off his shoulder. Damn, this man's gorgeous.

He catches my gaze in the mirror and grins. "Missed you in the shower."

"You never would've made it to work if I'd gotten into that shower with you."

His grin widens. "Work is overrated."

I shake my head, trying to stay focused and not fall under the spell of those sexy eyes. He could have me naked and in bed in seconds, completely forgetting about the stranger in the living room. "Um, there's someone here for you."

He frowns. "Who?"

"Milo. He said he's your brother?"

Dean's smile falls away and he bows his head, breaking eye contact and focusing on returning his comb to his toiletry kit. "Did he say why he's here?"

"I didn't ask." I glance over my shoulder. "I think it might be important."

"I'll take care of it." He steps around me and heads out into the living room without sparing me another glance, let alone the regular every-chance-he-gets kiss I'm usually treated to before he walks away from me.

Convinced that exhaustion is making me take this personally, I follow. The unexpected appearance of his brother is obviously an issue for Dean, so the least I can do is stand beside him.

The kid's sitting on the edge of the couch, twisting his hands, and he jumps up when he spots Dean. "Hey."

"You need something?" Dean asks softly.

"It's about Dad."

His expression goes cold. "Then my friend shouldn't have let you in," Dean says.

Friend. I don't know why I hate that word so much right now, but I push away my nagging feeling of dread. *Now isn't the time.*

"Then again," he continues, "if you would've been upfront about the fact that I don't want to hear that shit, she wouldn't have made that mistake."

The kid shifts from one foot to the other. "I'm sorry to show up like this. I just wanted you to hear me out."

"Not interested," Dean says, and I cringe at how callous he sounds. I'm sure Dean has a good reason, but this kid seems nothing but anxious to please him. "You know the deal. I'm here for you, but you don't get to use our relationship to drag me back into one with him. You can go now."

"Dad's *bad*," Milo blurts.

Dean flinches, but a moment later his face returns to a picture of detached coolness. "Sandy already told me. And, like I told her, that's a matter for you and your family to deal with."

Milo's hands clench and release at his sides. "He's your dad too."

"Nah," Dean says. "He's not."

Milo studies his shoes. I don't blame him. This cold, angry Dean is intimidating. "Today they'll be releasing him into hospice care. You're running out of time to say goodbye."

Dean doesn't reply. He doesn't move. It's as if the words froze him in place.

"I just thought you should know," Milo says, chancing another glance at Dean. He shakes his head and heads to the door, letting himself out.

I open my mouth to say something—but what? *Thank you for coming*? I'm not sure he did Dean any favors by sharing this information. Or maybe he did, but Dean doesn't know it yet.

We stand in silence at the sound of Milo's car starting up and backing out of the drive.

When he's gone, I turn to Dean, stepping close. "I'm sorry. I didn't know. I—"

Dean yanks me into his arms and squeezes me so tight I can barely breathe. Then he buries his face into my neck and takes several long, ragged breaths before releasing me again. "Not your problem," he says when he pulls back. He tucks a lock of my hair behind my ear. "Sorry you had to see that."

See what? A bit of family drama? Dean's known me and Kace long enough that he's seen more than his share of our family's drama. And sure, we don't have anything like this, but I wouldn't think twice about telling him if I had a fight with my mom or argued with Kace. "Do you want to talk about it?"

"No. There's nothing to talk about." He turns to the kitchen and heads toward the coffee pot.

"But it's your *dad*, Dean."

"Wrong." While I know the anger in his eyes has nothing to do with me, it burns a little anyway. "He might be my father, but handing over half his DNA doesn't make him my dad."

There's an accusation in his tone I don't understand. What am I missing here? "Should we call Stella and let her know?"

He fills his mug, taking his time before he replies. "No need. I'm sure she already knows."

"Wouldn't she have told you?"

He takes a gulp of his coffee, staring straight ahead at nothing. "She tried. I reminded her how I feel about it."

"Dean—"

"I don't want to have this conversation, okay?" he snaps.

I don't recognize the anger and frustration in his eyes right now, and I definitely don't want it aimed at me, so I just nod and let it go.

CHAPTER TWENTY-TWO

ABBI

I don't bother texting Dean when I get off work after nine. Considering the way he froze me out this morning, I'm afraid if I ask, he'll tell me not to come over. Deciding it's better to ask forgiveness than permission, I head straight there.

I find Dean on his back deck when I get there, and I immediately sit in his lap and wrap my arms behind his neck. Three weeks ago, this would've been unthinkable. I would've been far too fixated on my weight and awkwardness to do this. But tonight it's as natural as breathing. This man needs comfort, and I'm going to give it to him in any way I can.

He sets his glass down on the little wrought-iron end table next to him and then wraps his arms around me. "Hey, you," he murmurs, burying his face in my chest.

"Are you okay?" When he pulls back, his eyes are red, as

if he's been crying, and my heart feels like it cracks in my chest. I've known Dean a long time, and this is maybe the third time ever I've seen the evidence of tears. I stroke his cheek with my thumb. "I've been thinking about you."

"Under normal circumstances, I like the idea of you thinking about me all day, but this time I'm not really a fan."

"So I'm only allowed to think about you if sex is involved?"

He lifts one shoulder in a lopsided shrug and slides his hands under my shirt. "If I have it my way."

I want more from you than that. I want you to confide in me. But I can't ask for that. Not when this isn't supposed to be that kind of relationship. Even if it was starting to feel like more. Even if this hope in my chest is growing so big that it's smothering my doubts.

I brush my lips across his. "To be fair, I had sexy thoughts too. Those are never too far behind when I think of you."

Groaning, he tugs me closer, and his hands roam over my back, rough calluses against sensitive skin. "Even after you had to see me lose my shit this morning?"

Is that what he considers losing his shit? A little show of temper and then stonewalling me? "I can't pretend I understand what's between you and your d—father—but you're human. You're going to get upset sometimes."

He trails kisses across my collarbone, stopping at my shoulder, where he sucks lightly. "I just don't like you knowing that part of me. I don't like giving you any reason to think about it."

I want to know all parts of you. "What part? The one that clams up and won't talk?"

He huffs out a laugh and nips at my neck. "The one whose dad wasn't ever around."

I pull back so I can see his face. "Dean—"

"I know I can't change it, so I try not to think about it too much. This morning just shoved it in my face and brought up some unhappy memories."

"When did he leave?" I ask softly. Kace has been friends with Dean since they were really young, but I wasn't close enough to Dean to know about his family situation until . . . well, probably not until I dropped out of college and moved back to Orchid Valley. I was always aware his home situation wasn't as stable as ours, but I didn't think much about it.

"My parents got divorced when Stella was still in diapers, but he came back a lot on and off for years after that." He grimaces, and I can tell it really makes him uncomfortable to talk about this, but I don't let him off the hook. I think he needs to let it out. "Anytime I'd come home from school and see his Nissan in the drive, I'd be so excited. For a long time, I was convinced he and Mom would get back together if I acted just right."

"I think a lot of kids feel that way after their parents get divorced."

"Yeah, but he made it worse. He'd say, 'You be real good at school and keep your room clean for your mama, and we'll celebrate. We'll go to the zoo in Atlanta and have lunch at a fancy restaurant.' He never meant any of it—he didn't have two pennies to rub together, let alone money for a day in Atlanta with his kid. But all I heard was if I was good, I'd get more time with my dad. That's all I wanted."

My chest aches for him, but all I can do is squeeze his hand so he knows I'm here, knows I'm listening.

He shakes his head. "It's embarrassing to think about how many times I made myself sick over a baseball game because my dad told me he'd be there, and I wanted to impress him. I'd be so nervous I could barely join my team on the field, and then he wouldn't show anyway. Happened over and over again until one of my teammates finally called me out for being so nervous. 'Your dad isn't coming, you idiot,' he said. 'He's busy with his other family.'"

"I'm so sorry," I say, combing my fingers through his hair. "Was the kid being honest or just trying to upset you?"

"He was one hundred percent right. Dad and Sandy still lived in Orchid Valley back then. She had a couple of kids from a former marriage, and he was so busy being the perfect dad to them that he couldn't show up for me. And my mom . . ." He closes his eyes. "Shit, she's not a bad person, but she knew he was living with Sandy. She was a sucker for his promises, though, and she'd let him come back home, let him stay the night, let him sweet-talk her into thinking he might be coming back for good that time."

"I can't imagine what it must've been like—to learn that from a teammate and not your parents."

"It was shit, but it was also exactly what I needed." His arms tighten around me. "That was the end for me, though. I confronted Mom about it, and she admitted it was true and that Sandy was pregnant. I'd have a little brother, so Dad wouldn't be coming home anymore."

"Milo," I say.

"Yeah. Mom stopped believing his bullshit after that—not because he stopped with his lies and promises, but because she was a mom too. She might've been able to sleep with her ex-husband even though he was living with another woman, but she couldn't take the kid's father away."

Dean's mom is such a sweet woman. It's hard to imagine her letting a guy like that back into her life again and again. But then, Stella's made reference a time or two to her mom's terrible track record with men, so maybe I shouldn't be surprised. "I guess we have hard lines we won't cross, no matter how desperate we feel."

"That's when all of my grandmother's comments started." He cringes. "You probably never met my mom's mom, but she was a mean old lady, and once I stopped looking like a kid and began looking like a young man, she started in with the commentary. *Watch out for that one—he's a little version of his dad. Cheaters make more of their own. Hope no woman ever trusts him—he'll be just like his father.*"

"That's awful."

He huffs out a breath. "Yeah. I spent all my teen years worried she was right. I was *terrified* I'd accidentally cheat on my girlfriends someday, worried I'd never hold down a job and take care of my family—because that's who my dad is, and she loved to tell me how I was going to be just like him."

"I sure hope that shit doesn't haunt you anymore," I say. "You've more than proven yourself."

He studies me for a long time like he's trying to figure out how to say what he needs to. "I really try."

"So Milo knew about you? You acted like you've met before."

He nods. "He's an okay kid, and I help him out when I can. He just can't see where I'm coming from about the old man. He was always tracking me down when my father was in trouble. Not long after Kace and I started our business, my father contacted me and said he needed money for Milo, that Milo had been given this great opportunity to travel abroad with this international STEM program that'd supposedly give him access to any engineering college he wanted after he graduated. I made the mistake of believing him. Maybe he was a shit father for me, but I liked the idea of him being a good dad for Milo. And he had a whole plan on how he'd pay me back. It seemed legit." He swallows hard, and I can see it hurts his pride to tell this story.

"You don't need to be ashamed for being a good brother."

"But I wasn't. I was an idiot for believing anything that came out of my old man's mouth. Never mind that I didn't have the kind of money he was asking for. I borrowed it from our company—and Kace and I hit a slump after that and almost lost the business because of it."

My heart squeezes. "I didn't even know you and Kace were struggling."

He shrugs. "You were at school, and we weren't looking for sympathy. Amy was actually the one who gave us the money we needed for the capital to take on a new project and get afloat again."

"He never paid you back?"

"No. I paid the business back, of course, but I felt like an idiot for believing Dad's lies." Dean leans back in the chair, pulling me with him until my head's resting on his chest. "I know it probably seems cold to not want to see him before he dies, but I can't handle the thought of feeling the way he made me feel as a kid. Helpless and unwanted. Not good enough." His arms tighten around me like a vise. "I don't want to be reminded that he's my blood."

"You get to make this choice," I say against his chest. "No one else. If you don't want to go, there's no one who can make you. But for what it's worth, you might not feel that way if you went. You're not the kid you used to be. You're a grown man with a successful business and friends who love you. You don't owe him anything, but if it might help *you* to say goodbye, I think you should."

His warm fingers stroke circles on my back. "I'll think about it." He's quiet for a long time, and the songs of the crickets and katydids fill my ears before he says, "When he came crawling back for more money, he tried to convince me I was just like him—chasing money and a better life." Dean swallows. "And in some ways, that's true, but I don't chase it the way he does. I *work*. And I'd never walk out on my family like he did. That's why I don't have long-term relationships with women I'm not head over heels for. I've gotta make sure I get it right, because I won't be like him."

I can feel his heart racing beneath my cheek, and I want to cry. "There's not a doubt in my mind you'll be a great husband and father when you're ready."

"I can't change who my father is, but I can promise you I am nothing like him. I'll never, ever be like him. If I doubted that, I wouldn't let myself be with you."

I pull back and stare at him for a long time, my heart both full and aching for him. "I know that, Dean." I press my palm to his chest, right over the heart he just opened for me. "I know who you are."

His eyes glisten in the patio lights. I could stare at him all night—wondering at the strength and vulnerability of this amazing man—but I curl into his chest instead, hoping I can offer him just a little comfort.

We're quiet for a long time before he speaks again. "If I go see him, will you come with me?"

"Of course." *I'd go anywhere with you.*

DEAN

Once again, our schedules keep us apart more than I'd like, but at least Abbi stayed at my place on Tuesday and Wednesday night, and holding her while she sleeps centers me. We haven't talked about my dad since my little melt-down on the deck, but it feels good to have it out there—to have at least broached the subject of my family. Of the kind of father I grew up with and the kind I'm determined to be.

Abbi's matured a lot in the last four years. We both have. Maybe my upbringing is irrelevant to her now. Maybe she doesn't even feel that way anymore.

Regardless, I can't complain about how things are progressing. She texted me at work today and insisted I meet her at Smithy's for dinner and drinks. I didn't ask if she was sure she wanted to be seen in public with me. I didn't want to remind her that she thought this was a bad idea just a couple of weeks ago.

So here we are, scanning Smithy's dinner specials, sipping drinks, and in no hurry to go anywhere. Like a real couple. And I like it a lot.

"Hey, Abbi!" a brunette lady says, stopping at our table. "I just wanted to thank you for the cookies you made for Harbor View. My mother's in long-term care there, and they really brighten her day."

My phone buzzes on the table while they talk, and out of habit I flip it over to look at who's messaging.

Amy: I have a kid-free night, a bottle of

tequila, and a new lacy little thing. Any
ideas of how I could use all that?

I could just block her number, but that feels cheap. I
might not want Amy anymore, but I care about her and
don't want to cut her off completely. What I *want* is to
make things official with the woman across from me so I
can explain to Amy exactly why her little invitations need
to stop.

"What's wrong?" Abbi asks, and I realize the woman's
walked away, and I'm scowling at my phone.

I shake my head and close my texting app, putting the
phone facedown on the table. "Nothing. Just someone
selling something I don't want." I snatch the menu out of
her hand instead of grabbing my own from the end of the
table. "What are we eating tonight?"

She laughs. "Well, I don't know about *we*, but *I* am
trying to decide if I want the barbecue chicken flatbread,
the black-and-blue salad, or just a giant plate of fried
cheese."

I snap the menu closed and lean forward on the table.
"Sounds perfect. *We* will have all three."

A pretty pink blush creeps up her cheeks. "I don't need
all that."

"Uh, for one, we're sharing, so you don't *get* all that, and
for two, you're going to need your energy for the things I
have planned for you."

That pink glows brighter to a dusky rose. "Like what?"
she asks, all feigned innocence.

"If you make me start talking about it here, we'll never
make it through the meal." I smirk. "Or maybe that's what
you're hoping for?" I lean forward on the table. "I could

take you in the bathroom. I seem to remember you liked that."

The pretty pink turns red. "I trust Brinley's bathroom way more than Smithy's."

"Want me to call her?" I pick up my phone as if I'm actually going to do it. "I'm sure she wouldn't mind if we swing by."

Abbi just rolls her eyes and laughs, but unfortunately, picking up my phone to pretend I'm going to call Brinley means I see the latest text. Another from Amy.

> Amy: You used to like it when I'd text you wanting sex. You said I never had to apologize for it. Is everything so different now?

I swipe away the message without even bothering to pull up the texting app. I can't deal with Amy right now.

The woman in front of me is far too important to get anything less than one hundred percent of my attention.

&.

ABBI

Halfway through my second martini, and I'm feeling loose and carefree. Dean just excused himself to use the restroom, and I'm chilling in the booth thinking happy thoughts about getting him home and naked. My mouth practically waters when I think of the way his stomach muscles clench under my tongue as I lick my way down to his waistband.

My phone buzzes in the middle of the table, and I flip it over and read the text preview.

> Amy: Because I do want sex. With you.
> Right now.

I yank my hand away as if I've been burned. That's *not* my phone. That's Dean's phone, and Amy is texting him. Amy, whom he supposedly isn't involved with anymore—whom he supposedly hasn't been involved with for *weeks*—is texting him demanding sex.

My stomach lurches, my martinis suddenly not sitting so well.

My head is swimming, and I feel like the floor is falling out from under me.

Dean wouldn't cheat on me. He wouldn't—

But it's not cheating if you two aren't an actual couple, a little voice whispers.

I grip the edge of the table, as if holding myself steady might make any of this make sense.

"Abbi!"

I look up as Frankie Perez slides into the booth across from me, taking Dean's seat.

I can only blink at him. "What are you doing here?"

Frankie beams at me. His smile is so charming, but I wonder how I ever thought it made me feel warm. It's Dean's smile that warms me up from the inside out. "I told you I'm moving to town, remember?"

Right. That's why Dean was teaching me how to be good in bed. A maniacal giggle slips out of my mouth, and Frankie frowns.

"You okay?" he asks.

No. I'm not okay. I've fallen in love with a guy who's in love with someone else. I'm not okay. I should've known better. I should've known I'd never be enough. I shake my head, but before I can answer, Dean returns to the table.

He smiles at Frankie, but his brow is creased. "Hey there. You trying to steal my date?" He asks it like he's joking, but anyone who knows him well would hear the edge of annoyance beneath his words. I *don't get it*. How can he be so possessive of me and still be . . . whatever he is with Amy? *Are* they messing around? Did he never close that door?

Frankie's eyes go wide and shift back and forth between me and Dean. When his gaze settles on me, there's no missing the hurt and disappointment in his eyes. "Right." He practically jumps out of the booth. "Sorry. Didn't mean to interrupt." He shoves a hand toward Dean. "I'm Frankie, a friend of Abbi's. Just moved to town."

Dean's fake smile falls away, and his expression goes stony. "Frankie?" He turns to me, his jaw hardening. "You didn't tell me he was going to be here tonight."

I'm so confused. Dean knows Frankie? I shake my head. "I didn't know. I didn't even know he was in town yet."

Frankie looks as confused as I feel, but he finally gives up on Dean taking his hand and drops it to his side. "Um. Should I go?"

"Yes," Dean and I say in unison. Then I grimace, because we sound like total assholes. "We'll catch up another time," I tell Frankie gently.

"Looking forward to it," he says, backing away.

"I'm sure you are, buddy," Dean mutters. He pulls his wallet from his pocket and throws money on the table. "Let's get out of here."

"What's your problem?"

His eyes widen. "*My* problem?"

"Yes, *your* problem." I lower my voice, worried we're calling attention to ourselves. "You're acting like a dick for no good reason." *And you might still be sleeping with Amy, and I'm not okay with that.*

He grunts. "I finally get my girl to go out with me in public, and the guy she's doing all this for literally shows up to take my place. Seems like reason enough to be a dick to me."

"Let's go." Yep, people are turning to stare. "Make sure you don't forget your phone." I slide it to him, climb out of the booth, and march toward the door, my anger the only thing keeping the tears at bay. With every step, I feel Dean behind me, his glare burning into my back.

I don't stop when I hit the sidewalk, and I don't go toward the back lot where I know he's parked. I just keep marching all the way to my house.

When I hit the porch and finally turn to him, his stony expression has turned to granite. And really? *He's* pissed right now?

"How do you even know about Frankie, anyway?" Of all the things I could start with, I don't know why I start there. Maybe because that's the easiest part of this mess we're in.

His nostrils flare, but he looks away before he answers. "Stella told me you'd been working on your confidence. Of course, I already knew that. The part I *didn't* know was that you were fucking me so you could be better for *him*."

"I . . ." I don't know what to say. He's *hurt*, and I can't exactly deny that's how it started, but I've barely spared Frankie a thought. Of course, I didn't realize Dean was keeping things going with Amy. And I should have. I never should've believed he'd settle for me. But I did. I really, really did.

"You can't even deny it," he says, his voice rough.

"I could," I say. "I could explain this all started because of Frankie, but everything I wanted changed once I thought I had a chance with you." I try to laugh, but it sounds more like a strangled sob, and tears roll down my cheeks. "But I don't really see the point in defending myself—in fighting for this—when Amy's still sexting you."

The blood drains from his face, and I want to drop to the ground and cry. *This is really happening. I'm not wrong about what I saw.* "Abbi—"

"Don't." I shake my head. "I can't do this. I won't compete with her."

"It's not a competition," he says, and for the first time since Frankie introduced himself, Dean's expression is tender. "There is no competition."

But she has a reason to think she should still text you like that. I back toward the door. "I just can't do this. I'm sorry."

I fumble with my keys to get into the house, but he doesn't try to stop me.

Shutting the front door behind me, I lean back against it and sink to the floor, my body desperate to catch up to my heart. I knew this would hurt.

I don't know how long I stay there, but after a while, my phone buzzes in my purse over and over again. I turn it off without looking at the messages and crawl in bed.

CHAPTER TWENTY-THREE

ABBI

I'm dragging when I get to work the next day, but when I sit down at my desk, I force myself to unlock my phone and read the messages waiting for me. I look at the screen through blurry eyes.

> Dean: I don't know exactly what you saw or how, but I wanted to make sure you had the full picture. Here are screenshots of every text I've exchanged with Amy since before I first kissed you. I don't want to be with her. I want to be with you. But we need to talk about this.

Beneath that message are images of exactly what he promised: screenshots of the texts between him and Amy.

Evidence that he didn't reciprocate, that he even tried to shut her down.

"Abbi," Layla says, peeking her head into my office. The look of concern on her face tells me that my misery is apparent on mine. "I'm sorry to bother you, but I have a client here who wanted to get the chef's take on their menu choices for their reception next month."

I shove my phone in my purse and my thoughts of Dean to the back of my mind. I can't figure this out right now anyway.

I make it through my brief meeting with Layla's bride and groom, working on autopilot as I agree that, yes, chicken is served at a lot of weddings but that it's generally a crowd pleaser, too. After I leave them, I start my prep work in the kitchen, but I can't concentrate and am flat-out miserable, thinking about those texts.

I should've let him talk. I shouldn't have assumed the worst without hearing Dean out. As much as it might hurt to show him my heart and put my feelings out there, that's what I need to do. *This is why seeing that text hurt me. This is why I think we might have something worth fighting for.*

I excuse myself from work early. I can trust the staff to keep things running smoothly through the Friday dinner rush, even though I'd normally never ask them to.

Friday and Saturday nights are part of the job, but I have something more important tonight. I stop at the store and grab everything I need to make salad, lasagna, and garlic bread. My mom always says you need carbs if you wanna hash out something big. I pull up to his house before five. I don't think he's been getting home until closer to six lately, so I send him a quick text so he knows to expect me.

Abbi: I'm at your place. I'm going to make us
dinner and we'll talk. I'm sorry I thought
the worst.

When I let myself in the front door with the key he
gave me, I find it already unlocked. I glance toward the
drive, but there's no sign of his truck. Maybe he just forgot
to lock it this morning. But when I step inside, I see Trixie's
outside, jumping up on the sliding glass door on the opposite side of the living room.

Has she been locked out all day?

"I'm in the bedroom," a woman calls out. *I know that
voice.*

My stomach pitches, and when it settles back down,
dread and a sick understanding settle with it.

I drop the bags of groceries in the foyer and follow the
sound of Amy's voice to Dean's bedroom.

The sight that greets me is even worse than what I
imagined. Amy's sprawled out on top of the gray comforter,
completely nude except for a pair of lacy panties and
matching black heels.

Dean and I slept together under that comforter just two
nights ago. On Monday, he wrapped me in it when I was
wet from the shower and shivering. And on Tuesday he
didn't even get his shirt off before he spread me out on it so
he could drop to his knees beside the bed and kiss me
between my legs.

I never thought about who else he'd had on that
comforter. Never thought anyone else would find her way
there again but me. *Idiot.*

"Abbi," Amy says, jumping out of bed and grabbing her
robe off the chair.

The sound of my name snaps me out of my horror-induced paralysis, and I spin around and run for the front door. I feel her behind me.

"Wait."

I stop but don't turn. "Why?"

"You're the one?" she asks. "The one Dean started seeing to get me to give him a chance?"

Slowly, I turn around. She's put on a robe, but it's thin and just this side of transparent. "What do you mean?"

She shakes her head. "I never meant for anyone to get hurt."

"Tell me what you mean." My back teeth clang together. My jaw aches. She was lying in his bed like she belonged there. Like he'd invited her.

"He wanted a real relationship, but I wasn't ready," she says. "I told him he had to start dating someone else and if he still wanted me, then I'd consider it. Guys like Dean, you know, he's never really been the long-term type. He's never wanted that."

Except from Amy. He wanted it from her very badly. He even told me. He was jealous of what she had with Kace.

"I never meant for you to get hurt," she says again. "I had to be sure he didn't need me to be exciting all the time."

I wish she'd quit saying that. It implies there's a reason to be hurt. That this isn't some big misunderstanding Dean will clear up in a few words.

"You're a nice girl. I think he really cares for you, but you need to understand the only reason he ever gave you a chance was because he was trying to prove something to me."

"That . . . that doesn't even make sense."

"You wouldn't understand. You've never been the girl guys want the fling with—no offense, but you know what I mean."

Yes. Yes, I do. "You had your chance with him." I don't even know what I'm saying. I sound so pathetic.

"I think you and I have a lot in common," she says, and I want to smack her. The only thing we have in common is loving Hope, her daughter. She destroyed my brother when she left and then broke Dean's heart. And now she's breaking mine. "We both care about Dean a lot. But if you really want him to be happy, don't make this any harder for him by making a scene."

I squeeze my eyes shut. "I have to go."

❧

DEAN

I was so fucking relieved when I saw Abbi's text that I packed right up and headed home. I half expect to smell something amazing when I walk in the door, but instead I see piles of grocery bags lining the foyer. Trixie is outside, and I hear movement in the bedroom.

Shit. I don't want Abbi to think I expect her to cook for me. "Wanna just order in tonight?" I call out, dropping my keys on the foyer table.

"That sounds good, but sex first."

I spin around at the sound of a feminine voice that's definitely *not* Abbi's. Amy saunters toward me in a thin silver robe tied loosely at the waist. Her blond hair is piled on top of her head like she's channeling casual, but her eye makeup says *clubbing*. Dread takes my stomach in its fist. "Where's Abbi?"

"She came and went already. It's taken care of." She puts her hands on my shoulders and squeezes, and I'm so fucking bowled over by her audacity that I just stand there and stare. "You could've picked someone *other* than my ex-sister-in-law, by the way." She laughs, low and sultry. I used to think that laugh was the sexiest thing I'd ever heard, but tonight, in this context, it makes my skin crawl.

"What did you do?" I'm already reaching for my phone, but Amy snatches it from me.

"Don't complicate this, Dean. I'm here. *You win.* I'm giving you what you wanted. Strings, commitment, the whole nine yards."

"What I wanted?" *Came and went.* I'm gonna be sick. I grab my phone back and unlock the screen, expecting to see that I somehow missed a call from Abbi. There's nothing. "I don't know why you're here, but you'd better explain what you said to Abbi real fast."

"I thought I'd surprise you. You can imagine how awkward it was for her to find me naked in your bed." She makes a face of mock horror. "So awkward. I actually felt really sorry for her."

I squeeze my eyes shut. "Please fucking tell me she knew I had nothing to do with you being here. That you *were not invited.*"

"Of course I did! I told her you'd given me the space and time I'd requested, and you know everything else."

The dread gripping my stomach keeps hold of it as it crawls up my throat. "What do you mean, everything else?"

"I told her that I told you I needed you to date someone

boring before I'd have a serious relationship with you. That sometimes life with a mom isn't sexy and I wanted to know you could really handle it." She shrugs. "And Abbi Matthews? Point made, Dean."

I thought I loved this woman. I truly believed that. But all I see when I look at her right now is a small, self-centered bitch. "You never told me to date someone boring. We broke up because you thought my track record with supposedly boring girls was too weak, and I told you to fuck off."

The smirk that's been playing at her mouth since she appeared finally falls away. "You're telling me you didn't date her just to prove something to me? You were dating Abbi Matthews just because you *wanted* to?"

"Of course I *wanted* to." I shake my head. "Why is that so hard to believe?"

"You have a type, Dean, and it's not socially awkward, chubby chefs."

There's too much bullshit in that sentence to unpack. "Get out of my house."

Tears well in her blue eyes. "Why are you being so cruel?"

"Why am *I* being cruel? You just told the woman I love that I was dating her as some sick method to win *you* back? *That* is cruel."

Panic creases her face, and tears roll down her cheeks. Instead of feeling pity, all I feel is manipulated. "I don't understand why you're so mad at me right now," she says. "You told me you wanted us to be together. That you loved me. I'm here because now I want that too."

"I don't want that anymore." Fuck. I don't know if I ever

did. I think . . . I think I was just lonely and wanted Amy because she seemed okay with my baggage.

"Are you punishing me for making you wait?"

I bite back a curse and shake my head. "This isn't *about you*, Amy. I moved on. I'm in love with Abbi, and all I want is for you to get the fuck out of my way."

CHAPTER TWENTY-FOUR

DEAN

I don't bother with the car. I run the five blocks to Abbi's apartment, cell phone in hand, calling her over and over again as I go. She doesn't answer, and I only run faster. By the time I'm knocking on her door, I'm out of breath. "Abbi!" I shout. "Abbi, open the door."

I hear her soft steps. "Dean, just go away. I don't want to do this."

"Amy's gone. I'm so sorry she did that, and I'm sorry she said those things."

Her jagged inhale guts me. "It doesn't matter. Just go."

I press my palm against the door and squeeze my eyes shut. I need to hold her. I need to see her face and know I didn't lose her. "Please open the door."

"What was I supposed to think?" she shouts. "She was in your bed, Dean. The woman you *love*, the one who left you heartbroken and so sad and lonely that you were willing to screw *me*."

"I'm sorry." Jesus. It really couldn't look worse, but I deserve the fucking benefit of the doubt. "I swear I didn't invite her. I didn't want her there. Amy does what she wants."

"Well, now she wants *you*."

I lean my forehead against the door and close my eyes. "I don't want her," I whisper. She probably can't hear me, but it doesn't matter, anyway. I see who we are now. How this will play out.

"I suppose you want someone boring? Someone like me?"

Amy couldn't have played more into Abbi's insecurities if she'd tried. "I don't want to have this conversation through the door."

She sniffles. "I don't really blame you, Dean. This is on me. I knew it was too good to be true. And you know what? You never promised me anything. I won't hold promises you never made against you, but I can't look at you right now. I can't look at you and try to figure out if I can trust you." Her words are muffled by her tears. "This has run its course anyway, right? It was never supposed to be forever."

I feel like I've been punched. I straighten and step back. "Right. You wouldn't want forever with a guy like me. Bastard kid of a cheater."

Suddenly the door swings open. "What's that supposed to mean?" Her eyes are red. She's been crying, and I fucking hate that, but more than that, I hate that she believed— even for a minute—that I'd do that to her.

"You know what it means." My voice is gruff. "You're assuming the worst about me, and I'm supposed to fucking *grovel* when it's your assumptions that are the problem here."

Her red face contorts in frustration. "She was sending you dirty texts, then she was naked in your bed, and now I'm the bad guy because I thought something was happening between you?"

"You didn't even *ask* me. You didn't even give me the courtesy of a single question." Anger floods my veins, washing away all the hurt I've been feeling for the last twenty-four hours. "You truly believe I'd cheat on you." I shake my head, jaw tight. "But you didn't ask. You just assumed. You believed the worst because it went along with the narrative you tell yourself—the one about you and the one about me. All the bullshit you fed me about believing that I'm different than my father, but you didn't mean any of it."

"What are you talking about? This has nothing to do with your dad."

"Doesn't it?" I tilt my face toward the ceiling of her covered porch and draw in a deep breath.

She turns on her heel and walks into her apartment, leaving the door hanging open behind her.

I follow her in and don't bother closing it. I won't be here long. "Do you remember your twenty-first birthday?"

She stops inside her tiny living room. "What? Why?"

"Do you remember it?"

"Not well."

"You told me that night that you'd never marry a guy whose dad wasn't around when he was growing up. That you wanted your kids to be raised by a man who knew how to be a father."

Slowly, she turns around and stares at me, eyes wide. I

see the recognition there. She remembers. "I didn't mean—"

"You meant what you said. And you meant it when you said boys learn fidelity and honor from their fathers." I shake my head. I suddenly feel way too tired for this, but I need to get it off my chest, so I keep going. "That was four years ago, and I thought maybe you'd changed your mind. But then you assumed the worst when you saw that text from Amy, and even when I showed you the whole history —gave you the whole *context*—you once again assumed the worst when you saw her in my bed." I drag a hand through my hair. "I fucked up by not setting stronger boundaries for Amy, by forgetting to get my fucking key back. But *you* assumed the worst about me when three days ago you held me and promised you believed I wasn't like my father."

Her bottom lip quivers. "You were in love with her, and you and I weren't— We've never been real."

"You think this wasn't real?" I snap. "You think every touch, every moment I've spent with you hasn't been real for me?"

She folds her arms, putting up walls, pushing me away. "I'm sorry I assumed anything. But you have to understand what this is like for me. There's no reason you should love me like that. No reason you should *choose me*."

I swallow hard. "There are a thousand reasons I'd choose you over and over and over again. We all have insecurities, Abbi. We all have pieces of ourselves we don't want the world to see, but the difference between us is you walk around with yours visible to the world. It's no secret that you're not a size six." Her face crumples, as if I just hurled an insult. "Dammit, I don't fucking *care* what the number on your jeans is. Don't you understand? It's not a secret. I knew what you looked like when I told you I wanted to do this. I *liked* what you looked like then, and I like it now. You fucking turn me on and twist me up, and as much as I don't understand why it should matter when you're still so damn beautiful, I've tried to be patient because I know it matters to you. You carry these pounds like they're scars of some shameful past."

Tears roll down her cheeks, but I plow forward. "You know why I went home with Amy that first time? She'd confessed to me that she'd cheated on Kace. That she was a fucking mess over it and was terrified he'd find out someday. I *liked* that she had this black spot on her record. I liked that she'd fucked up. Because after the shit my grandmother shoved down my throat, and after what the girl I was head over heels for said to me on her twenty-first birthday, I believed only someone like her could accept my asshole cheater heritage. You aren't the only one with insecurities, Abbi. I know you struggle, and that people make assumptions about you and that it's not fucking fair, but at least the things people judge you for are out in the open. Mine are buried a little deeper. They come out and haunt me when I least expect it."

"I don't think of it that way," she whispers. "I didn't think of your dad for a second."

I shrug, but fuck, acting like it doesn't matter is killing me. "You still thought the worst—about me, and about what I feel for you." I walk further into the apartment until I'm standing right in front of her. I want to hold her so badly, but I won't. We're just going to hurt each other. "I want you. More than I ever wanted Amy. More than I ever wanted anybody. You're smart and sweet and sexy as fuck."

"Stop it," she cries. "Stop saying that crap."

My heart sinks. That's what she wants. It's *really* what she wants. And the realization only strengthens my resolve. "No. You're all the things you refuse to see in yourself. I *love* you." The words come out so rough that they sound like they're meant to cut. They sound like an insult. Hell, maybe they are. Right now, my own feelings are an insult to me. They're killing me. "I love you," I repeat, softer this time. "I've never felt for anyone what I feel for you. It's bigger and better and so powerful that no misunderstanding could destroy it. But I'm not sure you could say the same about the way you feel for me."

"Dean . . ."

I wait, desperate for her to say something that might make me believe we can salvage this so I can breathe again, but she doesn't continue, so I finish it for her. "Everything you feel for me is muffled by the hate you feel for yourself. Until you get that in check, I'm not sure you really can love me. And even if you do, your self-loathing is breaking us before we ever have a chance, and I refuse to let these insecurities of yours make me hate you. You are the most beautiful thing in my life, and these weeks we've been together have been some of the best, but I refuse to let the way you hate yourself turn my feelings for you into something ugly. Don't you see it? No matter how many times I try to prove my love, no matter how many ways I shower you in it, no matter how many times I try to remind you what I see when I look at you or how I feel about you, there's absolutely nothing I can say or do to make you love yourself. And you're going to have to love yourself before you can ever trust me."

The tears in her eyes spill onto her cheeks, and that

knife embedded in my chest feels like it plunges a little deeper.

"I love you," I repeat. "I'll walk out that door still loving you." I shake my head. This is all so fucking screwed up. It doesn't need to be like this. "Do you remember what you told me about how much you needed to feel beautiful? How much you needed to really believe it?"

She nods, and more tears spill over.

"Did you ever stop and think I might have some wounds that needed tending as well? That maybe after the way I was raised and the crap I was told, I needed someone to see I can be trusted as much as you needed someone who can see your beauty?" I huff out a breath and drag my hand through my hair. "Of course it would end like this. Look at how we began."

"I'm sorry," she says.

"Yeah." I take a final ragged inhale that feels like a blade being dragged down through my heart. "Me too."

CHAPTER TWENTY-FIVE

DEAN

There's a single booth in a dark corner at the back of Smithy's where I got drunk two nights in a row after Amy broke up with me. I find myself there again tonight, but I've barely had a sip of my beer. My stomach is too tangled to take anything in, and I already know there's no amount of alcohol that's going to make this better.

"Can I join you?"

I don't know how long I've been staring at my black phone screen, waiting for it to light up with a notification, but I pull my gaze away from it at the sound of Kace's voice. "Hey, go ahead."

Kace slides into the booth across from me and cradles his bourbon in both hands. "So, Amy showed up at my house earlier and had an interesting story to tell."

Closing my eyes, I blow out a breath. *Fuck.* Of course she went running to Kace. I don't even care, though. Right now, Kace knowing about me and Abbi is the least of my worries. "That so?"

"You and Abbi?"

I shrug. "I wanted to tell you, but Abbi thought . . ." I shake my head. "I was hoping I'd change her mind, but then she walked in on Amy naked in my fucking bed, and everything is a mess now."

Kace leans back in the booth. "Amy left out that part."

"Did she also leave out the part about me being in love with your sister?"

Kace blinks at me then sighs. "Yeah, I guess she did." He mutters a curse and stares out toward the crowded bar for a few loaded moments of silence.

"If you're pissed at me about Abbi," I say, "that's fine, but don't base shit on what Amy told you."

"Yeah, I know better than that," he says softly.

I take a sip of my beer and barely manage to get it down. Another glance at my phone. No texts. No calls. But why would she call when I laid it all out and walked away? I can't decide if I made a terrible mistake or did exactly what needed to be done.

"I'm sorry for the things I said when Stella suggested you and Abbi double-date with us. I had no idea." He coughs. "I just didn't think Abbi was what you were looking for."

I scoff. "Half the reason I never dated anyone seriously is because of my feelings for Abbi. It wasn't always conscious, but I never wanted to date someone looking for commitment when I was still hung up on someone else."

Kace stares at me and shakes his head. "I totally missed it. I had no idea."

"I didn't want you to know. It was all embarrassing,

anyway. I was ready to lay it all on the line and ask her out when she made it very clear I wasn't the kind of guy she was looking for."

"Shit. Did you tell anyone?"

"Smith was there the night she . . ." Hell, I don't want to go into it again. "He knows."

"You told Smithy and not me?" Kace squeezes his eyes shut. "I'm gonna have to sit with that for a bit."

"This is what I get for messing around with my best friend's ex. Karma's a bitch."

Kace shakes his head. "Nah. This isn't karma. It's Amy. Karma's got nothing on her."

"I think Abbi and I are through." The words are rough around the edges, as if they themselves are the dull blades that just pulverized my heart. Fuck, Kace is probably not the guy to talk to about this, but I feel like I'm falling apart, and I need to talk to *someone*.

When I lift my gaze from my beer, Kace is staring at me with narrowed eyes. "You're just gonna give up that easy?"

"You know what's crazy? When she saw those unfortunate texts from Amy and assumed the worst, I didn't take it personally. Not really. But when Amy was naked in my bed and Abbi thought I was planning to fuck her? That pushed me over the edge." I rub at the ache in my chest. It doesn't help.

Kace blows out a breath. "Did she ever tell you about Cody—her college boyfriend?"

"The reason she dropped out? Yeah. Hated that asshole." I shrug. "I guess I don't know much about him, but I know he did a number on her. I think he's the root of why she's insecure."

Kace nods. "Yeah, me too." He swallows. "Cody cheated

on her. He told her he'd never been attracted to her, that she was the kind of girl guys only went out with when they didn't have any other options, and that when guys had sex with girls like her it was never actually good, because the physical attraction was necessary for what he called *real release*."

"Motherfucker."

"Yeah. So she's carried that around. Her first love—her longest relationship—only stayed with her because he felt bad for her and said he'd never found her attractive. She was devastated. After that, every guy who showed any interest in her was suspect. What did he want from her? Why was he *really* giving her attention? She's . . . got insecurities."

I trace a line in the condensation down the side of my glass. "I know she does, but I thought I showed her the truth. I thought she was finally seeing herself for who she really is."

"When you carry something like that with you for so long, it's not so easy to change your mindset. We're talking years of programming."

I huff out a laugh. I get that. More than most people realize. More than even Kace knows. "Messes with your head."

"You give Abbi a compliment about pretty much anything other than her cooking, and she immediately comes up with a mental list of reasons you might've said it —none of which are because it's true."

"I just can't . . ." I swallow hard, second-guessing every-thing I said and thought in the heat of the moment. "If we're going to have any chance, I need her to trust me, and I don't think she can do that while believing that her appearance makes her fundamentally unlovable."

Kace takes a sip of his bourbon, puts the glass down, then picks it up and drains it. "You know you're like a brother to me, right?"

The backs of my eyes burn. Jesus Christ, I don't want to cry right now, and I'm afraid I'll lose it if I speak. I manage, "Same."

"I know my sister's not perfect, but I also know she's pretty fucking amazing."

"I know that." Hell, sometimes I think I see it more than anyone.

"So maybe she screwed up. And maybe her insecurities came out and did a good one-two punch to yours."

I cough out a laugh at his description. It's pretty accurate.

"If you two end up giving this a real shot? It'll happen again, and it'll suck. That's what happens in relationships. We screw up and we adjust and we screw up a little less epically the next time. Then sometimes we screw up in a whole new way just to keep things interesting." He chuckles, then his face goes serious as he studies me. "The key is trying to decide if it's worth it—if what you have together is worth it. I know you both are individually, but together?" He shrugs. "Only you two can answer that."

"Yeah," I say. "I get that." But we are, damn it. I know we are.

Standing, Kace smacks the table. "Give it some time. Sounds like you both have a lot to think about."

"Thanks," I mutter. I wait until he's gone before looking at my phone again. This time there's a message, but it's from Amy, not Abbi.

Amy: I've really screwed up with you,
haven't I?

I rub my temples. While I give Abbi the time Kace suggested, I need to deal with Amy. I'm thinking a firm explanation of some boundaries. Boundaries I should've set a long time ago.

※

ABBI

What does a girl do when she's brokenhearted? She calls a friend. But my friends all call each other and descend upon me *en masse*. Which is why, less than an hour after Dean walked away from me, I have a living room full of booze and sympathetic faces.

Brinley called up the forces—Stella, Savvy, and Layla—and filled everyone in on the arrangement between me and Dean, but apparently Stella already knew more than I confessed when she caught us making out in the dark hall at Brinley's.

"I had to check on my brother after I found out what was going on between you two," Stella says, pouring vodka into a martini shaker. "He's had a thing for you for years, so the whole arrangement worried me."

I scoff. "You're ridiculous."

Stella arches a brow. "You think I'm kidding? You dropped out of college and came home and started helping Dean and Kace with the business right when they needed it most, and my brother got all soft on you."

"I totally missed this," Brinley says. "How did I miss this?"

"Because he always swore they were just friends, but I knew there was more to it. It wasn't until this summer that I found out what happened the night of your twenty-first."

My stomach drops to the floor. "He mentioned that today." I feel like I want to cry all over again. I was drunk and ranting that night. Cody had called to wish me a happy birthday, and it had sent me spiraling, grasping for an explanation for everything that had gone wrong between us. "I forgot I said any of that."

"Said what?" Savvy asks.

Stella turns to me, and I hate that she's going to make me repeat the awful words, but I need to own it. I need to face the damage I did so I can fix it. Even if Dean never wants me back, he needs to know that I was talking out my ass that night. Nothing I said was true. I take a breath. "I was dealing with a bad breakup."

"Cody the gaslighting cheater?" Layla asks.

"Yeah," I say. "Cody's dad wasn't around much when he was growing up, and any time he was an ass to me and I called him on it, he'd use that as a defense. His dad never taught him how to deal with anger. He never had an example for how to be kind in a romantic relationship. He doesn't know how to be a good man because he never had an example, et cetera, et cetera."

"What an *ass*," Savvy says. "That's the shittiest excuse. There are so many *great* guys who grew up without a dad."

I nod, feeling even smaller.

Stella says, "And my brother is one of them."

"Aw, shit," Layla says. Unlike Brinley and I, Layla and

Savvy didn't grow up with Stella and Dean, so they don't know their history.

"Like I said, the night of my twenty-first, Cody had called, and I was feeling weepy and sorry for myself, and I was trying to come to terms with the fact that he and I were never going to get back together." I close my eyes, remembering. "I was sitting on the dock out at Lake Black-ledge, and Dean sits next to me to make sure my drunk ass doesn't fall in. We talked for a while and he said, 'I think you deserve a good guy.'" I draw in a ragged breath. I hate that I was so oblivious—not just to his interest in me but to his experience and his feelings. "I just thought he was saying nice things to the birthday girl, and I started ranting about the kind of guy I wanted."

Stella crosses her arms. I can tell it hurts her to imagine her brother living through this moment.

"I was thinking about Cody and his excuses and how I never wanted someone to hurt me like that again. I went on and on about how I wanted a guy who'd been raised with his dad around, because those were the guys who knew how to treat women. *Those* were the guys who'd be faithful and who wouldn't run when times were hard."

"Smithy said Dean had planned to ask you out that night, but you made him think he didn't have a chance," Stella says.

"Oh, no," Layla says. "Poor Dean."

I feel so low. So unworthy of what Dean and I almost had. "Until he brought it up tonight, I'd never really thought about it again. I was so self-involved and full of self-pity. It never crossed my mind how those words would make him feel." I press my palms to my hot cheeks. "I don't even believe it. I was just . . . I should never have said such an awful thing out loud."

Brinley squeezes my shoulder. "So when you saw texts from Amy and then caught her in his bed and assumed the worst, he immediately connected your assumptions to what you said that night about guys who are raised without fathers."

I nod vigorously, tears rolling down my cheeks. Stella pours the drink she's been shaking into a martini glass and passes it to me. "Thanks," I manage.

"You two just need to talk," Brinley says. "Explain yourself."

I sniffle. "He said a lot of things tonight that I need to think about. We do need to talk, but I need to figure myself out first. I need to . . . figure my life out."

Brinley cocks her head to the side. "Your life?"

More tears spill down my cheeks. "I want to open my own bakery, but I'm scared it'll be a bust and I'll have left you and a great job for nothing. And I don't want to lose you because you're such a great friend."

Brinley's face falls and she pulls me into her arms. "Girl, I'm your friend first. That doesn't change if you stop working for me." She laughs and glances to Stella. "Just ask her."

Stella nods. "True story."

"I don't know if I have the courage it takes to open a business. I need a business loan and a plan, and if I fail, everyone will see." I can't believe I'm talking about this right now. A reasonable person would've chosen a moment when she *wasn't* having an emotional breakdown to tell her best friend/boss she might be leaving.

"If you *fail*, you'll try again," Stella says. "Until you don't want to anymore or can't. And *if* that day comes, we'll all be here for you."

I squeeze her so tightly. I'm grateful for my friends. I'm so lucky to have them.

They keep me company until later than they should, given that we all have work tomorrow, but I'm lighter when they leave. That hardened, scarred part of me that Layla accused me of putting front and center has retreated to her corner, and the hopeful part of me—the one that's willing to give me some grace for my mistakes—has come out of hiding.

I look at my phone for the first time in hours and see a text message. My heart flips before I see it's not from Dean.

> Number Unknown: Hi, Abbi. This is Frankie, aka Date Destroyer. I hope you don't mind that I got your number from one of your employees from work. I just wanted to apologize for last night. I didn't intend to make things awkward between you and your date. Actually, I didn't realize you were seeing anyone. I wouldn't have been so forward if I'd known.
>
> I don't know how serious things are between you and that guy, but I wanted to take this moment when I'm feeling a little braver than usual and let you know that I really like you, and I'd love to take you out. Maybe that's stating the obvious, but I can never really get a read on you.
>
> Ignore this if you're not interested or if

you've got something serious going, but I
figured I'd rather try than wonder.

I laugh then cringe reading the message. Even Frankie,
this guy I thought I was totally flirting back with all these
months, wasn't sure if I was interested. Didn't Dean tell me
I practically had FUCK OFF written on my forehead?

Also, I'm totally going to have a chat with my employees
about giving out my number.

I carefully compose my reply, trying my best to keep it
honest but kind.

> Abbi: Hey, Frankie. I'm sorry about last
> night. That was awkward. I'm sorry things
> didn't work out between us. I was looking
> forward to going out with you sometime,
> but then life happened, and I found
> myself head over heels in love with my
> brother's best friend. I'm not sure what
> will happen there, but regardless, I'm in
> no place to be dating someone else. Take
> care.

I send the message then pull up the thread between me
and Dean. I should probably leave him alone, but I keep
thinking about how many times he said he loved me before
he walked out my door. I keep thinking that if he loves me,
maybe we can fix this.

I love you too, I type. Then I make myself delete it. I'll
tell him, but I need to fix myself first.

CHAPTER TWENTY-SIX

DEAN

*A*bbi was supposed to be here with me.

That's all I can think as I walk up to my old man's house. The thing is, I think she would've come if I'd asked her. Despite everything, Abbi would've held my hand as I saw my dying father. But I need to do this alone.

Dad's house is a run-down bungalow west of Atlanta. The area isn't great, his street isn't much better, and his house is definitely the worst on the block. Some people live like this because of the circumstances life delivered them. It's shit luck, and it's unfair and frustrating. My father lives like this because of the decisions he made over and over again. He's not an addict. He's not incapable of working. He's just always preferred trying to cheat anyone around him into paying his way. He's spent his life working so hard for a free check that he could've had an honest one many times over.

I don't know why I spent so many years worrying about being like him. I'm *nothing* like him. If anything, I'm his opposite. I live for hard work, for busting my ass to prove myself, and for taking care of the people I love. Genetics won't change that.

Sandy greets me on the crumbling concrete porch. Her thin blond hair whisks around her face in the light breeze, and her face is creased with the kind of stress that still shows even as she gives me a shaky smile. "Thanks for coming. Did you find a place to stay?"

I nod. "I got a room just off the bypass." I could've made an appearance and left, but I decided to come for a couple of days. Milo needs some help applying for college and wants to do a couple of campus visits too. I told Sandy I'd help, and I thought she'd cry. "It's the least I can do for my brother," I said on the call, and then I heard her soft whimpering on the other end of the line.

"He's in and out today, but I know he'll be glad to see you." She leads me into the house, where they have a hospital bed set up in the living room. The place smells of cat pee and death, and my stomach turns. Someone's placed a folding chair at the side of his bed, close to his head, and I lower myself into it. It's cold and hard and about as comfortable as I feel.

My father rolls his head to the side and looks at me through slitted eyes. "Dean?"

I nod, and my eyes feel hot. *Goddammit.* "Yeah."

"Milo said you'd come. I told him he shouldn't lie to a dying man."

"I didn't want to." He's too young to die. Too young to look this old. I guess cancer treatments do that to you. I stare at the pale hand by his side. My mind plays a hundred different cinema-inspired scenes in my head, and in every one I take that hand in mine and we share the most genuine, meaningful moment of connection we ever had. But this isn't a movie, and I'm not here for connection. I'm here because Milo needed to see me show up. Maybe our father stuck around for him, but sharing a roof with his youngest son made him no better a dad to Milo than he was to me. This man was absent for both of us in all the ways that counted. Now Milo needs to know there are people in this world who do *show up*, even when it's hard, even when things are rocky.

"Your mama come with you?" he asks.

"No. She said goodbye to you a long time ago."

"True," he wheezes. "You here to rub it in my face— what a fancy life you got?"

I shake my head. "Nah. It's not so fancy."

"Bullshit. I see pictures online of that business you run. Fucking mansions you're remodeling. Gotta be good money in that. You never thought to share a little of that good fortune with your old man?"

Oh, Dad. Even cancer can't change you. "I'll help Milo out when I can. That's enough."

"Selfish bullshit."

Sandy squeezes my shoulder, and I jump. I didn't even realize she was standing so close. *Thank you,* she mouths.

I used to have this whole speech in my mind for the time I saw my father again. *You remember when you used to say I was just like you?* I'd ask. *You were so wrong. You couldn't be more wrong. I'll live every day of my life to make sure I'm nothing like you.* He makes me angry enough that it'd be easy to let it slip out, but I see the grief on Sandy's face and keep it locked away. I'm not here for myself.

"I just wanted you to know that," I say. "Milo's a good kid. You don't need to worry about him."

My father's eyes drift closed, and I think he's asleep when he says, "I know. Takes after his brother." And it's the nicest fucking thing the old man's ever said to me, so even though I swore to myself I wouldn't, I sit by my father's deathbed and feel my face go wet with tears.

ॐ

ABBI

I've journaled for the last three days and had an entire hour with my new therapist, so I'm pretty much the local expert on self-love and acceptance now.

Maybe not, but I see a path toward a place that's better than where I am now, and that's more than I've been able to say in years.

I love that Dean looks at and touches me in a way that makes me feel truly sexy, but it only took one meeting with Dr. Katherine before I was painfully aware of the fact that I was giving him a job I can only do myself. Even though I have got my work cut out for me, I feel optimistic on Wednesday as I leave the bank. Optimistic about my journey to self-acceptance *and* about my potential future business.

I've been on a "data-collecting mission" this week: find out what it'd take to open my own bakery in downtown Orchid Valley. No pressure. No expectations. I just wanted to have the information I need to make an informed decision about what's next for me.

Of course, this mission resulted in me finding a beautiful bottom-floor storefront for lease and my amazing brother promising to help renovate it for me. It resulted in my mother asking to be a silent partner and part-time employee, which meant I had capital to discuss when I met with the bank today, and it resulted in my "let's see what's possible" becoming a real option.

I'm giddy and nervous. And all I really want to do is talk to Dean about all of it.

"Hey, Abbi!" Hudson calls. He waves then jogs across the street to where I'm standing in front of the bank. "I had a cancellation for tonight. Can I squeeze you in?"

I cock my head at him. So damn persistent. "Layla thinks you have a crush on me."

His eyes go wide and then he does the fish-mouth thing for a few beats before shrugging. "I mean, you're so cool. You've got a pretty smile, and I'm kind of obsessed with your cookies." He releases a rough, kind of dorky laugh. "You wouldn't believe the diet acrobatics I have to do to make those fit my macros."

I laugh. "I imagine that would be difficult."

"You know if you made them a little less fattening, it wouldn't be so bad. Have you ever considered—"

"Hudson."

He snaps his mouth shut. "Huh?"

"They're good *because* they're fattening. Not everything is meant to be lean and macro-friendly." *Not everyone, either,* I think.

"That's cool. I get it," he says, but I'm pretty sure he doesn't.

"Can I ask you a question? If you have a crush on me, why do you keep trying to get me to diet and work out?"

"'Cause you're so pretty," he says, as if this makes perfect sense. "You'd be a knockout if you worked on your body composition. You might not even have to lose much weight. You start eating better macros and lifting weights and—"

"Hudson."

"What?"

Oh, he's so sweetly oblivious. "If you like a girl, maybe just let her be. Most people don't enjoy flattery in the form of our bodies' *potential*."

"Oh." He cringes suddenly. "This is what my sister's trying to say when she says the exercise stuff is insulting sometimes?"

Maybe I had Hudson all wrong. Maybe he's less macho bro-dude and more awkward fitness nerd. "Exactly," I say.

"Sorry. I didn't mean to be rude."

"I forgive you, but I'm not looking for a new diet or exercise routine, okay? So maybe next time we talk, you could bring up something else instead."

He nods eagerly. "I could do that."

"Great." I smack him on the shoulder. "I need to go win my boyfriend back, so I'll talk to you later."

"Good luck," he says, but I'm already walking away.

&

Dean's truck's in the drive, and my heart races as I walk up to his door. I should knock, but I'm so scared he'll tell me to go away that I use my key and walk inside uninvited instead. I can hardly breathe, I'm so tangled up in nerves. He has every right to throw me out on my ass again. But I have to do this. I have to *try*.

I find him on his living room sofa with gaming headphones on, a video game on his big-screen TV and a controller in his hand. He has his glasses on, and the sight of them reminds me of the last time I stayed the night. The way we woke tangled up together, our hands moving before our bodies were fully awake. He reached for his glasses, and I didn't understand why he needed them. Even with something so obvious as that, I refused to believe he might *want* to look at me. That moment, that whole day, felt so much like a dream. When he brought me breakfast in bed, I just stared at him and tried desperately to enjoy the moment, but I couldn't. Not when the ugly voice in the back of my mind kept warning me it was about to end.

"Dean?" I say softly.

He turns to me, and his eyes go wide for a beat before he pulls off the headphones, pauses the game, and puts the controller down on the coffee table. "Hey," he says.

I bite my bottom lip. I wish I could just apologize and beg for another chance, but I know he needs more than that. He deserves more than that. "I have so many things to apologize for."

"Me too," he says.

I shake my head. "Me first?" He nods. "First, you need to know how sorry I am for everything I said the night of my twenty-first. I didn't even believe the things I was spouting that night. I should've just said what I was really feeling—that Cody hurt me, and I never wanted to be hurt like that again."

He swallows. "I don't understand."

"Cody's dad wasn't around much when he was growing up, and Cody would use that as an excuse any time he screwed up. I think his mom taught him to do that—

because *she* felt guilty that his dad wasn't around—and then Cody picked it up and it became a defense mechanism. I don't know why I said those things that night. I always knew it was a lame excuse he used so he didn't have to feel responsible for his mistakes."

Dean draws in a deep breath. "I didn't know that." Four words and some of the knots in my stomach loosen.

"And I didn't know you'd been carrying around my words all this time. I didn't know the details about your dad or about your grandmother." My chest aches and my eyes fill with tears, though it's way too soon to start crying. I have a lot more to say. "I hate that I added to that hurt in any way. When I thought the worst about you and Amy, it wasn't because of your dad at all. It didn't even have anything to do with you. *You* are kind and strong and loyal. I was the problem. I believed you were messing around with her because it was easier than believing someone as amazing as you would want someone like me."

Disappointment washes over his face before he closes his eyes. "Abbi . . ."

"Wait. Listen, please?"

Blowing out a breath, he nods and opens his eyes again. "I'm listening."

I take a deep breath and peel off my sweater. "I'm not sure I'll ever like my arms," I say, and before he can object, I push on, "but I like my hands." I stretch out my fingers. "It's a silly thing, maybe, but I've always liked my hands. Maybe it's from all those years playing piano or because I spend so much time watching them when I'm in the kitchen, but I like the way they look. Even though they get rough and dry from work, and even though I always keep my nails short and stubby. They aren't elegant like a lot of women's hands—but it's okay," I blurt. I'm already ruining this. "Because I like these hands just as they are."

He gives me a crooked smile. "I like them too. A lot." His voice is raw.

"Okay." I feel a little braver now that I've started. "My back. I've always liked my back. I like the smooth skin and the freckles sprinkled across it. I like that it's strong and I don't have to rely on my staff to unload a truck when inventory comes in. But I also like the way it looks. When you touched my back, when you were behind me and kissed your way across it, I never felt like I needed to hide anything or suck anything in. I just . . . felt good about it."

"You have a sexy back," he says, and I have to block out the impulse to find the lie in his words. That instinct will take some time to correct, but I'll work on it. For him. For *me*.

"Thank you," I say with a smile. "I've spent most of my life hating my breasts," I continue. Dean holds my gaze, but there's an undeniable sadness in his eyes. "That surprises a lot of girls, because any time size or weight comes up, they say I'm *curvy*, and I'm so lucky to have the breasts so many women shell out thousands of dollars for. But my breasts were always in my way growing up, and as much as our culture fetishizes that part of a woman's body, if you don't dress just right, they can just make you look even heavier." I look down at my hands, embarrassed all over again for bringing this up, but it's not like I'm telling secrets. "I hated that. I've always hated anything that makes me look heavier."

"Abs . . ."

Slowly, I lift my eyes to his. "But I *loved* my breasts when I was in bed with you. I liked the way your hands looked on them, and the way you'd touch me. You said it's impossible for you to love me enough to make me stop hating myself, and you're right. At the end of the day, that's my job and no one else's. But I *was* on my way there when I found Amy in your bed. Maybe I didn't believe I was beautiful, but I believed you thought I was, even if I didn't understand why. And maybe I didn't believe my size doesn't matter, but I did believe it doesn't matter to you. And honestly . . ." I swallow hard and give myself a moment to find the words I need. "I'll never be someone who oozes confidence or someone who believes she's the prettiest girl in the room. Most of the time, I just want to hide anyway. I don't want people to notice me, and a lot of that comes from not wanting them to see what I perceive as flaws, but I like when *you* notice me. I've always liked when you noticed me, even when I didn't think I deserved it, even when I thought it was some sort of weird mistake."

He grabs my wrist in one big hand and tugs me closer. "Will you come here?" I nod, and he pulls me into his lap. "There's no mistake. I love you, and you're beautiful. I was an idiot for calling you on your insecure bullshit when it was really more about *my* insecurities. I was wrong."

"But you weren't," I say. "Dean, you were absolutely right. I have burned down many good things in my life because I was afraid I'd lose them. I chose having some sense of control and pushing something amazing from my life over watching it slip away from me when I was trying to hold on. I was doing the same thing to us, and if you hadn't called me on it, I would've done it again and again. If you give me another chance, there's a good chance I'll do it again anyway, but I'm going to try so hard not to. I'm working on recognizing when my insecurities make me lash out, and I'm working on adjusting my reactions."

"I'm gonna mess up too," he says, shaking his head. "That's called being human. That's what relationships are about. We mess up and then we fix it and then we try again so we don't mess up as badly the next time." He grins. "At least, that's what your brother told me."

I let out a laugh. "He's all right."

"Yeah," Dean says. "Listen, it's hard for me to understand why you can't accept yourself, but if you'd just try to see what I see, I'll keep loving you every single day until you see it too. And even if you never do, if you can just promise me you'll be good to this woman I love . . ." He presses his palm to my chest, right between my breasts, and that spot that's been aching and hollow over these last few days fills with warmth and hope. "Be good to her. Be kind to her body and her soul. Because she's the best thing I've ever had in my life, and it makes me crazy when *anyone* tries to hurt her."

Hot tears stream down my cheeks, but I nod. "I love you," I say. "I love you, and if what you say is true and my love for you is limited by how I feel about myself, then you'd better watch out, because I'm working on how I feel about me, and you're going to have some crazy-big love coming your way."

"I love you too. So much it scares me a little when I think about you walking away. I've wanted you for so long, but I gave up because I was afraid I wasn't good enough for you. I've never wanted anything more than I want to be worthy of you."

"You are. More than worthy." I touch my forehead to his. "Can we try this again?"

He shakes his head, but I trust him too much to be worried. "No, we're going to try something better this time."

I wrap my arms behind his neck and kiss away his smile until he's groaning and shifting me to straddle him.

CHAPTER TWENTY-SEVEN

DEAN

*a*bbi squeezes my hand in hers as we climb the steps at her parents' house. "Don't be nervous. You've been here for dinner hundreds of times."

"I'm not." The lie slips out before I can catch it, so I shrug and add, "Not very nervous, at least."

We've been an official couple for a week and a half, and while in any other case I would run screaming from dinner with a woman's family so soon in a relationship, everything's different with Abbi. It's not so much that we're going fast as it is that we've already settled in. I love everything about *us* —the way she watches me when she thinks I won't notice, the way it feels to sleep with her in my arms, the easy rhythm we have at home. I love sitting across from her at Smithy's and making her laugh and watching her branch outside of her comfort zone to open her own business. I love cooking for her and letting her cook for me—the conversations and the sex. I really fucking love the sex.

I've never seen her so happy, and that might make me sound like one cocky sonofabitch, but *I've* never been this happy either.

"Dean Jacob!" Mrs. Matthews shouts when she meets us at the front door. "How dare you stay away so long?"

"Sorry, Mama," I say, giving her a quick squeeze. "I let time get away from me."

"I'll forgive it. If you don't let it happen again." She props her hands on her hefty hips and presses her lips together in a thin line as she looks me over. "Are you eating enough?"

I have to laugh. Mama Matthews always did like to make sure I was well fed, and she wouldn't have approved of the weight I lost during my Amy spiral. A couple of months of a whiskey-and-beer diet will do that to you, but I look down at myself, trying to imagine how I look from her point of view. I'm surprised she noticed, since I'm almost back to where I was last spring, but I suppose I shouldn't be. "Don't worry," I say. "Abbi feeds me well."

Abbi's cheeks flame red, as if her mom's going to infer everything *else* she's been doing for me.

Before she can say anything, Mama Matthews lets out an ear-piercing screech of excitement and claps her hands. "That's right, she does! Isn't this just perfect? I always knew you two would end up together. When my Abbi was fifteen and crushing on you so hard, I told her she just needed to wait, that one day you'd look at her and see her for the beautiful woman she was. Took you longer than I thought, but you got there."

I clutch Abbi's hand in mine. "I noticed a long time ago," I say roughly.

A booming voice reaches us from inside the house. "You're serious about my girl, right?" Abbi's dad calls. "None of this *casual* stuff you kids are all about these days?"

Abbi's pink cheeks go darker, and she casts her gaze down as her mom leads us into the house. "Yes, sir," I say, coming face to face with Mr. Matthews in the foyer. I lift my chin and meet his eyes. "Very serious."

Mr. Matthews studies me a long time then smacks me on the shoulder. "Of course you are. You're a good kid."

Leading us to the dining room, Mama Matthews chatters on about what she prepared for dinner and what she's going to send home with me now that she knows I'm "struggling to keep meat on my bones." A half-dozen side dishes are scattered around the large table already, but Mama Matthews excuses herself to grab the turkey from the kitchen, leaving Abbi and I alone in the dining room to take our seats.

I grew up thinking Kace and Abbi had the perfect family. Not that they were ever truly perfect. They fought, had disagreements and misunderstandings, but when it mattered they showed up for each other. That's the part that seemed so perfect to me. The Matthews were my example of stability. They showed me how a family could work. How I wanted my family to work. I still want that, and the easy acceptance from Abbi's parents is humbling enough that my throat is tight and emotion weighs heavily on my chest.

"Hey." Abbi turns in her seat and leans toward me. "Are you okay?"

I meet her beautiful brown eyes. Happiness and

contentment fill my chest, and for the hundredth time in the last ten days. I would've missed this if we'd never given *us* a chance—if I'd gone on believing Abbi could never want someone like me or if she'd continued to believe I couldn't really want her. Thank God the walls we erect around our hearts can be knocked down. "I'm amazing. You?"

"So good."

"I thought I'd get more of the third degree," I admit. "I got off easy."

"They already know you. There's no reason for the third degree." Her eyes shine with trust and love, and my heart swells.

"I love you." The words sound husky, like I had to squeeze them out around all this emotion.

"I love you too." She drags her bottom lip between her teeth. When it pops free, it's pink and swollen, and I can't help but steal a quick kiss that becomes not so quick the moment my lips touch hers.

"Man, that's my *sister* who you've got your hands all over," Kace says behind me.

I pull my mouth off Abbi's—and my wandering hand from her waist. I turn to where he and Stella stand at the head of the table. "Get used to it, Matthews."

My sister grins and jabs Kace in the side with her elbow. "He won't say another word. Especially since that would make him a total hypocrite." She flashes him a mock scowl, but her eyes are dancing with amusement.

Kace drops his mouth to Stella's and kisses her. "Good point," he murmurs against her lips.

"What's going on in here?" Hope asks, her curls bouncing as she runs into the room.

"Just getting ready to eat, kiddo," Abbi says, patting the empty chair beside her. "Sit by me?"

"Yay!" Hope skips around the table as Mama Matthews returns carrying a bottle of wine, her husband carrying the turkey behind her.

We all settle into our seats and the familiar ritual of Sunday dinner. Every once in a while, I reach over to squeeze Abbi's hand or touch her arm to make sure this is real. To make sure I'm not dreaming. She responds to each touch with a smile.

After dinner, her parents retire to the living room to watch their favorite Sunday night news show, and Hope goes to the toy room to play. Stella, Kace, Abbi, and I linger at the table, chatting and sipping wine. It's so comfortable and familiar, as if we've always been two couples.

Kace is telling Stella about the latest snag in his bathroom remodel when Abbi leans over and touches her lips to my ear. "Come upstairs with me. I want to give you a tour of my childhood bedroom."

I arch a brow. "I've seen it."

"You've never seen it knowing that's the first place I thought about you while I touched myself." Her eyes dance mischievously, and I push my chair back from the table so fast that it squeaks against the hardwood floor. Abbi's laugh fills the room and every nook of loneliness in my heart.

Yeah. Life is *really* fucking good.

EPILOGUE

DEAN

"*T*omorrow's the big day," I say, grinning at Abbi.

My girl has spent the last two hours pacing around her little bakery, looking for anything that might need cleaning or fixing before tomorrow. The display cases at the front are spotless, the counters are shiny, and all of her prepped ingredients are in the walk-in cooler for her four a.m. arrival tomorrow morning. I asked only once why she couldn't bake the items a day in advance. I will not make that mistake again. My girl has *standards*.

"I think I'm ready." Her eyes scan the kitchen for the millionth time.

"I *know* you're ready." I close the distance between us and slip my index fingers into the belt loops on her jeans. "It's going to be amazing."

"Thanks to all your help."

I shrug. Kace and I helped some, but anyone who was paying attention knows we were just following orders.

"Do you think people will expect fancy coffee? Maybe I should've splurged on the espresso machines and hired baristas. I might miss out on all that morning traffic. No lattes on the menu is like asking them to go to Starbucks."

I press a kiss to her mouth. "No lattes *yet*. You'll get there. And anyway, no one who's tasted your baked goods will give a shit about steamed milk."

Sighing, she gives me her first smile in hours. "I'm nervous."

"Understandable." I bury my face in her neck and nibble my way up. "I might know how to help with that." I unbutton her jeans, and she gasps as I slip my hand inside to cup her through her panties.

"What are you doing?" she asks, eyes already fluttering closed.

"Helping you relax." I flick her earlobe with my tongue as I stroke her. "Do you have any idea how hot you are when you get in here and turn your bossy voice on?"

She laughs. I love that sound. I love her. I love *this*. The talking to each other, the sharing plans and fears, the promises of tomorrow.

"Can I fuck you on this prep table?" I ask. I already know the answer and have to bite back my amusement when she pulls back to glare at me.

"It's been *sanitized*."

Withdrawing my hand from her jeans, I chuckle. "Better get into your office then," I say, smacking her ass. "I need to fuck you on that desk before you cover it with paperwork again."

Her lips quirk into a crooked grin. "You're gonna make

it so I can't sit at my own desk without getting turned on, aren't you?" She backs in the direction of her little office that's situated in the back corner of the kitchen.

I grin. "That's the plan. Any objections?"

"Not a single one." She runs, and I pick up the pace to catch up, kicking the door closed behind me so I can lean against it while I watch her strip.

I love this.

THE
END

📖

THANK you so much for joining me in Orchid Valley for Abbi and Dean's story. If you'd like to receive an email when I have a sale or release my next book, please sign up for my newsletter: lexiryan.com/signup

I hope you enjoyed this book and will consider leaving a review. Thank you for reading. It's an honor!

OTHER BOOKS BY LEXI RYAN

Orchid Valley

Every Little Promise (Brinley and Marston's prequel)

Every Little Piece of Me (Brinley and Marston's story)

Every Sweet Regret (Stella and Kace's story)

Every Time I Fall (Abbi and Dean's book)

The Boys of Jackson Harbor

The Wrong Kind of Love (Ethan's story)

Straight Up Love (Jake's story)

Dirty, Reckless Love (Levi's story)

Wrapped in Love (Brayden's story)

Crazy for Your Love (Carter's story)

If It's Only Love (Shay's story)

Not Without Your Love (Colton's story)

The Blackhawk Boys

Spinning Out (Arrow's story)

Rushing In (Chris's story)

Going Under (Sebastian's story)

Falling Hard (Keegan's story)

In Too Deep (Mason's story)

LOVE UNBOUND: Four series, one small town, lots of happy endings

Splintered Hearts (A Love Unbound Series)

Unbreak Me (Maggie's story)

Stolen Wishes: A Wish I May Prequel Novella (Will and Cally's prequel)

Wish I May (Will and Cally's novel)

Or read them together in the omnibus edition, *Splintered Hearts: The New Hope Trilogy*

Here and Now (A Love Unbound Series)

Lost in Me (Hanna's story begins)

Fall to You (Hanna's story continues)

All for This (Hanna's story concludes)

Or read them together in the omnibus edition, *Here and Now: The Complete Series*

Reckless and Real (A Love Unbound Series)

Something Reckless (Liz and Sam's story begins)

Something Real (Liz and Sam's story concludes)

Or read them together in the omnibus edition, *Reckless and Real: The Complete Series*

Mended Hearts (A Love Unbound Series)

Playing with Fire (Nix's story)

Holding Her Close (Janelle and Cade's story)

OTHER TITLES

Hot Contemporary Romance

Text Appeal

Accidental Sex Goddess

Decadence Creek (Short and Sexy Romance)

Just One Night

Just the Way You Are

ACKNOWLEDGMENTS

Every book is special to me. Every heroine I've ever written has a piece of me in her, but perhaps this one more than any other. For that reason, I feel more vulnerable sharing this story, but that's also why I wanted to. Thank you in advance, dear reader, for reading Abbi's story with an open heart.

I have to thank my husband, Brian, who embodies all of Dean's best qualities, and who helped me get to a point in my life where I can write an Abbi, where I can see the true harm she does with her self-loathing, and where I can see a path to a peace and self-acceptance for her. I am grateful to have such an amazing, supportive partner in my life. I love you, babe.

To my kids, Jack, and Mary—thank you for believing in me and inspiring me to be my very best. To my mom and siblings—thank you for all of your support and for making me want to write big casts of characters forever.

Thanks to all my writing friends who sprint with me and talk me off the ledge when the book looks like a disaster. To my hand-holding, hair-stroking, and pep-talking best bitches, Mira Lyn Kelly and Lisa Kuhne, my eternal gratitude to you and to unlimited texting plans. Thank you for understanding that I'm a delicate flower and never insisting that I toughen up (even if I probably should). To the Goldbrickers and the ladies in my Slack group, thank you for helping me remember the power of consistency.

To everyone who provided me feedback on this story along the way—Heather Carver, Samantha Leighton, Lisa Kuhne, Nancy Miller, and Janice Owen—you're all awesome. I appreciate you all so much!

I am so grateful for the best editorial team. Lauren Clarke, maternity leave may have meant you didn't get to join me for this book, but I heard you in my head while I was revising. Can't wait to read your comments again next time! Rhonda Merwarth, thank you for the insightful line and content edits. You push me to be a better writer and make my stories the best they can be. Thanks to Arran McNicol at Editing720 for proofreading. I've worked hard to put together this team, and I'm proud of it!

Thank you to the people who helped me package this book and promote it. Lindee Robinson took the gorgeous cover photo and Hang Le did the design and branding for the whole series. To all of the bloggers, bookstagrammers, readers, and reviewers who help spread the word about my books, I am humbled by the time you take out of your busy lives for my stories. My gratitude will never be enough, but it is sincere. You're the best.

To my agent, Dan Mandel, for believing in me and always believing the best is yet to come. Thanks to you and your team for getting my books into the hands of readers all over the world.

Finally, the biggest, loudest, most necessary thank you to my fans. Because of you, I'm living my dream. I couldn't do it without you. You're the coolest, smartest, best readers in the world. I appreciate each and every one of you!

XOXO,

Lexi

ABOUT THE AUTHOR

Lexi Ryan is the *New York Times* and *USA Today* bestselling author of emotional romance that sizzles. A former English professor, Lexi considers herself the luckiest girl around to make a living through storytelling. She loves spending time with her crazy kids, weightlifting, ice cream, swoony heroes, and vodka martinis.

Lexi lives in Indiana with her husband, two children, and a spoiled dog. You can find her on her website.